MAIL ORDER MOM

My Holiday Tails

Marina Simcoe

To my Captain

Mail Order Mom

This book is a work of fiction. Names, characters, places, and incidents are a product of the author's imagination. Locales and public names are used for atmospheric purposes. Any resemblance to actual people, living or dead, or to businesses, companies, events, institutions, or locales is completely coincidental.

New Cover Edition

Cover image source: Depositphotos.com

Spelling: English (American)

Editing by Cissell Ink

Proofreading by Nic Page

Mail Order Mom is a Science-Fiction Romance. It contains graphic scenes of intimacy. Intended for mature readers.

No part of this book was produced with generative AI. Written by the author.

Chapter 1

Susanna

Through the bent and dented blinds, I scanned the street outside my apartment for any suspicious elements. My basement window was so low, all I could see were people's feet. And all of them looked suspicious to me.

I wanted to lock myself in and stay here, relatively safe and sound, and literally underground. But my fridge was empty, as was my wallet. To put something in both, I needed to work.

I grabbed my purse and padded to the door. Pressing an ear to it, I listened for any suspicious sounds, as if the mafia thugs who stalked me would announce their presence.

All seemed quiet.

With a deep breath, I clutched the handles of my purse in my sweaty hands and opened the door. I climbed the set of crumbling concrete stairs up to the street and emerged from my underground hideout into the bright Manhattan morning.

The street was busy, like most streets in central New York. It seemed easy enough to get lost in the crowd. Only I knew that Bolshoy's people would find me. They always did.

The last time, one of them cornered me in the alley two doors down on my way from the ladies' fashion store where I worked.

They wanted the money my husband Tom stole from them. And they didn't give a damn that my dearest husband also stole everything from me—my trust, my innocence, and every single penny of my substantial inheritance. If I ever saw him again, I would punch him in the face then kick him when he fell.

Too bad he fled the country months ago, taking all my money, millions of his investors' funds, and whatever he owed to Bolshoy and his people.

Grabbing whatever he could before making a run for it, Tom had also snatched the busty secretary from his office. The two of them were out there now, probably enjoying the sun on a beach somewhere, while I was half-running to my job, scanning the street in fear for any sign of the dangerous people he was stupid enough to steal from.

It was a good thing I'd switched to wearing flats. The first day of working in retail in five-inch heels had almost killed me. Now, running was so much easier in my black, low-wedge shoes.

I reached the store, completely out of breath.

"You're late." Aileen pursed her lips. The owner and the manager of the store, she appeared to live here twenty-four-seven.

I threw a glance at the display on the cash register. "Just by two minutes."

"Five," she replied in an icy tone. "This clock is three minutes behind."

Resisting the strong urge to flip her a finger, I mumbled, "Sorry," on my way to the tiny employee-room-slash-office-slash-storage-room at the back to drop off my purse and coat. This wasn't one of the high-end fashion shops on 5th Avenue, even if Aileen liked to pretend it was just like them.

No wonder I was late. I had sat by the window for who knew how long, gathering the courage to leave my apartment. The sensation of the thug's rough grip still lingered on my throat from the last time one of them had caught me.

I kept telling them I had no money. But for some reason, Bolshoy believed I was an accomplice of Tom's and my two retail jobs were just a cover to keep a low profile. Like I would be living in a mouse-infested basement, eating frozen dinners, and working two jobs if I had access to the millions Tom had stolen.

Aileen had given me my very first job ever. I was born into money and raised in luxury homes with maids and nannies. I'd never been taught to do anything for myself. My mother wouldn't even let my sister and me make our own beds.

"There are less fortunate people in the world. We shouldn't take their jobs from them. We have to give them the opportunity to earn a living," she'd say in a dignified voice.

Mother thought herself a benevolent person by making others do things for her. She provided them with "means to earn a living" while looking down her nose at those she employed.

Customers of Aileen's often reminded me of my mother. Like her, they were snotty and self-important with no real accomplishments other than being rich. After two months of working in the store, I was still learning how to deal with them. Sometimes, I just felt like punching their well-exfoliated, made-up faces.

But I needed this job to pay the astronomical rent my landlord charged for that crawl space room I now lived in and to occasionally buy some food to eat too.

So, I smiled at the snotty shoppers and repeated like a parrot all day, "How may I help you?" and "Have a nice day."

Around noon, the bell above the door rang again, announcing the arrival of yet another customer.

I heaved a breath and plastered on a smile, then I saw my twin sister walking in.

Mara looked every bit like the customers I'd been dealing with on a daily basis. Louboutin heels. Hermes scarf tied artfully around her neck. Italian wool coat thrown over her shoulders, unbuttoned, because she'd taken a cab here, not walked like me. The handbag that people lined up for years to buy hung in the crook of her elbow.

Sliding her oversized sunglasses down her nose, she threw a glance around the store. The look in her blue eyes clearly conveyed she didn't want to be here.

Her gaze stopped on me. "Oh, there you are. I need to have a word with you."

She hadn't changed a bit. Though, just two months ago, she wasn't in a much better situation than me.

Mara's fiancé Jim would likely be at the beach with Tom and his busty secretary, right now. Jim and Tom were childhood friends, Ivy league graduates, and partners in crime—literally, as it turned out. I met them both through Mara.

Before he left, Jim had cleaned out her banking accounts just like Tom had mine. Unlike me, however, instead of taking two jobs to survive, Mara found a couple of wealthy men to pay for her expenses.

My sister and I never got along that well. And lately, she'd been treating me like a second-class citizen.

"I'm working," I snapped.

She trotted closer, expertly balancing on her sky-high heels.

"Come on, Susanna. It's important. I'll buy you lunch." She tossed another glance around the store. "It's not like there's anyone here, anyway." She tipped a chin at Aileen. "That old lady can cover for you."

Aileen squinted at her with so much disdain, another drop and she'd set my twin sister on fire.

It might be best to get Mara out of here before a fight broke out. It had been slow today. Lunchtime was close. My stomach growled, and the food truck parked on the street corner called to me. I was not in the position to turn down a free lunch.

"Fine," I said to Mara. "But only if you're paying. Aileen, can I take a break, please?"

Aileen must want Mara out of her store badly, because she didn't even argue about me taking my lunch break early.

"Thirty minutes," she sneered.

"I'll wait for you outside." Mara strolled out the door while I got my purse and coat.

After I'd joined her outside, we got gyros from the food truck, then walked to a bench nearby.

"This is not a place for a Takolsky." She curled her lip in distaste.

Takolsky was her last name. It had been mine too, before I changed it to Tom's—less glamorous—Riley.

"Which place? The store? Or the bench?" I snorted.

She sounded like our father. He always had a firm opinion about all the suitable and unsuitable places for his family to be. And no, a second-rate fashion boutique would never be considered a proper place for one of his daughters to shop, not to mention to work. Come to think of it, this chipped, worn bench wouldn't be much to his liking, either.

"You know what I mean," she brushed me off. "This is not what you should be doing with your life, Susanna."

By "this," she meant having any form of gainful employment, of course. She tossed a disgusted look back at the boutique as if it were some dirty strip joint.

"Well, gyros cost money," I argued. "So does a place to live. And since all wealthy men in Manhattan are taken..." I waved a hand in the air and took a bite of my gyro. God, was it ever good! I stifled a moan of pleasure, savoring it. Lunch time had been the highlight of my day ever since I'd first discovered this food truck.

Mara neatly unwrapped the paper from one end of her gyro too. "You didn't even try to find a wealthy man. The moment Tom left, you were applying for jobs."

"I didn't really feel like trading one asshole for another, you know."

"Well...not all men are assholes," she said hesitantly. I looked at her cynically, and she faltered. "Fine. Maybe in this city, they are. But you don't need to stay here."

I'd been thinking about leaving. A new start would be nice. Except that Bolshoy's people would find me wherever I went.

"This thing with Tom and Jim will have to end one day," I said. "Then, I'll leave. Maybe."

Mara's expression grew somber. Bolshoy had been threatening her too.

"Do you think it will ever end?"

"I hope so." I sighed.

She crumpled her napkin, her hand trembling. "They said they would cut off my head."

With a spike of compassion, I patted her arm. "They say a lot of nasty things. But sooner or later, they must realize we have no money to give them."

She sniffled and took a bite of her gyro. I ate mine, too, in silence.

"Jason believes there are some legal steps I can take," she said after a little while.

"Who's Jason?"

She perked up. "Jason Moore. He's running for senate next year. Huge prospects."

"Is he one of the guys you've been dating?"

She nodded, brushing a long strand of hair behind her ear. It was blonde, just like mine, only Mara's was much better styled, of course.

"With him, it's getting serious, though." Her eyes lit up with hope. "I think he may propose soon."

"Congratulations," I said flatly.

It was hard to muster any excitement—another man with "huge prospects." We'd been there before.

"Anyway," she sounded enthusiastic, "I have a proposition for you."

"What kind?" I asked suspiciously. Historically, all of Mara's ideas had been largely self-serving.

"Two months ago, I applied for a marriage program," she said.

"What?" I did not expect that. "Like a dating app?"

"Not really. It comes with a bit more commitment than just dating. You practically need to stay with the guy for a year before you can leave."

I blinked at her. "Is that even legal? Why on earth would you agree to something like that?"

She rolled her eyes at me. "To get off planet, of course. Away from the mafia and their threats. To save my fucking head, Susanna."

"Off planet?" It dawned on me. "Please tell me you're not talking about one of those alien wife recruitment things?"

"Why not? What's so bad about marrying some powerful alien dude and jettisoning off to another planet where no thugs would ever find you?"

"Well, if you put it that way..."

It sounded tempting, to leave not just this city or this country but the entire freaking planet. Talk about a new start!

Except that it came with yet another man attached.

"Think about it," Mara continued, her enthusiasm building with every word. "No more looking over your shoulder. No more fear. No struggle, no working two jobs just to make ends meet."

"That'd be nice..." I brought my gyro up for another bite, then stopped, staring at her. "Wait a minute. Are you talking about me?"

She chomped at her gyro with the energy of biting someone's head off. "They matched me with one—"

"But you don't like him?"

That wouldn't be surprising; my sister wasn't easy to please. Her list of requirements for a man wasn't long, but it was very specific.

She threw her hands up in the air dramatically, half-eaten gyro clutched in one.

"Susanna, you have no idea. The guy is from Aldrai!"

Aldrai was one of the four populated planets Earth had made contact with in the past few years. Neron, Tragul, and Ivodi were the other three.

"So?" I shook my head.

"Have you seen the Aldraians? They're ugly as sin! The horns, the bumps..." She shuddered. "They say they have tails too. Only those must be the most disgusting things ever, since they hide them all the time."

"Why did you apply, then?" I shrugged. "You knew what they looked like, didn't you?"

She rolled her eyes again, then tossed her unfinished food into a nearby trash can, landing a perfect hit. I couldn't help but admire her aim.

"Besides," I added. "You should be able to either accept or decline a match. If you don't like him, say you don't want him. Swipe left, or whatever they do for that."

She hung her head between her shoulders. "Yeah, well... I already accepted it. A month ago, right when they matched me."

I stopped chewing my very delicious lunch to stare at her in shock. "Why?"

Mara leaped to her feet, clearly agitated. "I was scared, okay?" She plopped back on the bench next to me again. "I wanted to get out. I didn't even read the info they sent me about him. Besides, things weren't going that well with Jason back then. I didn't care."

That was so typical for my sister, doing whatever she wished at any given moment without thinking about the consequences.

"But now you care?"

She made a face at me, as if I were the one forcing the unwanted alien on her. "Things have changed. Jason is about to propose. If I leave, I'll mess it up between us."

"The mafia may get to you before Jason makes up his mind, you know," I pointed out.

She winced, drawing the ends of her coat closer together around her.

"They've kind of cooled off a bit, don't you think? I haven't seen anyone following me lately."

I hadn't been approached by anyone for a while, either. That didn't mean we hadn't been watched. Either that, or I'd been growing insane with paranoia. Living in constant fear sucked.

"Well, at least you have a chance to leave, now," I told her.

"No!" she yelled, as if I'd slapped her. "I can't possibly marry this alien guy."

"Why not? Just because of how he looks?" I knew my sister preferred handsome men, but she could be persuaded to overlook the flaws in a man's appearance if he had some valuable assets, like yachts or private jets.

"Susanna, he's some kind of truck driver!" she said dramatically, as if revealing to me that her match was a serial killer.

"Okay. But that could've been expected, couldn't it? I would imagine people of all walks of life would apply."

She wrung her hands, shaking her head.

"It's just my luck. The first human woman who participated in the program was matched with a Voranian from the planet Neron."

"Do you find Voranians more attractive than Aldraians?"

She curled her lips in disgust. "What? No. Voranians look like goats. Ravils are cute, but their planet, Tragul, doesn't have a marriage program with us." She heaved a heavy breath. "Ivodians are pretty good-looking too. But there has only been one Ivodian ship that came here for brides, and who knows when the next one would arrive. Anyway, that first woman from Earth got married to the head guy of the entire Voranian Army. She's like a celebrity in Voran now. And what do I get? A farmer! How unfair is that?"

"You said he was a truck driver." I finished my gyro and sighed, wishing it'd lasted longer.

"Same difference," she dismissed. "It states in his application he's a captain. I thought that meant he'd be a captain of a plane or a spaceship—"

"On spaceships, they call them commanders, I think." I opened my bottle of water and took a drink.

"Well, he drives some kind of machine they use to..." she waved both hands over the pavement, "...to turn dirt or something. Apparently, that qualifies him to call himself a captain." She sounded exasperated. "He drives a tractor for a living, Susanna. How can I possibly marry him? Me, Mara Takolsky! Dad would roll over in his grave if he knew."

Dad must've rolled a few times by now, from the moment his beloved protégé Tom turned out to be a thief and scoundrel, to all our possessions being sold at auction to cover some of the debt Tom and Jim had made in my and Mara's names.

"I can't be a farmer's wife!" Mara wailed. "I can't spend the rest of my life wearing housecoats, milking alien chickens, and taking care of his bratty kids."

"He has children?"

She faced me, her eyes wide in horror. "Four of them! Imagine that." She shook her head with another shudder. "It could be worse, I suppose, since Aldraian marriages are super prolific. They say they get like a dozen babies from each pregnancy."

"Why does he only have four, then?"

"I don't know. Who cares? Just be happy it's not twelve," she groaned, rubbing her forehead.

It definitely didn't sound like the lifestyle Mara would fit into. I felt sorry for her. But even more so, I felt sorry for the poor alien guy who would have to deal with her displeasure if she ever came to his planet.

"Can you get out of this?" I asked.

She looked outright miserable when she said, "No, I signed all the papers already."

"Because you believed him being a captain meant something more exciting than driving a truck?" I wasn't impressed with her lack of responsibility. Though, it didn't surprise me, either.

She pursed her lips as her chin trembled. "At the very least, I'd hoped that captain was a rank in the army. That he lived in the city. But Aldraians don't have any real cities. Even their capital looks like a bunch of hills." She sobbed, dabbing at her eyes with her napkin. "He lives in the countryside. Imagine me out in the country? On a farm?" A real tear rolled down her cheek, soaking into her napkin. "He's expecting me to board the ship to Aldrai next week." She gazed at me imploringly. "Susanna, I just can't do it..."

Oh, I knew that look well. And its meaning.

"So, you want me to do it for you? Is that why you came here?"

She clasped her hands, pressing them to her chest. "Could you please? It'd be a win-win solution. For everyone."

I arched an eyebrow. "Would it, now?"

"Look..." She perked up, her tears drying up instantly. "What do you have to lose? A shitty job or two and an equally shitty apartment."

My sister had never been to my apartment, but she was obviously familiar with the housing situation in New York. It was no secret one couldn't afford much of a place working retail jobs, no matter how many of them one had.

"So, you think I'd do just fine as a farmer's wife and raising four kids?" I asked skeptically.

She scooted closer to me along the bench. "We both know you have more patience than me. You've been working in that clothing store for months now. Personally, I would've scratched the eyes out of that old crone at the cash register long ago. But you keep taking every pissed-off look she gives you."

"I need that job to pay my rent."

"Exactly! That's what I mean," she exclaimed cheerfully. "You adapt easily. You accept the situation, no matter how shitty it is."

"That's not a compliment," I noted, unimpressed.

She just waved her hand again. "You know what I mean. You're also much better with kids. You wanted some of your own, remember? With Tom?"

Right. I had. Until I found out he'd had a vasectomy back in college and never bothered to tell me, even after we'd both agreed I would get off the pill and start trying for a family.

I heaved a sigh. There had been so many lies in my eleven-month marriage. Now it felt like there hadn't been even a shred of truth.

"Oh, and you were always so nice to our little cousin Billy, too, when all I wanted was to rip the brat's head off," Mara continued. "Could you do it, please? For me?"

Her pleading tone brought up the memories of so many other times I'd taken her place before. Like every time she'd failed a school test I'd passed. She'd beg the teacher for a retake, then send me to take it for her. The dates she'd promise to go on but then change her mind. The group meetings in college she found too boring to attend.

We looked so much alike people could only tell us apart by the clothes we wore, and switching clothes was easy.

Sometimes, it'd been fun to pretend I was my twin, since my own social life wasn't nearly as vibrant as Mara's. Other times, she would manage to make me feel sorry for her.

Now...

"It's not just a date, Mara. I'd have to live with that man as his wife."

"But it's only for a year, according to the contract," she said quickly. "After that, you can say it's not for you and come back. A lot can happen in a year, right? They may find Tom and Jim by then and recoup what they stole. Or Bolshoy could finally get it through his thick head that we don't have his money and leave us alone. And don't worry about the wife part." She wiggled her eyebrows with added meaning in her eyes. "The alien dude doesn't want sex."

"What?" That was weird. "Did he just say it like that?"

She shrugged. "Pretty much. It states right in his application. That was one of the reasons I signed the contract in the first place. I mean, who would ever want to have sex with an Aldraian, right?"

"I don't know. I've never seen one."

"Lucky you." She made a face as if she'd bitten into something sour. "Anyway, you can fuck him if you wish for all I care, but trust me, that no-sex clause is a blessing."

I pondered everything she'd told me so far. The man's situation started to intrigue me, bringing questions. "Why does he need a wife, then? If he doesn't want sex? And what happened to the mother of his children?"

"She died. Years ago. His kids need a mother. He has two daughters...blah, blah, blah..." She took a drink from her water bottle. "Being a stepmom is so not my thing. I prefer the role of Cinderella with Prince Charming and the cool shoes."

"How about the hard work and abuse part of Cinderella's story?" I snorted, unable to picture Mara humble and industrious.

"Yeah, no," she dismissed. "I don't need any of that. I've had my struggles. I'm about to land my very own Prince Charming, who already buys me a lot of fancy shoes. I can't leave Jason for some alien farmer-ogre with a bunch of bratty kids. Can't you understand, Susanna? Please help me."

I bit my lip, mulling over her proposal.

I held no illusions; Mara's motives were purely self-serving. She didn't care if I worked myself to death at as many jobs as twenty-four hours a day would allow me. She wouldn't be here if there weren't benefits for her. But she was right. There were some advantages in her plan for me too.

I'd never worked with kids before, but it couldn't be much harder than serving the cranky, well-to-do women with superiority complexes who were Aileen's customers.

A change could be good for me, considering the circumstances.

And yes, getting away from Bolshoy and his people would be a huge bonus.

"Maybe I should consider applying myself?" I wondered out loud.

Mara gasped. "Why would you do that? When I already found one for you?"

I shook my head. "I would go on my own, Mara. As myself. But I'm not going to pretend to be you."

"Well, that can't happen, Susanna." She spread her arms, staring at me in disbelief. "The ship is leaving next week. I got the ticket for it this morning. All documents are done in my name. The papers are signed. What difference does it make whether you go as me or you? No one would know, anyway. We look so alike, our own mother couldn't tell us apart."

Maybe if our mother had spent more time with us instead of letting a bunch of nannies raise us, she would've found it easier to tell us apart. Instead, she made us wear color-coded clothes—pink for Mara, purple for me. Though, I'd always liked pink more.

"To aliens, humans all look the same already," Mara insisted. "But with us, we could alternate sleeping with him, and the guy would still think he only has one wife."

I kept shaking my head.

"Maybe, if you could bring me along—"

"Susanna!" She slapped her knees impatiently. "Are you really that dumb? Or are you just not listening to me? I don't want to bring you along. I don't want to bring anyone. I don't want to go! I want you to go instead of me."

"I'm afraid I can't help you with that, Mara."

She groaned in frustration. "But why? What do you have to lose?"

Mara was right. I had nothing left other than the seventeen dollars in my account that had to last until my next paycheck.

I'd lied for Mara before. However, I'd also been lied to, a lot. Lately, it seemed my entire life had been nothing but lies. And I was tired of it.

"I'm not pretending anymore, Mara. I'm trying to give an honest life a shot, here."

She gazed at me with so much disappointment, like she'd caught me committing a fashion crime. "Oh, you're stupider than I thought."

I was getting tired of her insults too.

"You know what? Maybe you should try to clean up your own mess, for once. Honor your commitments."

"Great." Mara scoffed. "Now, you're talking about honor. How very grand of you." She got up, hanging her overpriced and over-hyped bag on her arm. "I hope you enjoyed your gyro. Who knows where your next meal is going to come from?"

Watching her leave was a relief.

Maybe it was a mistake to turn down the opportunity to leave Earth and all my troubles behind. But I'd be going to another planet, pretending to be my sister, pretending to be interested in making a fake marriage work. I'd be living a lie. Again.

I couldn't do that to the unsuspecting alien truck driver. But more importantly, I couldn't do it to myself. I had nothing left in this life but my integrity. Giving that up would truly leave me with nothing.

"Well," I said to the pigeons that were scouring the pavement for crumbs, "maybe I should look into that marriage program myself. What do you think?"

However, the thought of putting myself out there in search of a romantic relationship made me sick to my stomach. I had given it my all with Tom, and I had nothing left to give to another man, either human or alien.

Chapter 2

Susanna

My phone rang the moment I opened the freezer that night in search of yet another frozen creation for my dinner. I bought enough in bulk each paycheck to last until the next one. Budgeting was an important skill I'd never needed to learn before but had mastered it quickly now.

Glancing at the screen, I saw it was my sister. Wondering what she wanted this time, I hit the green button.

"Mara?"

"Susannaaaaa!" Her loud wail almost made me drop the phone. She sounded as if she was being murdered.

I yanked it away from my ear, shoving the freezer door shut.

"What's going on? Mara? Are you okay?"

"They sent me his head!" she bellowed.

"What head? Who?"

Was she drunk?

"The mafia!" she screeched. "They shipped Jim's head to me."

I stared at the rusty scratch on the fridge's door, stupefied.

"Just the head?"

"Yes!" she yelled hysterically. "He's dead!"

"Holy sh..." I sank onto the threadbare pull-out couch that also served as my bed. "They cut off his head?"

"Yes! They said I'm next..." The last words were drowned by her loud sobs.

My hand covered my mouth in horror.

This couldn't be happening.

"Are you sure it's *his?*"

"Of course I'm sure! I know my fiancé, head to toe. Oh, this is so gross," she wailed. "He has a bad sunburn on his nose. Do you know how gross sunburn looks on a dead body?"

"No, I don't." And, frankly, I didn't want to know. I should feel sorry for Jim. He wasn't even thirty years old yet, but he'd brought it on himself. In the process, he'd gotten my sister entangled in this mess too. Right now, all I felt toward Jim was anger. "Did you call the police? Or that Jason guy of yours?"

"No." She broke into tears again. "I'm calling you."

"Why me? What the hell am I supposed to do about a dead...head?"

"They said they'd kill me if I went to the cops. I don't know what to do, Susannaaaaa," she bawled loudly.

"I really don't know, either." I wished so badly I didn't feel as helpless as I was at that moment.

"You're my sister!" Mara's tone turned demanding. It'd been two decades since we were toddlers, yet my sister still believed she could get anything she wanted in life just by throwing a tantrum. "You're in a very similar situation, too, you know."

"Am I?"

We'd both been lied to and manipulated by the men we thought we could trust. In that respect, Mara was right. We were in exactly the same situation.

Someone knocked on my door. Loudly.

To my already strained nerves, the sound came like a gunshot. I jumped on the couch, jolting in fear.

"Someone is at the door," I whispered, crouching to hide behind the armrest as if they could see me through the door.

"Don't open it," Mara whispered back.

Of course I wouldn't. But the door was so flimsy, a good kick would be all it took to break in.

"It won't stop them from getting in," I whimpered, scared out of my wits.

Another knock shattered the silence of my musty-smelling living space.

"Delivery!" a male voice yelled from behind the door.

"Don't fall for it," Mara urged me.

As if I would!

Thankfully, next came the sound of footsteps going up the concrete stairs back to the street level.

"He left," I informed Mara over the phone.

"Are you sure?"

I wasn't, but what would be the point for whoever it was to stay at my door after pretending to leave? If Bolshoy wished to get rid of me, his thugs could easily kick the door in and wring my neck, shower this place with bullets, cement my feet in a bucket of concrete, or whatever gory things the mafia did to those who wronged them.

Carefully, I creeped to the door, staying low. Keeping the chain on the door, I cracked it open.

There wasn't a soul behind my door, just a cardboard box on my worn, rubber doormat.

"There's a box," I told Mara.

"What is it? Did you order something?" she asked.

The cardboard box was a perfect cube, like something one would ship a soccer ball in. Or...one's husband's severed head.

"You're next!" was written in red letters on the side of the box.

I slammed the door shut.

Bile rose in my throat, my knees weakening. Clasping the phone in my hand, I leaned against the door, then slid down to the floor.

"Susanna?"

The musty air of my apartment suddenly proved impossible to breathe. It rushed in and out of me in pants.

"Mara, we need to get out of this city... Out of the state... The country... The planet. Did you decline that ticket to Aldrai?"

"No, I couldn't decline. It's too late. But I asked Jason to do something about it today. He has connections high up in the government—"

"Call him right now; ask him not to do anything." I scraped a hand over my face, trying to collect my thoughts scattered by panic. "No. Ask him to get a second ticket. For me."

"Are you going?" She sounded shocked.

"Yes. We both are. Tell them you need to bring a companion for moral support, to help with the kids, or whatever—"

"But, Susanna, I can't go, remember?" Mara whined. "Jason is about to propose. I *feel* it—"

"Jason won't propose to a dead woman, will he? And you *will* be dead if you stay here."

I would be dead too. My thoughts whizzed back to the box outside and the words written in something suspiciously red on it.

"You're next!"

Another bout of nausea rose in my throat.

"We're getting out of here, Mara. We have to. The sooner, the better. And as far as we can."

Chapter 3

Susanna

"Is this what you're going to wear?" Mara critically eyed the clothes I'd laid out on my bunk.

I rubbed the back of my neck, stretching my shoulders. We'd woken up from our five-month-long cryosleep yesterday. I still tried to work out the stiffness from my muscles and get my joints moving the way they should.

"This." I pointed at my knee-length black-and-white dress. "Classic is good, right?"

Mara curled her lip, obviously unimpressed. "You know they invented 'classic look' for poor people who can't afford to buy the latest fashion every season. 'Vintage style' is for those who shop second-hand, by the way. Like there's any class or style in wearing someone else's used clothes."

I just shrugged. "I am 'poor people' now, remember? You are too, by the way. We had to borrow the money for the second ticket."

"I'm *not* poor!" she scoffed. "I may be temporarily down on my luck, but I might've solved the situation by now, had you not dragged me away from Jason."

I closed my eyes, taking a deep breath and calling on my patience. It'd been less than twenty-four hours of us sharing the spaceship cabin, and I already felt like jumping the ship to escape my sister's company.

Thankfully, we'd spent most of the journey cryogenically frozen. Five months in this close of quarters would've been real torture.

"Mara, I convinced you to get away from the bad guys with guns and knives who were literally after our heads. If Jason really cares about you, he must be happy you're alive. And he'll wait for your safe return when things calm down a bit."

She brushed me off with a regal gesture of her hand. "Fine. Whatever. We're getting off this space tin can soon. Some very important people will be meeting us at the spaceport. Government representatives, I imagine. It's not every day that Earthlings visit Aldrai. It's kind of a big deal for them there. The first impression is everything." She raised her chin and declared with pathos, "You're representing Earth, Susanna."

"Why can't I represent it while wearing this dress?" I pointed at the outfit on my bunk bed.

"Listen, we may be..." her lips quivered, "...*poor*. At the moment. But there's no need to broadcast that to every alien out there. Fake it until you make it." She cocked her hip with a glamorous flip of her hair over her shoulder. It was impossible not to admire her confidence. Then she tossed a reproachful look at the offensive garment I was about to wear. "This isn't even Chanel."

I had sold all the clothes that Mara would find acceptable. All I had left were the outfits I'd worn to work. These were still decent enough pieces, but of course, they all were way below Mara's impossibly high standards.

"Do you honestly think the Aldraians will be able to tell the difference between a Chanel dress and this one?" I asked.

She propped her hands on her hips.

"Maybe they can. It's awfully presumptuous of you to assume all aliens are complete savages. A few may be civilized enough to appreciate a decent outfit." She rummaged through one of her suitcases. The cabin was too small to accommodate all her luggage. We'd only managed to fit two of the dozen or so bags she'd brought.

"Since you're going to be seen with me, I need to salvage this somehow. Maybe we could at least dress it up a little? Take these shoes, these sunglasses..." She handed me the items as she took them out of her bags.

"We don't have time to do anything about your hair, but here..." She pulled out a pearl-gray scarf. "Hermes. Pure silk."

She tied the scarf around my head, letting the ends drape down my back, then propped a pair of sunglasses on my nose.

"Voilà! You look like a blonde Audrey Hepburn. Chubbier than her, but still *classic*, just like you wanted."

I let the "chubby" comment slide. Mara and I had worn the same size clothes all our lives. Yet she never failed to emphasize my "extra" weight.

I glanced in the narrow mirror on the door of the cabin. One thing my sister was really good at was creating "the look." If I tied the scarf over my head, I'd look like a babushka from middle-ages Russia. When she did it... Well, it looked classy.

"Thanks," I muttered.

"You're welcome. I can't let my own sister embarrass me in front of the entire alien planet, now, can I?"

THE MASSIVE METAL DOORS of our spaceship opened, and the wide ramp descended for us to disembark. A puff of fragrant air rushed in. It smelled like freshly cut grass and exotic flowers—a scent I hadn't smelled in like...well, never. This was an entirely new planet, after all.

Bright sunlight burst through. I adjusted Mara's sunglasses on my nose, taking a step out of the ship to follow the human representatives of the Liaison Committee who came on the ship with us.

It was a warm, sunny day, with our spaceship landing in the middle of a meadow with artfully arranged hedges and flower beds. Green and colorful, the space hardly looked like a spaceport.

"It's pretty here," I whispered to Mara as the two of us tottered down the ramp in our high heels.

"Oh no!" she gasped, staring at the group waiting for us on the stone path below. "They're even uglier in person."

The Aldraians ranged in color from pale wood to dark walnut and every earthy shade in between. There was a clear difference between male and female Aldraians. The women were closer in appearance to humans, except for the three pairs of breasts in the front. They had no horns, and their long hair closely matched the color of their skin. All the women present were pleasant to look at.

Mara's comment must've been about the males. Huge and muscular, they could be easily mistaken for rock formations. The hard lines and corners of their bodies made them appear as if roughly hewn from pieces of granite. I wouldn't call them outright ugly, but they sure looked different.

As I studied the Aldraians, they all turned toward us. Their scrutinizing gazes weighed heavily on my shoulders. I straightened my back and adjusted my sunglasses.

"Fake it until you make it," I repeated Mara's words in my head, calling on whatever confidence I possessed.

The group included a non-Aldraian. Slightly smaller than them, he was covered in dark-gray fur. He had long, slightly curved horns and a pair of hooves instead of feet—a Voranian from the planet Neron.

He moved his gaze from me to my sister, then back again. I guessed his confusion. We both wore sunglasses. But even if we didn't, I doubted he would be able to tell who was who. The man clearly needed help.

I quickly touched my hand to the now fully healed scar behind my ear, the place where the translator had been implanted. On Earth, only those involved in interplanetary travel had them. However, people from other planets usually had the translators implanted from birth. All of those standing in front of us must have them too.

"She's Mara Takolsky." I flipped my thumb at Mara. "I'm Susanna Riley, her sister."

"Oh, you're the nanny," he stated politely.

Was that what I was?

To obtain the ticket for me, we had to give the reasons for my accompanying my sister. One was to help her look after the children of her new husband.

I guessed I could try to be a nanny. As long as I remained far away from Bolshoy's people and my head remained on my shoulders.

"I'm the nanny," I confirmed.

The furry man with hooves took my sister's hand in both of his.

"Welcome to Aldrai, Madam Xavran Rax," he addressed her by her new married name. "I'm Alcus Hecear, the Voranian representative of the Liaison Committee."

Mara arranged her features into a magazine-shot worthy expression. "It's so very nice to meet you," she cooed.

Alcus Hecear got hold of my hand next, enclosing it between his in a similar manner. As he bowed his head, I shrank back a little, afraid of being stabbed by his long horns.

"Welcome, Nanny Susanna Riley."

"Thank you." I returned his bow with an incline of my head. Like the Aldraians, this man was unusual looking. But his manners were polite and friendly. "I'm glad to be here."

"Allow me to introduce Madam Councilor Vrux," he said. "She's the head official of the Aldraian branch of our Liaison Committee."

An Aldraian woman with a high, dark-brown ponytail smiled at us. "Welcome to our planet. I hope you like it here."

"Thank you." Mara gave her a polite half-smile.

"It's so beautiful," I said, sweeping the green hills around us with another appreciative glance.

"It is," Alcus Hecear agreed. "Aldrai is a gorgeous planet. Its people have been working hard on making it so."

Councilor Vrux added, "If you need anything at all, you can contact me either directly or through Captain Rax." She gestured at a man who'd been watching us from a distance.

He stepped forward. This one was possibly the biggest one of them all. I had to tilt my head back to see his face as he approached.

"Allow me to introduce your husband in person, Madam Rax," Alcus Hecear announced in a formal tone. "Captain Xavran Rax."

"Oh..." Mara stared at the Aldraian through her sunglasses.

I did too.

With skin the color of pearl-gray granite, he looked like a golem carved from a piece of a mountain. Several horns graced his head, forming a sort of crown. His eyes were dark, almost black, hiding his expression as effectively as our sunglasses did.

"Well, hi." Mara finally found her words. "How do you do?"

"I'm well, thank you." He tipped his head swaying his crown of horns.

"Um, hi..." was all I could manage to say.

There was strength in his appearance, a power I wished I could lean into. Like he would rip off the heads of anyone who'd dare to wrong his loved ones. It made me want to inch closer to him, for safety...

I blinked, shaking off the out-of-place fantasy.

The captain was a large man. That was all I really knew about him so far.

He was dressed casually, in a tan-colored shirt with leather buckles on the shoulders and on the sides, a pair of dark-brown pants, and light shoes. A pair of beige bracers with rows of bumps on the back enclosed his forearms.

"This couldn't possibly be the entire welcoming crowd." Mara gestured at about a dozen Aldraians meeting us. "Where is the main ceremony taking place?"

The captain rolled back his massive shoulders decorated with clusters of short horns and bumps. "I requested no ceremony."

Mara's face fell, her expectant expression leaving it. "No ceremony? But..."

Dressed in her finest, Mara was quite a sight. She could easily grace covers of any high fashion magazine on Earth. I understood her disappointment at not being able to show it all off to a larger crowd.

"There's no time for that nonsense," the captain said gruffly. "We need to get back before the kids come home from school."

"Oh, right... The kids." She sighed, then added softly for only me to hear, "How banal and prosaic."

He turned to face me next. "Greetings, Madam Riley."

I tried not to fidget under the gaze of his dark eyes. "Just Susanna, please. You can call me by my first name if you wish."

"Thanks," he replied rather flatly.

Mara pursed her lips, obviously displeased about missing out on the party she believed she was owed.

"My aircraft is that way." The captain gestured to the left with a hand the size of a shovel.

"You have a plane?" Mara's voice lifted with obvious interest. Maybe not all was lost for her with this "farmer." "Do you own a jet?"

"A jet?" With a brief nod to the Voranian and the Aldraians, the captain headed down a cobblestone path toward a tall hedge to the left.

Mara trotted after him. "Well, what do you call a private airplane here?"

I followed them.

"An aircraft," he repeated. "I have two. One is for me. One for my nanny."

"Me?" My mouth fell open. Why did a nanny need a private jet?

Mara stopped in her tracks suddenly. "Hey! What about our things? Our luggage?"

The captain didn't slow down, leaving me unsure whether to remain with her or keep walking with him.

He glanced back at us over his shoulder.

"The luggage from your cabin has already been loaded into my aircraft. Three suitcases." He lifted a hand with three long thick fingers outstretched.

"Just three?" She stomped her foot.

He stopped, turning around. "Are there more?"

"Of course there are more!" She threw her hands up in the air. "I came here for a year, not a weekend."

He lifted one heavy eyebrow ridge. "It'll have to be delivered later, then. I've no space for more."

"Not enough space?" she retorted. "What kind of jet is it?"

His broad chest rose with a deep breath. I wondered if he was counting in his head to calm down before speaking. That was what I often did when dealing with Mara or with cranky customers.

"I never said I have a *jet*, whatever that word means to you," he said slowly. "I have a personal aircraft with limited cargo space and no time to unload any more luggage. It'll have to be delivered later."

His argument was valid. Sadly, Mara had never been one to respond to the voice of reason.

"When?" She wouldn't give up.

This time, however, her tantrums appeared to be no match for the captain's stubbornness. He calmly turned around and proceeded down the path.

"Later," he tossed over his shoulder. "You'll have to make do with what you have."

Mara's chest rose and fell rapidly, her hands fisted at her sides. Clearly, she was not used to this attitude from men. I expected her to yell at him, but maneuvering the cobblestone path in her stiletto heels stole her concentration for a moment. Cobblestones never went well with high heels.

The captain moved fast, pumping those thick, muscular legs of his. Mara and I had a hard time keeping up.

"Is there a problem?" He glanced over his shoulder to see what was holding us back.

Shifting his gaze down to our shoes, he frowned, but slowed down enough for us to catch up.

We turned around the hedge, entering a field of colorful objects parked in neat rows. They looked like large birds with their wings folded. As we approached one, I realized it was a vehicle with a glass cabin in the front.

The captain pressed a button on one of his arm bracers, and a glass panel slid open on the side of the green-yellow-and-purple vehicle right in front of us.

"These are so pretty—" Gaping at the colorful aircraft, I lost focus on the cobblestones. My heel slid, getting trapped in a gap. Knocked off balance, I lurched forward, flailing my arms.

With a curse under his breath, the captain grabbed me around my waist, saving me from falling on my face.

"What are those stupid things you're wearing on your feet?" he grumped, his huge arm clamped around me from behind. "We'll never get out of here at this rate."

He lifted me off my feet.

"Oh!" I made a choked sound, too shocked to protest.

He heaved me under his arm, my shoe dangling from my toes.

"Here." He offered his other hand to Mara. "Hold on to me."

Wide-eyed, she took one look at me hanging over his arm as if I were no heavier than a cat and didn't argue. She silently grabbed onto his other hand for support and trotted alongside the captain toward his vehicle.

"You'll get in here." He lightly shoved her toward the open side panel, pointing at the back seat next to our suitcases piled inside on top of each other.

Then he carried me to the other side and opened the panel there. "And you go in here." He deposited me into the cushy seat inside, then climbed into the driver's seat next to me. "We'll be home in less than two hours. Buckle your seatbelts, ladies."

Chapter 4

Xavran

If he didn't know Stefan, his male nanny from Earth, he would've thought humans were unbearable. He might've even sent these two back. But since he got along well with Stefan, he figured there was hope for the females too.

Somehow, in the process of stuffing them both into the aircraft, he'd lost track of who was who. They were wearing slightly different clothes, but he rarely paid attention to fashion. And now he couldn't remember. Was the chatty one in the back his new wife? Or the clumsy one sitting next to him?

Not that it mattered much. He hoped for an amicable, working relationship with both women, but nothing more than that with either.

They were both now quiet. Even the chatty one sat quietly behind him, probably sulking that he'd left their cargo behind.

How much stuff did a human female need to survive? He hoped they weren't considerably less resilient than their male counterparts. The last thing he needed was to hire a bunch of caretakers for his new wife and nanny.

He slid a glance at the one sitting next to him. Taking her shoe off, she inspected it. She appeared to be frowning, judging by her creased forehead and pursed lips. The giant black eyeglasses concealed the rest of her face.

"An extremely impractical choice of footwear," he voiced an observation.

She fingered a tiny scratch on the absurdly high heel of the shoe. "I'm afraid I have to agree with you on that one."

Their conversation caught the attention of the woman in the back.

"Did you ruin my Louboutins?" she hissed, leaning forward.

"It's just a small scratch," the clumsy one replied apologetically, rubbing at the scratch as if hoping to erase it from the shiny leather. "I'm sure it can be fixed."

"Yeah? And do you see a shoe repair place anywhere here?" The chatty one attacked her sister.

He felt sorry for the clumsy one, who kept fingering the scratch.

"We have skillful cobblers in Diria. They'll fix it in no time," he offered. "Or better yet, they'll make you a pair of better shoes," he couldn't help adding.

Impractical footwear wasn't an exclusively human habit. Some Aldraian women in Arqa, the capital city of Aldrai, wore weirdly shaped shoes too. Not that he approved of that silliness, either.

"Better shoes?" the chatty one scoffed, sounding defensive. "Better than Louboutin?"

"What's *Louboutin?*" The highly sophisticated translating system that flawlessly conveyed the meaning of foreign metaphors, idioms, and even slang, failed to translate that word. Which only confirmed what he already knew—the chatty one spoke a lot of nonsense.

"Mara, come on," the clumsy one reprimanded her sister, and the one in the back settled down with a huff.

If the chatty one was Mara, his new wife, then the one next to him must be the nanny.

She turned to him. "It's not important. Louboutin is just another word for these shoes."

Just what he thought—gibberish.

He steered the aircraft out of the city and laid a course home, back to Diria.

Both women silently stared out the glass cockpit. This part of Aldrai was beautiful. He loved seeing it too. The rolling green hills and bountiful flowers that bloomed year round were the results of efforts from generations of his ancestors.

Like his forefathers, he took pride in his work, terraforming the inhospitable desert to the south. He did his part in transforming the desert into luscious green landscapes like the one below.

"What a gorgeous planet," the nanny marveled.

"I never get tired of looking at it myself," he admitted.

"I heard you don't build houses?" Mara enquired.

"Not in the sense that people on other planets do. But we do put a lot of work into our living spaces."

They fell silent again. After a while, both women appeared to be dozing off to the soft, monotonous whirring of the engines.

He threw a furtive glance at the nanny slumping in the seat next to him. Leaning against the glass, she appeared to be asleep. Light-colored wisps of hair made their way out from under the cloth on her head. He couldn't help a glance at her stomach. It looked odd without the extra two pairs of breasts that the Aldraian women had.

She'd probably find him odd too. Probably ugly as well. There was a reason Aldraian-human marriages had been predominantly those of human men with Aldraian females. Generally, other races didn't find Aldraian males visually appealing, thinking them too large, too crudely shaped, and overall too awkward.

He wondered if specifying that he didn't want sex in his marriage helped him secure the match as fast as it did.

Either way, he was looking forward to finally having some female help. With his two girls heading into their teens in a couple of years, it'd be good to have a mother figure to guide them through the transition to womanhood. He often felt over his head on his own, especially as far as female matters were concerned.

Diria came into view. The sheltered town hall in the center was surrounded by open garden homes as far as the eye could see. His home was on the very edge of the town, the closest one to the lake.

He brought the aircraft lower, then landed it in front of the gate. The landing was as soft as it could be, but the slight jolt from the aircraft's contact with the ground woke the females up.

"Are we there?" The nanny tried to rub her eyes, clearly forgetting she had the glasses on. She knocked them off, and they landed in his lap.

"Sorry..." She grabbed for them, groping his cock through the fabric of his pants in the process. "Oh!" She dropped the glasses back on his crotch, her cheeks flushed crimson.

The sensation of her fingers groping him jolted through his body with a charge of heat. His heart pumped faster for a beat or two. He forced the excitement down just in time before his cock rose and pushed her glasses up.

"Here." He picked up the glasses and handed them to her.

"I'm so sorry," she exhaled, meeting his eyes. Hers were clear blue, like the sky.

"Lovely," he couldn't help thinking.

"What's your name?" he heard himself ask.

They had been introduced, but all the names were scrambled in his brain at the moment. Besides, he wanted to hear her voice again. This one didn't speak nearly as much as the other woman.

She cleared her throat. "It's Susanna."

"Susanna," he repeated.

He liked how her name slid off his tongue. It brought the sensation of having a piece of sweet dessert in his mouth.

She bent over to put her shoe back on.

"Leave it." He pushed the buttons to open both side panels. "Take the other one off too. We walk barefoot in our homes."

Chapter 5

Susanna

I'd thought the planet was gorgeous from the air. But up close, Aldrai simply blew my mind. The captain's place was incredible. There was no house! None at all. The gate led us into beautiful live gardens separated by tall hedges.

The captain took us along a path of cobblestones made from rubberlike material. It compressed slightly under my weight, massaging my bare feet.

"Your room is here, Susanna." The captain opened a lattice gate draped with live flower garlands.

I walked through the gate as he took Mara farther down the path to her "room."

The space I'd entered looked every bit a magical garden from a fairy tale, surrounded by dark green hedges with lime green vines of colorful flowers. Some "flowers" took off as I approached, turning out to be flying insects with colorful wings and flowing tails. I stilled, and they settled back down, one by one.

"This is just..." I laughed to myself. "So beautiful!"

I spun in a circle, taking in my new living space. There were no rugs or cobblestones here. Instead, luscious green grass tickled between my toes.

A large bed stood on a wide, flat mound in the middle. The trunks of four tall trees served as bedposts. Their thick, green canopies provided cool shade. Long branches swayed softly in a breeze above, and I could only imagine how comfortable the sleep here would be.

I felt like a forest fairy in this fantastical space.

The bathroom was yet another open space, with a pond for a tub filled by a series of waterfalls cascading from an artfully constructed rock wall.

"Wow!" I whistled to myself. "This is just beyond words."

The water was nice and warm to the touch. I wished I could rip my clothes off and dive in. But I felt I should at least speak to our host first, to thank him and to ask what was expected of me. After all, I was a nanny here, not a guest.

I also needed to return Mara's shoes to her before she started missing them and got too cranky.

I left my suitcase behind another lattice partition in a space with shelves that looked like a closet. Then I grabbed Mara's heels and headed out of my "room."

Cool, silky grass felt much nicer under my feet than any shoes ever would. I stepped onto the path outside the gate and watched the cobblestones compress under my feet.

"I could certainly get used to this," I muttered under my breath.

I took a few bouncy steps in the direction where the captain had taken Mara.

My attention was on my feet as I walked and...slammed full speed into a wall. In a place with hedges, I hadn't expected a hard, massive wall to rise suddenly in my path.

The impact was crushing.

"Oomph!" I staggered back.

The wall turned out to be the wide, hard chest of the master of this place.

"Careful." The captain grabbed me by my arms, stopping me from falling backwards.

"God, my head is ringing." I flattened my hand over my forehead. "Why are you so hard?" I poked his chest with a finger.

I must've hurt my head badly. Why else would I poke a stranger? Especially one as unapproachable as the captain appeared to be.

Especially after I'd accidentally groped him in the aircraft.

The thought immediately turned my face burning hot. The memory of his thick length in my fingers rushed into my mind uninvited.

"That's a lot of dick for one man."

Why, oh why was I thinking about his dick?

And now, I couldn't look him in the eye.

He remained in my path.

"It's hereditary. The males in my family tend to be larger than average," he said. It took me a moment to realize he was replying to my question. "Lots of physical labor also doesn't make me any softer."

At least he sounded at ease, unaffected by my awkwardness.

I ventured to lift my eyes to his face. Like the rest of him, his facial features appeared hard and angular, as if chiseled from a slab of rock. I wondered if all of him was solid like that. His dick had felt thick but not overly hard when I grabbed it.

"Why am I still thinking about that?" I groaned inwardly.

His dark eyes remained unreadable as he stared at me. But his lips stretched into a smirk. It could hardly be called a smile, just a shift of his mouth slightly to one side. I didn't find it hideous at all. It made him seem more approachable, almost as if he were inviting conversation.

"Lots of physical labor? Of course," I said. "You work in the fields, right? On a farm?"

I could totally imagine him hauling rocks around or uprooting trees. All those muscles of his could surely handle that type of work.

He crossed his arms over his chest, making his biceps bulge out in a nearly illicit manner.

"I work in a desert on the frontier. Or at least I used to until last year. That's actually something I need to speak with you about. Would you care to join me in the kitchen?" He gestured in the direction behind me.

"I was going to return these to Mara." I lifted the pumps in my hand. I realized this was basically admitting I had no suitable shoes of my own and had to borrow from my sister. It was embarrassing. But it was also true.

"They're hers?" He squinted at the shoes, looking at them as if they were a pair of dead frogs. "Leave them here. Mara wanted to rest after the flight, anyway. No need to disturb her."

"Alright." I dropped the shoes by the gate to my room.

The captain headed down the path. "Are you hungry? I'll make you something to eat."

That was new. No one had ever fed me unless I paid them.

I followed him into yet another open space. This one had a long, heavy table in the middle with a round counter to the side. There was something that looked like a grill and another intricate water feature, which served as a kitchen sink, I imagined. Some of the things on the shelves above it, I didn't even try to name or place.

"Sit down." He pointed at one of the massive log chairs by the table. "Do you eat meat?"

I nodded.

"How about grains? Bread?" he asked.

I nodded again.

He opened a large wooden door built into a tall, grassy hill next to the counter and appeared to lead underground. From one of the many narrow shelves on the inside of the door, the captain took out a terra-cotta jar and a basket wrapped in cloth.

From the basket, he produced a loaf of light-brown bread and cut off a slice, then put a few strips of meat from the jar on it.

"Eat." He slid the open-face sandwich to me. "Humans need to eat more often than Aldraians do."

"How do you know?" I took a bite. "Oooh, this is good." The bread had a grainy texture, and the meat tasted like cured cold cuts, juicy with marinade.

He smirked again. I guessed smirks were all he had in terms of smiles. Not that I minded. They were still better than frowns.

"Pickled *cuqrel* and *vehnun* bread," he said. "It's good that you like it because it's one of the staple foods on Aldrai. Easy to find anywhere and nutritious for both humans and Aldraians."

"How do you know what's good for humans?" I took another, much bigger bite of the sandwich. Space travel had left me starving, and the hunger grew stronger as I ate.

The captain poured two glasses of water, one for me and one for himself. He then took a seat across the table from me. "I did some research on your kind before deciding to apply for a human wife. Also, my current nanny is human."

"She is?" That was unexpected. "You already have a nanny?" Wasn't that supposed to be *my* job here?

"*He,*" he corrected. "My nanny is a man."

"A man?" I took a drink of my water to wash down the sandwich. "A bit unusual, but not impossible, of course."

"Stefan came here under the marriage program like your sister," he explained. "He's the husband of one of our Town Councilors."

"So, are you going to have two nannies, then?" I'd be more than happy to let Stefan take over completely. As far as kids minding went, I felt way out of my element.

"No. Stefan's quitting. His wife is pregnant. They're expecting her to go into labor by the end of next month. As of next week, Stefan wants to look after her full time. I was going to search for his replacement, but then your request to join your sister came in, just in time."

"Just in time..." I echoed.

My thoughts flashed back to that horrible night when Tom's severed head was delivered to my door. After ending the call with Mara, I'd called the police while she got a hold of Jason. I'd only caught a flash of Tom's russet hair, mussed and smeared with blood, when the police officer had opened the box. But it was enough for the image to haunt me ever since.

"Thank you so much for allowing me to come," I said sincerely. "You'll never know how much it means to me. To both Mara and me."

He tilted his head.

"You're welcome. I wouldn't want to deny my wife the company of her sister. Moving planets comes with many challenges and adjustments. It helps to have the support of a loved one. I know multiple pregnancies are rare on Earth, and twins tend to grow especially close."

"Right." I decided not to point out that every norm came with exceptions, and twins didn't always get along. At least Mara and I didn't.

The captain's thoughtfulness wasn't lost on me. He appeared to be taking this marriage seriously, even if it wasn't real. Despite his gruff attitude and stubbornness, he'd taken the time to learn about humans and wanted to make his wife comfortable in her new surroundings.

I sincerely hoped his efforts wouldn't be wasted on Mara.

"Stefan has been amazing with the children," he continued. "We'll miss him, but I'm glad to have a female nanny now. It'll be better for the girls."

"The girls?" Shoot, I knew nothing about the kids I was supposed to take care of. "What are the kids' names?"

"The girls are Ene and Illal. I also have two boys, Ivex and Xilvo."

I repeated their names in my head several times, committing them to memory. Unwittingly or not, the captain was sheltering me from the murderous mafia. The least I could do was to remember the names of his kids.

"How old are they?" I asked.

"Eleven."

"All of them?"

"Yes. They came from the same pregnancy and were born on the same day."

The muscles in his jaw flexed with a hard glint in his dark eyes. This wasn't the expression a loving father would have when speaking of his children's birthday. I wondered what caused that flash of anger, but it wasn't my place to ask.

"Anyway." He shrugged his massive shoulders, as if shaking off something unpleasant. "The children will be here any minute. Stefan will show you what to do for the next few days. I'll also stay in Diria until the end of the month."

"And then? Are you planning to leave the town?"

He shifted in his seat, moving aside his half-empty glass of water.

"I'm trained as a *crozan* operator. That's what I do. Or *did*. Until about a year ago, when my mother got sick and couldn't help me with the children anymore."

"I'm sorry to hear that. I hope she's feeling better."

"She died," he replied flatly. The look in his eye hardened.

"Oh... I-I'm sorry," I repeated.

He nodded.

"After that, I took a job in the office of the company I work for." He winced, not looking happy about that decision. "It allows me to stay in Diria and be with the children at night after Stefan leaves for the day. With Mara and you here, I can return to my job on the frontier. The desert is a long flight from here. I won't be able to come home every night. The typical working schedule on the frontier is three weeks on the job, one week off. If you agree to match your work schedule with mine, it would be ideal."

I didn't know exactly what a *crozan* operator did or what "frontier" meant on Aldrai, but my job requirements appeared clear enough—look after the kids while their dad was away.

"Sure, of course." I just really hoped I'd be good at this job. Looking after four children for weeks at a time was a huge responsibility. Knowing my sister, I couldn't count on her help with that. I'd be on my own.

"Thank you." He nodded, tipping his horns. There were quite a few of them on his head—a row of short, slightly curved horns ran down the middle of his head, front to back, like a mohawk. In addition, two longer ones curved on either side above his ears.

Short horns and bumps also covered his shoulders. Hard bumps grew over his elbows. When he turned his back to me to take the dishes to the counter by the water feature, I noticed a raised bump over each of his vertebrae pushing against the light material of his shirt.

With his body mass and all those horns and hard places, this man could work as a wrecking ball if he so chose. It was a miracle I'd survived bumping into him earlier without breaking any of my bones in the process.

"Yours is an unusual situation, Susanna," the captain said, returning to his seat. "Until now, humans have come to Aldrai only as spouses. As my wife, your sister has unlimited access to everything I own. As my employee, you will have a bank account in your name, where I will deposit your pay weekly."

This was a nice surprise. I hadn't counted on being paid while hiding from the mafia.

"Thank you." I nodded, then added with a smile, "Word of advice, don't mention 'unlimited access' to Mara."

"She likes to shop?" He gave me the knowing smile of a man well-familiar with how bad this habit could be in some women.

"We both do." We were sisters, after all. In so many ways, I was just like Mara. Except that unlike her, I'd gone through the boot camp of aggressive saving and budgeting while trying to survive on my own. "Just give her an allowance, for now. To see how it goes."

He looked contemplative for a moment.

A soft whirring sound filtered from the distance. The captain's face lit up. He tilted his head back. I did the same, scanning the sky above us.

A brightly colored bird in the sky descended lower and lower, growing in size.

"And here they are," he announced excitedly.

Chapter 6

Xavran

He heard their cheerful voices before the front gate opened and his family raced in. All four of his beloved little people ran through the front garden, tossing their school bags under the nearest hedge.

"Hi, Daddy." Illal, the sweetest one, rushed to him first. She wrapped her arms around his middle.

"Come here, youngsters," he boomed, opening his arms wide. Ivex and Xilvo bounced into the hug next, finally joined by Ene.

He hugged them all at once. The one advantage of having fewer children than most was that he could do this—an all-family hug.

"How was school?" He released them with some reluctance.

"Good."

"Fine."

"The same."

He didn't know why he bothered asking. He knew all about their achievements in school from the daily charts of their performance and progress reports. He never got any meaningful answers when he asked, but he still did every day he was home.

"Bring your bags to your rooms," he ordered, pointing at the pile under the hedge. "Then I want you to meet someone."

Mara remained in her room, probably taking a nap. Susanna was in the kitchen.

Stefan entered after the children and closed the front gate.

"Is this the new nanny?" The man smiled, his gaze directed behind Xavran's shoulder.

Xavran turned around to see Susanna standing in the archway of the exit from the front garden.

"Hi." She waved at Stefan, her focus quickly shifting to the kids, who started picking up their school bags. "Nice to meet you all." She gave another wave, looking somewhat stiff. Meeting his rambunctious foursome must have overwhelmed her.

He moved to her side, unsure of how to show his support to make her feel more relaxed. "Yes. This is the new nanny, everyone. Her name is Susanna."

"Oh, you're so pretty," Illal cooed, enclosing Susanna in a hug.

"Thank you." Susanna smiled, finally relaxing a bit.

Two tiny dimples appeared high on her cheekbones with that smile, which made her expression rather adorable.

She wrapped her arms around his little girl. The concern in his chest lifted a little.

"I'm Illal." His daughter introduced herself then her siblings. "My brothers, Xilvo and Ivex."

The boys adjusted their school tunics and nodded, saying in unison, "Nice to meet you."

He felt pleased with them using their manners.

"And this is my sister Ene." Illal gestured at his other daughter.

"Nice to meet you," Ene muttered, refraining from hugs.

SUSANNA

Some may find adult Aldraians ugly or at the very least intimidating, but the little ones were simply adorable.

Illal had the sweetest smile. Her long, tawny hair was pulled into a high ponytail, the ends of it reaching down to her waist.

The two boys seemed as rambunctious as any human children would be. Under the strict stare of their father, however, they obviously were making an effort to behave. The horns on their heads were only two-three inches long. I itched to touch them, they were so cute.

Ene, the second girl, gave me a stare that was both curious and slightly resentful. Her light-gray hair was cut short. Separated into sections, it was tied into pigtails in the same spots on her head where the male Aldraians had their horns—several in the row from her forehead to her nape and one above each ear.

I wondered if this hairstyle was in fashion or if she was making a statement.

"Bags in your rooms," the captain barked out the order again.

Grabbing their clear shoulder bags, they obediently trotted out of the room, one by one.

"Are you hungry, guys?" Stefan called after them.

"Starving!" the boys yelled back.

"They're always starving." He smiled, coming to me. "I'm Stefan."

"Susanna." I shook his hand.

Stefan's wide smile seemed to have a permanent residence on his face—a rather stark contrast to the stern expression of his employer.

"How do you like Aldrai so far?" Stefan asked, and I realized he wasn't speaking English. With the translator working so flawlessly, I had to pay very close attention to catch that. It sounded like a Slavic language, but I couldn't tell exactly which one.

"From the little I've seen of Aldrai so far, I love it," I replied.

He ran his fingers through his cropped, light-brown hair.

"Aldrai is gorgeous. I've been here for close to a year now, and I still find it breathtaking." Stefan followed the kids out of the room. "Come, I'll show you around the kitchen a little. I'm sure Xavran didn't."

The captain scoffed, but said nothing, silently stomping to the kitchen with us.

"Aldraians don't eat lunch. Some only have one meal a day—dinner," Stefan continued, talking on the way. "The kids get breakfast at school and a snack when they get home."

"The snack is a human habit," the captain noted. "My children didn't need it until Stefan started making it for them."

"Guilty as charged," the nanny easily agreed. "I got them into this habit. Aldraians eat very little throughout the day. Dinner is their main meal."

He washed his hands under the waterfall feature in the kitchen, then opened the wooden door that was built into the hill.

"This is the cold room. Xavran keeps it well stocked," he said.

I peeked inside. The underground air felt chilly. A staircase led down into a space that was much larger than it appeared from the outside. Every wall inside was covered with floor to ceiling shelves of various sizes. And every shelf was laden with jars, boxes, and baskets filled with items like cured meat, bread, grains, and things I couldn't name.

Stefan selected a jar and a box from a shelf above the stairs.

"Aldraian meal preparation is intense," he explained. "They pickle, ferment, and marinade anything and everything. Xavran makes his own sauces and marinades for all of that, and some recipes take weeks to complete."

I turned to the captain, trying to imagine this mountain of a man pickling and marinating. He had looked like he knew his way around the kitchen when he'd made the sandwich for me earlier.

"You can cook?" I asked anyway.

He just grunted in reply.

"He does, and he's excellent at that, too," Stefan spoke for him. "When he's home, he makes dinner. But I strongly advise you to stay out of his way in the kitchen. Xavran gets grumpy as hell when he's disturbed while working his culinary magic."

The captain shrugged his wide shoulders, looking slightly uncomfortable at being the topic of conversation.

"I better go." He tipped his head at Stefan. "You're in good hands now, Susanna."

He exited the kitchen.

"He's not much of a talker," Stefan said.

"I don't know…" I stared at the archway through which the captain's large figure had disappeared. "He spoke just fine with me earlier. He told me all about his expectations and such."

Stefan's eyebrows rose in surprise.

"Well, that's rare. Usually, I have to drag words out of him. But he is a good man, fair and just. He's great to work for. Anything you want, just ask him. He'll make it happen."

He opened the jar, cut four slices of bread, and made sandwiches like the one the captain had made for me earlier, only much smaller.

"The kids demand food when they get home," he explained. "But if you feed them too much, they won't eat dinner."

The children bounced into the kitchen, one by one.

"Did you wash your hands?" Stefan placed a sandwich in front of each of them. Like the captain earlier, Stefan wasn't using any plates. "Are you hungry?" he asked me.

I shook my head. "No, I just had a sandwich."

"Okay, good." He started putting the things away. "I usually stay until Xavran comes home from work. I have dinner at home with my wife. But you'll live here, right?"

"Yes. I'm…um…on a live-in basis, I guess, with room and board."

"Right. Well, like I said, Xavran likes making dinners. You don't have to worry about those for now."

Thank God for that. Aside from a fried egg or avocado toast, I rarely cooked. I made a mental note to find some recipes somewhere for when the captain left for his job in the desert.

"So, I'll be leaving soon," Stefan said, putting away the leftover bread and meat. "But I'll come back first thing in the morning to get the kids ready and take them to school. Do you drive?"

"Like a car? Yes." I lingered by the table near the kids. Absorbed by their sandwiches, they didn't pay me much attention.

Stefan nodded. "Good. Then you'll learn how to fly the aircraft too."

"What?" I gaped at him. "I can't fly!"

"It's easy, trust me. Those things practically fly themselves."

Chapter 7

Susanna

After their snack, the kids ran back to their rooms to change and play, or whatever it was kids their age did on this planet.

Stefan left for the day, and the captain seemed to be starting dinner in the kitchen. I followed Stefan's advice to keep out of his way and headed out of the kitchen.

"Where are you going?" he stopped me.

"Um, unpack?"

"Haven't you done that already? And if you haven't, you can always do it later. Yours was the smallest suitcase of the three, anyway."

I hesitated by the exit. "I thought you preferred working alone."

His dark eyes narrowed. He appeared to be lost for words for a moment.

"Do you like wine?" he asked unexpectedly.

That was sudden. Was it a trick question?

"Sometimes," I replied tentatively.

He produced two clay goblets from a shelf above the water feature and put them on the counter next to the grill.

"Here." He got two jugs from the cold room under the hill. "This one is Voranian wine." He splashed some dark purple liquid into one goblet, then used his teeth to pull the cork from the second jug. "And this one is Aldraian." He poured magenta pink liquid into the other goblet. "Which one do you like better?"

I sat on a high bar stool on the other side of the counter.

"Let's see." I took a small sip of the first one. The Voranian wine was dry and slightly bitter, but it had a bouquet of sophisticated flavors and a nice aftertaste. "It's good." I took a taste from the other goblet. The Aldraian wine was milder and sweeter. The bouquet of flavors was not nearly as complex.

If all the fancy wine tastings I'd been to had taught me anything, the Voranian wine would appeal to more sophisticated tastes. But the Aldraian wine was easier to drink.

Lately, I far preferred ease to sophistication.

"This one." I took another sip of the pink wine.

Once again, the crooked grin made an appearance on his normally stern face. He filled my goblet with the Aldraian wine, then emptied the other goblet in one gulp.

"I knew it! Stefan likes our wine too. You humans like sweet things, don't you?"

"Generally, yes," I agreed, thinking of candy and chocolate.

He poured himself some Aldraian wine, too, before recorking the jug.

"I also know you do this on Earth." He clinked the edge of his goblet against mine. "Welcome to Aldrai."

The alien man just toasted me. I laughed. This entire experience felt surreal. I still couldn't believe I was actually on another planet.

"Thank you." I took a sip of my wine. "Did Stefan show you how we toast?"

"No." His lips glistened in the light of the setting sun, stained by wine as mine must be. "This was in the videos I watched during my research about Earth and humans."

He knew so much about my world, even though he'd never been there. And here I was in a world I knew absolutely nothing about.

I decided to ask Stefan tomorrow where I could read or watch something about Aldrai and Diria, the small town where we were.

As the sky grew darker, soft yellow lights flicked on along the top of the hedges and in the canopy of the tall tree in the corner of the kitchen. A woven seat with cushions hung from a thick branch of the tree, and I wondered if that was the place where the captain liked to sit after dinner sometimes. I most definitely would if I had that in my house.

He uncovered the grill and turned it on, then brought a huge black cauldron from the cold room.

"Is this dinner?" I asked.

"Hm." He nodded, heaving the cauldron onto the grill and centering it over the fire. "Will be ready in about an hour."

I didn't bother asking what was in the cauldron. The local names and terms weren't translatable by my device, anyway. It was best to wait and find out.

"That's it? That's all you have to do to make dinner?" I took a swig of my wine. Sweet fuzziness was slowly spreading through my insides. Weariness drained from my muscles. Any lingering awkwardness dissipated too. "You make cooking look easy," I teased.

He laughed. The sound reverberated through his wide chest with a growl so low it resonated in my chest with a pleasant tingling sensation.

"I fished the ingredients for this dish out of the lake two days ago," he said. "I cleaned them, then marinated in the sauce that took hours to mix and weeks to ferment. But yes, the cooking part is easy."

"Impressive." I nodded with appreciation. "Did you say you fished? Are we having fish for dinner?"

"Sort of." He fixed the lid over the grill, enclosing the cauldron, then walked over to my side of the counter with his wine goblet.

"Did you work as a nanny back on Earth?" he asked casually, taking a seat on the barstool next to me.

No one had asked me about any previous nanny experience before. Would he send me back home if he found out I had none?

I could lie. It was unlikely he would want to check my references at this point. But I resolved to avoid lying at all costs. This was my new start.

"No. This is my first job as a nanny," I confessed. "I worked in a clothing store before."

Now, I was glad to have any working experience at all. Had he asked me just two months ago, I would've had to admit that I'd made it to the ripe age of thirty without having to work a day in my life.

"Do you think you'll manage?" There was concern in his voice.

"I'm a fast learner," I assured him. "I have the patience and determination to succeed."

Not to mention a whole lot of motivation not to go back to Earth.

"If you need anything to make it easier for you, just ask."

"Thank you," I replied with genuine gratitude.

"Personally, I think my children are the best in the world." He smirked. "But I know they can be a handful. Stefan would tell you."

"They're adorable. I hope we'll get along." I meant it with all my heart.

He took a drink from his goblet. "Your family name is different from that of your sister's. What does it mean?"

"It's my husband's last name. I took it after we got married."

His dark gaze flicked to mine. "You're married?"

For a man who Stefan claimed rarely spoke, the captain seemed to be rather talkative with me.

I stared at the shimmering pink of the wine in my goblet.

"Was. I *was* married. I'm a widow now," I said slowly.

A widow. The word sounded strange and heartbreakingly sad. Never in a million years would I have believed it'd apply to me so soon.

He leaned onto his elbow propped on the counter. His expression grew even more somber, his stare unmoving on me.

"Do you have more family?" he asked, thankfully, not one of the questions I feared. I wasn't ready to speak about Tom's death.

I shook my head. "Mara is the only close relative I have."

"Are your parents gone, too?"

"Yes. They died in a plane crash. Six years ago."

My father was the owner and the pilot of that plane. Having a private jet with a crew available to take him anywhere he wished hadn't been enough for him. He'd wanted to learn how to fly too. He had bought a turboprop plane, taken some flying lessons, then crashed it with him and my mother on board.

The old anger stirred inside me, like it did every time I thought about their unnecessary deaths. The only good thing was that no one else got hurt. Dad had wanted to bring another couple on that trip to show off his new piloting skills. They canceled at the last minute, thank goodness.

"I'm sorry to hear that," the captain said.

"Thank you." I rubbed my chest. "I never was close with my parents, but their deaths affected me deeply. They didn't need to go so soon. Both were healthy and too young to die. They could've lived for many years to come had my father been a little more cautious and slightly less self-assured."

I couldn't believe I'd just said it out loud. For the first time ever. And to a man I'd just met.

Maybe being not much of a talker made the captain an exceptionally good listener? Was that the reason I'd suddenly blurted out to him things I'd never said to anyone else before?

Either way, finally telling someone exactly how I felt about my parents' deaths lifted some of the weight I'd carried ever since that plane crash.

I took another drink from my goblet which was almost empty now. Maybe it was the wine that had made me talk?

"My father died on the job," the captain said unexpectedly. "He was a *crozan* captain, just like me. There was an accident. Four of his crew died. He was one of them."

He clutched the goblet in one giant mitt of a hand. The other one rested on the counter between us. I got the sudden urge to hold it. Despite the wine, however, it felt like I'd poked and groped him enough already when he'd never given me any indication he liked being touched in the first place.

I kept my hands to myself this time.

He took another drink. "My mother had a sickness we didn't know about until it was too late."

And I couldn't fight the urge to hold his hand anymore. Reaching over, I covered it with mine. "You're an orphan then, just like me."

He glanced my way as our hands touched.

"I'm sorry you lost both of your parents," I answered his questioning stare.

He turned his hand so that my fingers slid into his palm. He then squeezed them gently.

"I do have eleven brothers and sisters, though. All of them are well and living," he said in a lighter tone.

"Eleven? Wow!" I knew about the large families of Aldraians, but it still felt incredible.

"Yes. Six sisters, five brothers, forty-seven nieces and nephews. Though all of them live quite far from here, deeper into the terraformed territory. When we get together, we rent a town hall to fit us all in."

"It must've been fun growing up?"

"It was," he said, staring right in front of him. A faint smile played on his lips, softening his hard features. It made him look uncharacteristically vulnerable somehow.

Now, I felt like giving him a hug, or stroking his face, or...doing something equally inappropriate.

Ok, no more wine.

I shoved aside the empty goblet.

"Well..." I slid off my barstool. "I better go tell Mara dinner will be ready soon."

He glanced at the grill. "Not for another thirty minutes yet."

It appeared like he didn't want me to leave.

Well, I also liked talking to him. So much so, I feared, I might forget he was my employer. I'd already told him much more than a boss needed to know about a nanny.

"Mara can take much more than thirty minutes to get ready." I smoothed the skirt of my dress. It looked wrinkly after the flight here. "I should get changed too."

He slid his gaze down my body, purposefully slow, then turned away quickly. "Well, go then. But come back soon."

I found Mara's room just past mine along the path. She was napping but woke up when I entered with a knock on her gate. "We're having dinner soon. In half an hour."

She sat up in bed, sliding her eye mask up to her forehead. "Dinnertime? Already?"

"Did you get some rest?" Her lavender-colored sheets with puffy pillows piled up high looked like heaven. I wouldn't blame her if she wished to stay in bed.

"Not nearly enough." She yawned. "I'm not even hungry yet."

"Suit yourself, but you probably should meet the kids, at least."

"Why?" She plopped back into the pillows.

"To make some effort to fit in?" I shrugged. "One way or another, we have to spend a year here. You're like their stepmom, now."

She tossed a pillow at me. "I swear if you call me that word again, I'll smother you with one of these pillows!"

I jumped aside, evading it. "Hey! It's just a polite thing to do, to meet the people you're going to be living with under the same roof."

"What roof?" She groaned, lifting her arms up to the open sky above. "They don't even have roofs on this freaking planet. It feels like...camping." She shuddered.

"How would you know what camping feels like? We've never been." I picked up the pillow she'd tossed at me and threw it back to her. "I doubt people put huge beds like that in their camping tents."

"The bed is nice," she agreed. "The bath was decent too. Not sure that would make an entire year here bearable, though." She sighed heavily, crawling from under the covers. "Fine. I'll come to dinner, meet the little brats..."

"The kids are cute, actually, and seem well behaved. At least when their dad is around."

She winced. "Their dad... Is he going to be there?"

"Well, he made the dinner. I expect him to eat some too."

"As long as he keeps quiet, I guess," she muttered, stumbling to the lattice in front of her closet section. "And keeps that smirk off his face."

I felt the strong need to defend the man. "The captain is actually a nice person. You should take the time to get to know him a little."

"What for? Why me? Just because I'm his wife on paper? He said he doesn't want sex, anyway."

"Okay, there is a long way from getting to know someone to having sex. I didn't say you should sleep with him. But you could at least talk with him a little. We're living in his house, after all."

"What house?" she groaned again, disappearing behind the lattice to get changed. "I'm sleeping literally under a tree, like a homeless person or some forest creature!"

Giving up on having any cohesive conversation with her, I left her room and went to mine.

I got rid of the scarf on my head, brushed my hair, and pulled it back into a ponytail. Then, I changed into a wide, flower-print polyester skirt and a white, short-sleeved blouse with pearly buttons in the front. Even this outfit felt a bit too formal for this garden-home that called for flowy frocks, summer dresses, and shorts. Sadly, other than the work clothes, I only had a sweatshirt and a pair of sweatpants I wore back home. It'd always been too cold down in my basement apartment.

By the time I returned to the kitchen, the captain's family had already gathered at the table. All five of them stared at me. I realized this was the first time they saw me without the scarf on my head.

"You have a ponytail, like me!" Illal exclaimed, flipping her hair back.

"Mine is not as long, though." I touched my ponytail that reached only past my shoulder blades.

"It'll grow," she assured me. "Just don't cut it short like Ene did." She tipped her head at her sister, who glared at her, then at me.

"Long hair is stupid," Ene snapped. "Who needs it, anyway?"

"Well, hello, everybody!" Mara's voice rang from behind me.

My sister sauntered in, wearing a shimmering maxi dress and strappy stiletto sandals.

"That's—" I was going to introduce her, but stopped myself, unsure what the captain had told his children about Mara. Did the kids know she was his wife and legally their stepmother? Were they supposed to call her "mom?" That seemed wrong.

"Mara," the captain introduced her for me. "Meet Mara, children."

Their gazes shifted to her, then to me again.

"How are you so alike?" Ivex asked.

"We're twins," Mara explained, tossing her unbound hair over her shoulder. "We were born on the same day."

"So were we," Ene commented. "But I'm nothing like my sister."

True, despite sharing a birthday, the captain's children didn't look identical. Their coloring was very different too. Ivex was the color of the golden-blond sand on a beach. Illal was a shade or two darker—light brown. Ene was light gray, like their father. And Xilvo was the darkest shade of walnut.

Both boys also had coal-black eyes, like their dad. Illal's eyes were bright orange, and Ene's were pearl-gray, just like her hair and skin.

"Susanna and I are not *that* much alike," Mara protested. "We never wear the same clothes."

"You're even the same color," Xilvo gushed excitedly. "Everywhere. You have the same eyes, the same hair."

"That's weird," Ivex agreed.

"And boring," Ene said.

"Ene," the captain reprimanded sternly.

"Sorry," the girl apologized, but I caught her furtively roll her eyes the very next moment.

"We're identical twins." Mara pursed her lips, taking the seat at the head of the table, on the opposite end of the captain's. "So, what's for dinner?" she asked, clearly trying to change the subject.

The captain returned to the grill.

"We're having cauldron dinner tonight!" Xilvo announced excitedly.

"Cauldron?" She curled her mouth, looking puzzled.

"Mara, this is Xilvo," I introduced the boy, since no one else had. "And this is Ivex, Illal, and Ene."

"Sure. Nice to meet you all." She waved in their general direction.

The captain opened the grill, and I stepped to the counter.

"Do you need help setting the table?" I asked. There was nothing but a glossy tablecloth on the tabletop.

"No need." He removed the lid from the kettle. An appetizing aroma wafted from the dish.

"Smells good," I said.

Xilvo bounced in his seat impatiently. "I love Dad's cauldron dinners!"

With a grunt, the captain heaved the huge kettle off the grill, then carried it to the table. Here, he turned it over and dumped its contents straight onto the tablecloth.

With a startled gasp, Mara shrank back. I just stood there, staring at various sized creatures spilling from the cauldron. Some looked like clams, or rocks, others had legs and tails, all slathered in a thick, creamy-red sauce that smelled...delicious.

"Yum!" Xilvo grabbed something that looked like a giant pill bug with a flat segmented body and several long, skinny legs.

"Xilvo, wait for everyone to join," his father stopped him.

The boy dropped the bug back on the table and furtively licked the sauce off his fingers.

"Is this a joke?" Mara jumped to her feet. "This is just..."

Her face paled as she glanced at the pile of "food" on the table, then turned away, pressing a hand to her stomach. Clutching her throat with another hand, she ran out of the kitchen.

I felt like following her. The slimy pile on the table looked inedible, no matter how great it smelled.

The captain's expression darkened. The children stared after my sister, confusion clear on their little faces.

It occurred to me, this might be the first time they ever had a human for dinner. Stefan never stayed long enough to have it with them.

The dish wasn't a joke or a prank. This was what they ate. And they kindly invited us to share it with them.

The captain silently turned around and took the empty pot to the water feature to wash it. The kids just sat there, staring at the food but making no attempt to eat.

If they waited for Mara to return, they'd be sitting here for a very long time, growing hungrier. She wasn't coming back.

It was awkward and gloomy, and I couldn't leave them like that. The best I could do in this situation was to eat a damn bug myself.

At the very least, I could try.

"It smells so good." I took the seat vacated by Mara. "Do we eat using our hands?"

"Yes." Xilvo perked up. He grabbed again the bug he'd dropped. "I'll show you."

He folded the bug's flat body lengthwise, cracking the outer skeleton, then pulled a slab of white flesh out. It looked flat like a pancake and flaky like fish. Xilvo tore off a piece.

"Then you dip it." He dunked the piece into the sauce spreading in a puddle on the tablecloth. "And eat it." He stuffed the meat into his mouth and chewed, closing his eyes. "Mmmm. The best!"

The captain finished washing the pot and now watched us from his spot by the sink.

"All right. Let's see." I picked a bug out of the pile.

Come to think of it, it didn't look any more repulsive than a crab or a lobster. It was just gray outside, instead of red.

I crushed its shell, like Xilvo had done to get to the white meat inside. Once it was out of the exoskeleton with all those legs and antennae, it looked like an ordinary piece of fish, or a flat lobster tail. I tore a strip off and dipped it into the sauce.

It tasted even better than it smelled. The flavor must come from the sauce, not from the meat. Either way, it was good.

"Mmm." I mimicked Xilvo's expression, utterly surprised by how much I liked the taste of the dish. "It is good."

"Your sister doesn't know what she's missing," the boy observed pragmatically, tearing another piece from his "pancake."

"Right, she doesn't." I smiled, dipping the next piece into the sauce. "Maybe I'll take her some later."

The captain returned to the table and took his seat. The other children started eating too, with crunching and munching sounds coming from every direction.

My hands were quickly covered in sauce up to my wrists, as I dug for more "bugs" in the pile and crushed them to get the tender white meat out.

"You have sauce on your nose." Illal pointed at my face.

If I used my hand to wipe it off, I'd make it worse. I wiped my nose with my forearm instead, then licked the sauce off my arm.

My gaze crossed with the captain's on the other end of the table. This was by far the least "classy" dinner I'd ever attended. But it was possibly the most fun. I giggled and shrugged, crushing another bug.

The captain watched me with an amused expression.

Xilvo picked up a round shell-rock from the pile. "Do you know how to eat this, Susanna?" The boy obviously had taken the role of my guide this evening.

"No. What are those?"

"*Qualis* mussels. You take them like this..." He gripped each half of the round shell with one hand. "Then wiggle them a little." He rotated his hands in opposite directions. The halves of the shell fell open, revealing a gray core. Its wrinkly surface reminded me of the human brain. Or a walnut. Depending on how one looked at it. "Want to try it?" Xilvo offered the core to me.

I decided to think of it as a walnut not a brain. Dipping it in the sauce, I took a bite. The texture was denser with this one, but the sauce made it taste just as delicious.

"It's good." I smiled.

"I told you." The boy nodded confidently. "Dad's cauldron dinners are the best."

The captain listened with one of his crooked half-smiles while effortlessly crushing the shells in his giant hands.

There wasn't much to clean after dinner but our hands. The captain had already washed the pot. He just wrapped the empty shells into the dirty tablecloth and put the whole thing into the garbage shoot.

"Where does the garbage go?" I asked, watching him.

"In the composter below. It's then used to enrich the soil for the plants to grow."

"Oh, the tablecloth is biodegradable, then?"

He arched a brow ridge. "Isn't everything?"

On Aldrai, it appeared it was.

As the captain was putting away a few leftover mussels and "bugs," I asked if I could have one. I then cracked it, sliced the meat into thin strips, and put some sauce in a small dish before taking it to Mara's room.

She sat on her bed, dressed in her silk pajamas, a cleansing mask smeared on her face.

"What's this?" She eyed the plate suspiciously.

"Dinner." I handed it to her.

As far as food went, Mara had the endurance of a monk and could go for weeks sustained by nothing but vitamin shakes or vegetable juice if she suspected she'd gained a pound. But this was a new planet. Our bodies had gone through a lot already, and I honestly didn't remember the last time any food had passed her lips.

"You need to eat," I insisted.

She wrinkled her nose. "Please don't tell me it came from that pot."

I didn't say that. I knew my sister. She had the willpower to fast for days as part of the many diets she had done in her life, and now was not the time for that.

Instead, I brought the dish to my nose and smelled it with an expression of utter pleasure on my face.

"It's really good," I said. "Try it. It tastes very much like the lobster from that French restaurant where we had lunch with Petra, the German heiress, remember?"

She lifted a strip between her fingers, then took a tentative bite.

"Not bad. Fine, you can leave it here."

Chapter 8

Susanna

Today had been overwhelming. Everything was new here—the smells, the tastes, the textures. All I'd done was eat and talk, but as night fell, I felt exhausted.

Alone in my room, I stripped off my clothes, then finally sank into the bathtub carved from a solid slab of rock. The warm water caressed my skin, reaching up to my neck when I lay down. The tub was long. Stretching out, I could barely touch the other end of it with my toes.

Something poked at my ankle. I shifted my leg. Another slight poke came to my thigh.

Alarm jolted me, and I sat up.

Slick, silvery bodies slithered in the water. Their reflective shapes stood out against the dark rock of the tub. Two of them, each about the length of my hand, tapped against my leg with their heads, two more propelled from the wall of the tub toward my other leg.

With a screech of panic, I leaped out of the tub, splashing water all over the place.

Heavy footsteps, muted by the rubber cobblestones, thudded outside of my room.

"Susanna?" The lattice gate flew open, and the captain barged in.

I dashed for the exit, running into him. "Snakes!"

He grabbed me.

"Snakes? Where?"

"In the tub!" I gripped his shirt, shaking out my legs. The sensation of the creatures slithering against my skin wouldn't leave me. "Long, silver things…"

"Do you mean *nals*? The fish?"

"I don't know what they're called. Ugh!" I kept shaking my legs. "Gross! So, so gross. Fish?" The word finally registered with me. "Why are there fish in the bathtub?"

"To clean it," he said, matter of fact. "*Nals* are harmless. Probably just curious, since that tub hasn't been used for a while."

"You have fish living in the bathtub?" I just couldn't wrap my mind around that. "You don't take them out before taking a bath?"

"No. Why would we? They mostly keep to the walls and eat soap suds."

His calm tone had soothed my panic.

"Is that a common thing on Aldrai?"

"Yes," he assured me.

"Okay, well... They scared me." I exhaled slowly, the tension and stress receding. "Sorry. I've been too jumpy lately."

Lately? When did it all start? When my cheating husband left me for his receptionist after stealing millions? When the mafia guys got me on their radar, scaring the shit out of me on quite a few occasions? Or when I got my husband's head delivered to me, along with the threat of me being next?

I dropped my shoulders and pressed my forehead to the captain's chest, feeling drained and exhausted. I clung to his side, my hands fisted into the soft material of his shirt, his clothes getting soaking wet from my naked body.

Naked!

I froze. I was hugging my new boss while being completely naked.

And... He was hugging me back. His arm went around my shoulders. The other hand rested on my hip.

"Sorry..." I mumbled, prying my fingers open to release his shirt.

Instead of letting me go, however, he pulled me closer.

"It's all right," he murmured. "You're safe."

He meant I was safe from the fish, of course. But the word resonated with me.

Safe.

I didn't think I'd ever known the true meaning of it until now, when I was wrapped securely in his burly arms.

Hugs weren't common in my family. When something undesirable happened, my father would curse, my mother would purse her lips, then both would get on their phones and make things happen.

We dealt with it. That was the Takolsky way, the only way I knew. That was how I'd been trying to solve my situation. Alone. When all my friends had turned away from me after Tom's investor scandal, I dealt with it completely on my own.

No one had hugged me and told me I was safe or that it'd be alright. No one comforted me.

I knew the captain's words applied purely to the fish in the tub, but for me, they reached so much deeper. For the first time in a long time, I truly felt safe.

I pressed myself to him. He slid his large hand down my back. His palm was rough and warm. Strong but gentle, like he could hold my heart in it without breaking it.

The warmth of his big body seeped into me through his shirt. The strong, fast beating of his heart thudded against my cheek pressed to his chest. And it felt...intimate.

"What happened here?" My sister's voice shrilled from behind the hedge. "Who yelled?"

The captain stiffened, and I jerked away from him.

"It was me." I grabbed my skirt from the floor to cover myself up. "I yelled."

Mara sleepily waddled into my room, dressed in her silk pajamas. The matching eye mask was on her forehead, a sheen of night cream spread evenly over her face.

"You're just dead set on keeping me awake today, aren't you?" she grumped at me, not sparing a glance at the captain. "All I want is to get some sleep."

"Sorry. There's fish in the tub—"

"So? They do that here. Didn't you know?" She gave me a sleepy glare. "Maybe you should read something about Aldrai. Honestly." Shaking her head, she left.

I clutched the skirt to my chest.

"How are you feeling?" the captain inquired in a neutral tone, and I kind of missed his rumbling murmur of earlier.

I gave him an apologetic smile. "I feel rather stupid for causing the commotion."

"It's not your fault. You didn't know."

"No. Mara is right. I should learn more about this planet. Things just happened so quickly back on Earth. I had no chance to do any research. I need to catch up. Well... I..." I adjusted the skirt, trying to cover as much of my body as possible. "I'm sorry for waking you up."

He had every right to be annoyed with me, just like Mara.

"I wasn't sleeping." He shook his head, shifting his weight to another foot. It was hard to tell whether he was eager to leave or lingered because he wanted to stay.

"I promise to learn everything there is to know about the fish and everything else that differs from Earth," I assured him.

He opened his mouth, then closed it again, rubbing his left horn.

"Good night," I said.

"Right. Sleep well." He finally left my room.

Once the gate closed behind him, I tossed aside my skirt and climbed back into the tub. I kept an eye on the slithering shapes under the water. They swerved around me for a few moments, then spread out to the sides.

I inhaled deeply, leaning back against the warm rock of the tub. Its rough surface reminded me of the captain's hands—warm and solid.

It finally settled in my mind that fear, stress, and paranoia were things of the past. I had a safe place to live now, a stable job that I could keep for years if I learned to do it well, which I was determined to accomplish.

For once, my future was looking up.

It was good.

Chapter 9

Xavran

It was bad.

The unsettling tingles rushed up and down his body. His cock swelled with heat and pressure. His tail twitched, tenting his pants from the back.

Not good. Not good at all.

He'd spent over a decade in full control of his body. All it took was one human woman pressing her sweet naked body to his, and he almost lost it. She had felt so good in his arms. It took everything he had to let her go.

The sensation of her soft skin, damp after her bath, tormented his memory.

His cock throbbed painfully and urgently, demanding a release. The easiest way would be to head straight to his bedroom, lower the privacy shield over his bed, and use his own hand to calm his throbbing member.

The problem with that solution was that he'd be thinking about *her* while he pleasured himself. With the way things had gone that day, he'd end up roaring her name at the top of his lungs while coming.

Susanna.

Even her name felt like a forbidden pleasure on his tongue when he whispered it.

After making sure the children had settled into their beds for the night, he put on a pair of shoes and stomped outside. The night was thicker out here, away from the lit living space. He chose a direction and took off in a jog along the path that snaked between the garden-homes of Diria.

Touching himself while thinking of Susanna, he feared, would be like training his body to associate *that* kind of pleasure with her. Instead, he chose to work the lust out of his system by physically exhausting his body. He'd run until all the images of her curves would disappear from his mind.

Seeing her flat, breast-less stomach was bizarre. Sadly, it turned out to be the exciting kind of bizarre.

He had caught the sight of her breasts, noting they were considerably fuller than those of the Aldraian women. It had been all he could do not to reach for them and touch them. His hands flexed as he imagined cupping her full breasts, kneading them, toying with her hard, pink nipples...

"Stop that!" he ordered his mind that kept conjuring all those tantalizing images.

"And you, too!" That was for his cock that started stirring and swelling again.

He moved faster, running between the hedges of his neighbors. Inescapable, the images of Susanna's naked body chased after him.

What was it about that woman that wouldn't let him get her out of his mind?

She'd stirred curiosity in him. There was a vulnerability in those blue eyes of hers. He had sensed something fragile and broken in the way she'd clung to him, trembling and scared.

That afternoon, he'd kept asking her questions, and the more he'd learned, the more he wanted to know.

He'd also felt the unexpected desire to share. He'd known her for less than a day, yet he'd already blabbed more about his life to her than most people knew. Their conversation went well beyond the new hire briefing he had intended. It'd been most certainly more than a job interview. It had felt like...a date.

He nearly tripped on the path, waving his arms to regain his balance.

That conversation in the kitchen had been very much like a date. He'd even served her wine, hadn't he?

Dammit!

That couldn't happen again. He had no intention of romancing his new nanny, or his new wife, for that matter.

Susanna simply proved to be a good listener. Something inside him craved her attention. When she gazed at him with those eyes the color of the sky, he couldn't stop talking.

Obviously, he'd been alone for too long, starved for female company. He needed to regain control of the situation in his own home.

After running for what felt like hours, he returned to his gate. Out of breath, his chest aching and his legs numb, he stumbled into the front garden. All was quiet; only the flying insects made soft clicking sounds with their wings and the breeze whispered gently in the hedges.

The moment he thought of Susanna, however, his blood rushed to his groin again. His cock stirred anew, despite his exhaustion.

Clearly, he had to go back to work as soon as possible. The less time he spent with his new nanny, the better.

Maybe, he could also start some home project to occupy his mind and body until then, since both preferred to focus on Susanna so much. Maybe he could move that hedge in the kitchen farther out, as he'd planned to do when he first got this place. By moving it into the ravine, he'd open up the view onto the lake...

The lake where the crash happened eleven years ago.

He turned his head to the north, where his late wife's room lay untouched since her death. That was the one part of his home that needed remodeling, badly. Other than the routine maintenance provided by the automated, built-it systems, no work had been done there.

For years, he hadn't been able to bring himself to even enter that room, not to mention touching any of her things left in there.

Chapter 10

Susanna

"Okay. Your turn." Stefan gestured at the pilot's seat.

We'd just dropped the kids off at school and returned to the aircraft parked nearby. Even though the school was in the same town, we'd flown here. According to Stefan, there were just a few hundred households in Diria. But with each family space being the size of a park, the town sprawled for miles in every direction. The school was on the opposite end of Diria, and walking to it would've taken forever.

Now, Stefan wanted me to fly the aircraft back home.

"Are you crazy?" I gaped at him. "Do you want to die?"

"No, I don't!" He laughed. "I have a lot to live for. But you're not going to crash."

I glared at him skeptically. "I'm not so sure about that. I'm not a pilot."

"Neither was I. But flying these things is super easy. You said you drove a car back on Earth."

"Yes, but—"

"Then you can fly these." He grabbed my arm and nudged me to the pilot's seat. "Jump in. I'll show you."

I hesitated.

"This was how my parents died," I mumbled under my breath.

I hadn't meant to blurt that out like that, but the situation was close enough to feel unsettling.

"What?" The smile slid off his face. "Oh, I'm so sorry, Susanna." He scratched the back of his head. "Somehow it made sense in my head to just put you in the seat and let you do it."

I glanced at the pretty aircraft. It was the same size and color as the one the captain had flown us in on our arrival day. The feathery material of its wings framing the shiny glass panels of the cockpit made the resemblance to a bird uncanny.

"Was that how *you* learned to fly it?" I asked. "Just sat in the seat and went for it?"

"Yep." He nodded. "Like I said, these things fly themselves. All you have to do is just let them."

His unwavering confidence gave me some reassurance. In my new job, I'd have to take the kids to and from school. I needed to know how to operate the aircraft if I wanted to do my job properly, even if that meant pushing myself out of my comfort zone once again.

"Well, fine," I conceded. "But just to warn you, it looks like I, too, have something to live for now. If we crash and die, I'll be very pissed at you." I climbed in and put the seat belt on.

Stefan got into the passenger's seat and closed both door panels. "We won't crash. Just make sure you don't touch anything randomly."

I jerked my hands up, holding them in front of me, like a surgeon who'd just had them scrubbed and prepped for a surgery.

"But how do I fly it without touching anything?"

"I told you these things practically fly themselves." He clicked his seatbelt on.

My arms grew sore from my straining not to move them.

"What if I do touch something? Accidentally?"

"If it's something you shouldn't have touched, it may cause an emergency."

I halted my breath, freezing with worry.

Stefan chuckled. "Relax. In case of an emergency, the aircraft lands on its own. We'll be fine."

"Lands? Where?"

"On the ground. Wherever we are."

"Oh." I blinked at him. "So, since we're flying over the town full of homes with no roofs, we may end up in someone's bed?"

"Only if their protective shields aren't functioning," he said, not eliminating that possibility. "Normally, the shields would come up, and we'd just sit on top of their bedroom."

"Good to know," I mumbled, staring at the screens of the control panel. The floating blobs of Aldraian written language made no sense to me, whatsoever.

"First, you turn this one on, here." Stefan pushed a button.

"Text-to-speech activated," a mechanical voice sounded from the panel.

"Then, you'll need to select your destination." He scrolled the screen in a spinning circle, with the system announcing, *"School, town hall, office, home..."*

"Home." Stefan touched the corresponding blob.

The engines whirred to life. The light, colorful wings unfurled. With a soft lurch, the aircraft lifted off the ground.

"Whoa!" I hovered my hands over the panel. "What do I do now?"

"Nothing." Stefan swatted my hands away. "I told you, don't touch anything. It's programmed to take us back home."

"That's it?" The ground fell away from under us, the neat squares of the school's classrooms growing smaller.

"That's it." Stefan lay back in his seat. "You can put your hands down, now."

I carefully lowered my hands into my lap. "The captain did something more when he flew us to Diria from the spaceport."

Stefan shrugged. "He was showing off. Some Aldraians like to hand-fly their aircraft for the 'real flying' experience. I'd say why reject technological advancements that allow us to do nothing?" He grinned.

I ventured another glance down. The landscape moved under us smoothly. The system was obviously in control.

"Well, that seems easy," I marveled.

"Told you."

I relaxed a little, shifting back in my seat. "So, does the captain always hand-fly it?"

Stefan nodded. "More often than not. But he's been trained as a machinery operator. I guess he likes it. I'm a teacher and have no problems with letting machines do the flying for me."

"You're a teacher?"

"Yes," he replied proudly. "I taught Polish Language and Literature in grade school back home. Since there's obviously no demand for that on Aldrai, I took the job of a nanny while Esstal, my wife, was still at work."

That was Polish, then, that Stefan spoke. Not that it mattered. Our translators worked so seamlessly, they erased the language barrier completely.

"Is Esstal no longer working, then?" I asked.

"She is, but only from home now. With the babies growing, it's too hard for her to make it into the office every day like she used to."

"How many babies are you expecting?"

"Six." He smiled broadly, happiness radiating from him like sunshine.

I whistled. "That's a lot!"

"An entire family at once." He nodded enthusiastically. "Ours will be still significantly smaller than an average family on Aldrai. But that's why the marriage program was created in the first place—to reduce the number of babies per mother while increasing the frequencies of pregnancies."

"How frequent are they now?"

"Not very. Few Aldraian women get to experience childbirth because pregnancies are so rare among them. When mixed with humans, however, it happens more often and with fewer babies. That's why human spouses have become so sought after here."

"They are?"

"Well, when I applied, I got eight matches in less than a week."

"Eight? Really?"

"Yes." He nodded. "But it took me weeks to choose the right one. The marriage program is pretty strict. It doesn't allow for casual dating or frivolous 'let's-try-and-see-how-it-goes.' They want at least a full year of commitment. So, I wrote to all eight women and exchanged a lot of photos and videos with each of them. Esstal stood out from the very beginning. There is just something about her that felt..." He waved his hand in the air, his expression turning dreamy as he searched for a perfect word to describe his wife.

"Right?" I suggested.

"That's it." He snapped his fingers. "She was *right* from the start. Exchanging letters with her felt like having a real conversation. I could be myself, and she accepted me. It's always been so easy to talk to her. You know what I mean?"

I nodded because I did. I had that very feeling just yesterday during my conversation with the captain. It felt...easy, just like Stefan said. Not that I considered the captain as a match, of course. But I'd been thinking about him. So many questions remained about that man.

He hadn't been around that morning. Stefan said he went to the office early, which surprised me because I thought he was supposed to be off for a while.

"Stefan, do you know what happened to the captain's first wife?" I asked. "She was an Aldraian, wasn't she?"

She had to be. The marriage agreement with Earth was barely a year old.

"Yes, she was," he confirmed. "Historically, Aldraians rarely marry outside of their race, the main reason being that they aren't biologically compatible with anyone but humans."

"If they both were Aldraians, how come they only had four kids?"

Stefan inhaled slowly.

"Well, I don't know much about what happened. In town, they say there was an accident. His wife crashed her aircraft into the lake over there." He gestured at the large body of water glistening outside of Diria, in the direction we were flying.

"You said these things don't crash." I gripped the edge of my seat.

He shook his head. "No, they don't. Normally. But who knows what exactly happened that day? Apparently, Xavran wasn't in the aircraft with her, but he got to the scene of the accident before anyone else did. She was in the last month of her pregnancy. The doctors only managed to save four babies."

"Oh no…" I pressed a hand to my chest, to the spot where my heart ached for the captain. That explained his frown when he'd spoken about the birth of his children. Their birthday would forever be the day his wife and the rest of his children died. "This is horrible. But why did it happen? How did she crash?"

"I honestly don't know. Xavran doesn't speak about that. Ever. The records were never made public, either. But there are a lot of rumors." He lowered his voice. "Some are worse than others."

I leaned closer. "What do you mean?"

"Some say Xavran was more involved in his wife's death than he wants everyone to know."

"What? No." I recoiled from him. "Do you believe that?"

He shrugged. "Like I said, these are just rumors. Personally, I suspect his late wife's family are behind them. They never got along well with Xavran, and lately… Well, they aren't allowed into his home. He only lets them see the kids on holidays and stuff."

I thought about what he'd just said. This was shaping up to be a rather difficult situation.

"Did the captain love his wife? Do you know?"

"I believe he did. Some say he was madly in love with her."

Fully absorbed by our conversation, I hardly noticed as the aircraft descended. Only when it jolted softly from the contact with the ground, I realized we'd landed.

"Wow. That's a lot to take in."

"You don't need to worry, Susanna," Stefan assured me. "I wouldn't let you stay and work for Xavran if I didn't believe you'd be safe in his home. He's a good man."

A good man.

I wished to believe that with all my heart. But my heart had terribly misled me before. There once was a time when I believed Tom was a good man, too, that he was honest and incapable of stealing.

Opening the door panel on my side, I unclipped my seatbelt. "Has there been an investigation?"

"There has. The authorities deemed it an accident and closed the case," Stefan replied, climbing out. "Like I said, you have nothing to worry about." He opened the front gate for me but didn't enter himself. "I need to go home for a couple of hours now to prep for dinner. It's my turn to cook tonight. I'll get back around lunchtime and take you grocery shopping. Okay? We'll go to school early this afternoon. I want you to meet the kids' teacher and the moms of their classmates. Between the four of them, they go on a lot of playdates."

"Okay." This was real. Classmates, playdates, other moms. All the things that came with a normal childhood. "Looking forward to it."

Chapter 11

Susanna

I found Mara sitting at the giant table in the kitchen. The captain was nowhere around. The jug of Voranian wine stood open in front of her, a goblet clutched in her hand.

"Are you okay?" I came closer and propped my butt against the table.

She took a swig from her goblet. "Where did you go?"

"To take the kids to school."

"Oh, right. I keep forgetting about the kids..." She slammed the goblet on the table with force. "I'm so fucking bored here. Where is the alien?"

"Who?"

"My *husband*." She made a face, looking disgusted by the very sound of that word.

I smiled. "You know we're on Aldrai now, right? Here, *we* are the aliens."

"Whatever." She waved me off. "So? Is he working the fields or something? Where is his farm, anyway? Is it big?"

For someone who studied the Aldraian lifestyle enough to know about the fish in their baths, Mara remained completely clueless about her own husband. Granted, their marriage was just a sham, but we all were sharing the living space. We should make an effort to get to know each other a bit.

"He doesn't have a farm," I said.

She frowned. "Great. He doesn't even have a farm."

"He works on the frontier, in the desert. He drives a large piece of machinery, called a *crozan*—"

"Riiiight," she drew out the word. "He's a truck driver..."

"It's not quite a truck he drives—"

"Whatever," she cut me off, hiding a yawn behind her hand.

I sat next to her at the table. "Listen, the captain is not a bad person. I enjoyed talking to him yesterday. He's a good listener and an excellent cook."

He also might have something to do with the death of his wife, but I decided against telling her that. Stefan assured me those were just rumors. And Mara already held a hefty amount of animosity towards her unsuspecting husband.

"Maybe you could... You know..." I wasn't sure myself what I wanted her to do. Be a little nicer to the captain? Did I want their marriage to become a little more real? Was it even possible, considering how completely different these two were? They really had no touching points on anything.

"What?" she prompted impatiently. "I'm not sleeping with him, if that's what you mean."

That was definitely not what I was getting at.

"You certainly don't have to do that," I said.

She yawned again. "If you like him so much, why don't you sleep with him yourself?"

"That is *not* what I was talking about. At all."

"Why not?" She rested her elbow on the table before dropping her head into her hand. "You obviously don't find him gross. I know you haven't gotten laid in a while. He probably has his urges, too, like all men do. If you fuck him, at least I won't have to worry about him barging into my room to demand I fulfill my 'marital duties' or some shit like that."

"What?" I exclaimed. "He would never do that!"

"How do you know? He may be playing hard-to-get with his 'no-sex' condition, but he seems very much interested."

"Does he?"

"Of course he does," she insisted. "He's a man, after all. Didn't you notice how he looked at you last night? I thought you were interested too. Wasn't that why you made up all that drama with the fish in the tub?"

"I didn't make it up!" Like I would make a fool of myself on purpose.

She squinted her eyes at me, suspiciously. "Why else would you run naked around him, then?"

"Oh God," I groaned. "Was that how it looked like last night? Do you think he'd assume I was trying to seduce him or something?" My face turned hot at the thought.

She shrugged. "It's not a bad move if you want to play that game. I thought for sure you hooked up last night."

"I... No! We didn't." I sucked in a breath, getting up from my seat. "Trust me, I don't want to play any games." Either with my feelings or the captain's.

But was she right? Could he really be feeling something for me?

"Suit yourself." Mara emptied her goblet then stared inside it, as if hoping to find more wine in it somehow. "If I was even remotely attracted to that alien oaf, I would let him fuck me. What else is there to do in this shithole, anyway? You may as well have some fun."

I fidgeted with the edge of my blouse. The idea of the captain finding me in any way attractive didn't feel unappealing. Not at all. Though it probably should feel inappropriate, since he was my employer. Oh, and my legal brother-in-law too.

"He is *your* husband," I reminded Mara.

"Oh, please," Mara groaned. "Stop saying that. I'd be just too happy if you took him off my hands, like I wanted you to all along. Honestly. Where is he, anyway?"

"I didn't see him this morning, but Stefan said he went to his office."

"Who's Stefan?"

Right, she hadn't met him yet.

"He's Captain Rax's nanny."

"A male nanny?" She scoffed. "Well, that's even worse than a truck driver."

Irritation spiked in me at her quick judgment. She reached for the jug to refill her goblet, but I took it away from her. "Why don't you go for a walk or something?"

"A walk *where?*" She rolled her eyes. "Is there a shopping mall or at least a coffee shop here?"

"I don't know. I've only been to the school so far."

She groaned dramatically, then shook the last droplets of wine from her goblet on her tongue. "I'm going to die from boredom in this place."

"Better than from decapitation," I muttered, taking the jug back to the cold room. Two silver discs on the counter by the grill caught my attention. "What are these?"

"No idea." She shrugged. "A drone dropped them off a while back."

I picked up one of the discs. It was the size of a dessert plate, thin but with some weight to it.

"I wonder what it is?" I turned it in my hands.

"These are tablets." The deep male voice came from the entrance to the kitchen. "For you and your sister."

My heart skipped a beat at the sound of that voice.

The captain walked into the kitchen.

Thankfully, he didn't look like he'd heard any of our conversation, especially that part about anyone sleeping with him or me trying to seduce him.

I chased those thoughts away and attempted to collect myself. He was my boss. My heart had no business making somersaults in his presence.

Mara pressed her hand to her chest. "Oh, you scared me. How did you manage to sneak up on us with your size and all that weight?"

He stared at her with a somewhat confused expression. "I wasn't trying to sneak up on anyone. Didn't you hear my aircraft?"

"We were talking," I explained. "The Aldraian aircraft are pretty quiet. Morning, Captain."

"*Xavran*," he corrected, coming closer. "Ranks are only used at work on Aldrai."

Oh, this wasn't good. It might be easier for me to keep things professional if I thought of him as Captain Rax, my boss, not Xavran, the big guy who gives the best hugs in the world...

"I prefer *captain*—" I tried to protest, but he wouldn't have any of that.

"But I don't." He stepped right up to me. "Say my name."

Tingles rushed down my arms, either from the way he said it, or from how close he stood, or both.

I glanced at Mara. She wiggled her eyebrows, looking amused.

"Say it," he insisted.

I raised my eyes to his. They were so impossibly dark, but when I looked closely, I could see the even-darker pupils in the middle. They were so dilated right now, they took over nearly the entire irises.

"Xavran..." I uttered in a half-whisper. My voice came out breathy, making his name sound intimate.

His throat bobbed with a swallow. His gaze remained on me, holding me prisoner. I couldn't move a muscle. I couldn't even blink.

"How does this thing work?" Mara's voice sounded like a gunshot in a library, shaking me out of whatever spell Xavran's dark eyes had put me under.

She was standing by the counter, flipping one of the discs in her hands.

When had she moved there from the table?

How long was I staring at Xavran?

And what the heck was the matter with me?

He calmly walked over to the counter and took the disc from Mara.

"Place your hand on it." He waited for her to comply.

She spread her fingers, pressing her palm to the smooth surface. The disc lit up with a silvery gray light.

A pleasant, mechanical voice sounded, *"Welcome, Mara."*

"Neat," she giggled, perking up. "It knows my name. What else can it do? Does it have videos? Movies? Can I talk to people?"

"You can connect to my entertainment system." Xavran showed her how to connect to his personal network and the available public networks. "This is the library of books and videos. Movies are here. The social net is here. The town news—"

"Great!" She grabbed it from him. "I'm in my room if you'll need me, but I really hope you won't." She took off, leaving me one on one with him.

He took the second device from the counter.

"Is this one for me?" I asked.

He glanced at me briefly. "You wished to learn more about Aldrai. This should help. I requested the devices to be programmed to communicate in audio, so your translator will pick up the sound and convey the meaning to you."

"Thank you. That was very thoughtful." I didn't expect him to act on what I'd said last night. He wasn't obligated to fulfill my wishes, but I was grateful he did. Learning more about this place would make my life easier.

He took my hand in his, making my breath hitch.

"Just like that," he said softly, placing my hand on the disc.

"Welcome, Susanna," the device greeted me.

I smiled. "It works."

"It does." His voice sounded above me. He stood so close to me, my shoulder was pressed to his arm, his fingers still circling my wrist.

If I turned just a little, I could rest my head on his chest...

He cleared his throat again, making his chest vibrate. He then let go of my hand.

"How was your morning?" he asked, stepping away from me.

Maybe he was "interested," like Mara put it, but he clearly chose not to pursue anything. All I could do was behave the same.

I released a breath, rolling back my shoulders. "Good. We went to school. Stefan showed me how to fly the aircraft—"

He snapped his gaze to my face.

"*Always* let the machine fly," he said with emphasis. "Never try to do it yourself."

Stefan had said that Xavran's wife died in a crash. Just like me, he must have some misgivings about air travel too, now.

"I promise I won't try to fly it myself. Stefan told me the same." I nodded. "He's taking me grocery shopping later."

"Good." He tipped his chin at the disc in my hand. "Do you need help with that?"

"Yes, please." I handed him the device.

He went with me through the same things he'd shown Mara. He did it in the same way, too—polite but distant. There were no smiles, crooked or otherwise, from him this morning. He almost seemed on guard with me. I couldn't figure out the reason for that change, but in the end, it was probably for the best. It would be easier for me to maintain a professional distance between us if he did the same.

"Stefan said you went to the office this morning?" I asked. "Is everything okay?"

"Yes. Why wouldn't it be?" Yet his prominent brow ridges shifted closer together, forming a frown.

"You said you weren't going back to work until the end of the month."

"Right." His jaw flexed. "Well, I went to see if they could schedule me in earlier than planned."

"When?"

"Hopefully, in a few days."

"Why so soon?" I couldn't shake the feeling that it might have something to do with Mara and me being here. Did he dislike sharing his space with us?

He shifted his weight to another foot, somewhat awkwardly. "Seeing how well you're doing, I figured you won't be needing me here anyway."

"But it's only been a day."

"I know..." He heaved a long breath. "That's all it took..." His gaze traveled to me again. There was wonder and confusion in his eyes, as if I were a puzzle he needed to solve. He blinked after a moment. "You're doing great, Susanna. Stefan is only a call away. I'm still here too, for the next few days."

"Sure. No worries. I'll be fine. The kids and I, I mean," I assured him. Because what else could I do? Cling to his leg to keep him from leaving? He couldn't babysit me forever. My job was to help him, not the other way around.

Though his decision to leave earlier bothered me. Combined with his behavior this morning, it seemed strange. He looked tense.

Was it something I did?

Then I remembered literally jumping on him last night. Naked. And now, the man was fleeing his own home rather than continue sharing it with me. He must think I was an idiot, or worse—a sex-crazed woman who knew no boundaries.

I rubbed my forehead, searching for a way to apologize.

"I'm really sorry about last night," I started. "I overreacted about the fish—"

He jerked his head up, giving me an odd look.

"It's fine," he said, slowly backing to the exit. "No need to apologize. I understand. It's the fish."

He turned to leave, and I noticed the back of his pants move, as if he had something hidden in there. Something long.

He left. But the tension lingered.

"Way to make things weird, Susanna," I muttered under my breath.

Grabbing my disc, I went to my room. There was still some time before Stefan's return. I could read or watch some videos about Aldrai to learn more about this world, so that I wouldn't nearly jump out of my skin when normal alien things happened to me again.

One thing I really loved here was my new bed. After the moldy couch in my basement back on Earth, the huge, comfy mattress under the canopy of the living trees felt like heaven. The fragrance of fresh grass and blooming flowers made it simply magical.

I stretched my legs over the silky covers and propped a pillow under my back, leaning against one of the trunks that served as the bedposts.

Scrolling through the blobs of the Aldraian language, I let the system read the titles and options to me, adding to a list the articles to read and videos to watch.

One section I found was titled *"Adults Only."* Curiosity prompted me to click on it.

"Just a glance," I promised to myself.

It contained a collection of what looked like sex videos, available through a public network.

"Well, since I'm already here..." I clicked on a video.

The first shot was of a naked Aldraian woman. Her long chestnut hair was unbound, streaming freely down her body. She had smooth, glowing skin the same color as her hair.

The most unusual thing about her was the three pairs of breasts on her front. The first pair was placed a tiny bit higher than those of humans, and the last pair was just above her waist. Small and perky, all six bounced slightly as she walked barefoot along a picturesque meadow with large flowers that appeared to grow bigger as she approached.

She sauntered toward a giant flower bud. It was purple and as huge as a tent, its petals closed tightly. The flower opened, revealing an Aldraian man sleeping in the bedding in the middle.

The flower looked real, not a prop. I immediately took a mental note to find more information about the giant flowers of Aldrai.

The man woke up, clearly excited to see the naked woman. So excited, in fact, his erection popped up immediately, standing up nearly vertically. He scooted aside, inviting her to join him on the flower bed.

The woman climbed inside on her knees and positioned herself between the man's knees. Wrapping his arms around her middle, he pulled her closer, then licked one of her breasts. She arched her back, and he dragged his tongue up and down three of her nipples, first on her right, then on her left. That many breasts presented that many more options.

The woman moaned dramatically. The camera zoomed in, showing her at an exciting angle.

This clearly was some kind of Aldraian porn entertainment site I'd stumbled upon. It'd do little in terms of research for me, since I had no plans to explore Aldraian sex life. I should just close the video and watch a documentary on the Aldraian school system or something equally useful.

But I couldn't look away. Maybe it was the flower, or the fact that the man and the woman were so beautiful together, or maybe I was just nosy and horny, but I found it impossible to stop watching them.

The woman slid her slender fingers up the man's erection. He tossed his head back with a muffled groan, then suddenly flipped down on his face and spread his arms and legs on the sheets like a starfish.

The woman didn't seem to be concerned by her partner's odd position or his sudden immobility. She straddled the back of his legs, then placed her hands on...the appendage that writhed and curled over the man's butt.

"What the..." I hit the pause button, then squinted at the image.

Did the guy have...a tail? Or was it a second dick?

Either option was equally unbelievable.

Then I recalled Mara saying something about Aldraian tails long ago, still back on Earth when she had tried to convince me to come here instead of her. She'd said Aldraians kept their tails hidden.

Xavran didn't have a tail, though, did he? Hidden or not, I would've noticed it if he did, wouldn't I?

Then I remembered the back of his pants moving as he was leaving the kitchen earlier today. That would be exactly where the tail would've been located—had he had one.

He did have a tail!

"Wow..." I minimized the video of the two Aldraians having a good time in the flower, then ordered to the device, "Look up Aldraian tail."

The search results that came up were even more scandalous than the video of the couple in the flower.

It looked like Aldraians indeed had tails, males and females alike. They kept them hidden in their clothes, however, all the time. It appeared they only displayed their tails in a sexual manner. Nearly every single video that had an Aldraian with his or her tail out had some kind of adult content.

The woman on the flower video licked along the entire length of the man's tail, then sucked the tip into her mouth. She rolled the tail between her palms, making the man groan.

He rolled over onto his back again, his hard-on bobbing in the air like a jack-in-a-box.

The Aldraian penis presented an interesting sight on its own. Raised bumps were placed along its entire length. The bumps were slightly darker than the rest of his skin. When the woman pressed on them, they compressed like little sponges, leaking clear, thick liquid.

"Interesting," I muttered.

The woman spread the liquid over the man's entire length, then slathered some on his tail. Straddling his hips, she lowered herself on his length in the front as he slipped his tail between her butt cheeks.

Double-penetration? By one man? Well, that was...

"Interesting," I repeated, flabbergasted.

Chapter 12

Susanna

I was glad Xavran wasn't around when Stefan came to pick me up to go shopping for groceries. I didn't think I could look the captain straight in the eye without imagining all the things I now knew he was packing in his pants.

The grocery store was under the open sky, as expected on Aldrai. Stands with fresh produce, water tanks with live seafood, and an expansive butcher shop gave it the feel of a farmer's market combined with an aquarium.

"Are these the things we ate for dinner last night?" I wondered out loud, spotting the flat round creatures in one of the water tanks.

"Possibly," Stefan replied. "There are lots of them in Diria Lake, just behind Xavran's home. And he's an avid fisherman."

"They're rather repulsive to look at." I watched the creatures crawl on the bottom of the tank, their many legs scurrying beneath them. "But they taste pretty good."

"Xavran is an excellent cook. I've had his dinner leftovers for lunch. Delicious!" He kissed his pinched fingers in a chef's kiss. "I suggest you learn as many of his recipes as you can before he leaves town."

That was a good idea. I made a note to research food sites and find videos about Aldraian meal preparation processes. With Xavran gone soon, I'd be left with four children to feed, in addition to my sister. Just like me, Mara had never cooked a meal in her life.

After the shopping, we went to school where I met the kids' teacher as well as a group of parents of the children's friends. Everyone was polite and friendly, and I responded in the same manner.

"If you need anything just ask," a few of the mothers said. "It's not easy to move worlds."

It shouldn't be. But it didn't feel as hard as I would've imagined. I could learn this.

I could do this job.

So I thought.

Until the kids came out running.

Illal ran to me with a hug. The boys nodded in greeting. But Ene turned away, sulking. She wouldn't even return my "hi."

"Did I do something?" I asked Stefan quietly as we all boarded the aircraft.

He shrugged. "Change isn't always easy on kids. She'll get used to you. Eventually. Just be kind and patient."

My patience got tested when we got home, however. Stefan went straight to the kitchen to make the kids' snack. They tossed their school bags under the hedge in the front garden. As I learned yesterday, it wasn't what they were supposed to do.

"Pick up your bags and take them to your rooms, please," I told them.

Both boys groaned and rolled their eyes but picked up the bags and marched out. Illal lingered, her bag in her hands. Ene wouldn't even touch hers. Chin up in challenge, she stomped toward the exit.

"Ene, you forgot something," I called after her.

She paid me no attention, as if I hadn't spoken at all.

"Ene. Your bag..." I touched her shoulder.

"Leave me alone!" she shrieked so suddenly, I jumped. "You can't tell me what to do. You're not my mom!"

I jerked my hand away, frozen in shock.

She took off, running in the opposite direction from the kitchen and her room.

"What did I do?" I asked Illal.

"It's not you," she said with a solemn expression on her little face. "Ene cried during the break today. Again."

"Why?"

"Girls make fun of her short hair."

"Well, that's ridiculous." I scoffed, feeling offended on Ene's behalf. "She can wear her hair any way she wants. If she likes it short—"

"She doesn't." Illal bit her lip.

"Then why did she cut it that way?"

"She didn't. Kessra did."

"Who?"

"Kessra. A girl in our class."

That sounded worse and worse with every answer I got.

"Does the teacher know? The principal? How about your dad?"

"No." Illal shook her head vehemently, her long ponytail swaying behind her back. "Ene doesn't want anyone to know. She just went to the bathroom with her craft scissors and cut whatever Kessra had missed to make it more even. Then she put it up in bunches. But now Kessra is making fun of her. She says Ene looks like a boy."

"That girl cut your sister's hair without permission? Now, she's making fun of her? What a little b—" I barely managed to stop in time before the swear word would've left my mouth. "Your father needs to know about this," I fumed, planning a retaliation. "The school most definitely has to know too. And Kessra's parents—"

"No." Illal grabbed on to my skirt. "Please don't tell anyone, Susanna. Ene will get angry with me for telling you. She's so upset already."

I immediately felt deflated. The entire thing felt way over my head.

"Well, then... How do we fix this?" I didn't think twice before asking for advice from an eleven-year-old, "What do I do, Illal?"

"I don't know." She shrugged.

So much for relying on help from a kid.

"Maybe I should try talking to her?" I asked hesitantly. Maybe I could get Ene to agree to let me speak to someone more qualified to handle this than me. "Where did she go?"

"To Mommy's room, probably," Illal replied casually.

"Where?" I really hoped I'd misheard her.

"Mommy's room. Ene always hides there when she's upset. It's that way." She waved in the direction where her sister had disappeared to.

I didn't recall Xavran saying anything about any rooms that way.

"Can you show me, please?" I asked Illal.

"Sure." Dropping her bag on the floor again, Illal took me down a path behind the hedge that I'd thought was the northern border of the garden.

"Here it is." She pointed at the opening in the hedge. It could be easily missed because of another hedge growing right behind it. One had to walk around it to enter the room.

This part of the gardens looked somewhat neglected compared to the rest of Xavran's well-maintained home.

Illal stopped at the entrance, visibly hesitating.

"Are you coming in with me?" I asked, not hiding the hope in my voice. It felt eerie to be here on my own. I wasn't looking forward to finding out what was in that room.

"No. I don't want to go in." Illal shook her head. "I need to put away my school bag, remember?"

Off she ran.

I rubbed the back of my neck, fighting the strong desire to follow Illal and leave, when the soft sounds of sobbing came from behind the hedge.

"Ene?" I asked quietly, stepping around the scruffy hedge and into an equally neglected space behind it.

Ene sat on the floor, her arms folded on the bed, her head dropped on them, her small shoulders shaking with sobs. The sight of her so small and sad, in this dark, obviously abandoned place, broke my heart.

"Ene?" I rushed to her.

"Go away!" she yelled, without lifting her head.

I wished I could do as she demanded and just get out. I really had no idea what I was doing here, in the first place. But she was clearly miserable, and I couldn't just leave her.

I shifted from foot to foot, clutching my hands in front of me and respectfully keeping my distance.

"I thought you could use some company," I said tentatively. "Crying is not fun. But crying while all alone is even less so."

"I'm not crying." She sniffled, lifted her head, and wiped her face with the old bedspread.

How long had this bedding been on this bed? Green saplings were growing through the fabric, it seemed to be becoming part of the nature around it.

Ene sniffled again, tossing me a glare from under her brow. "You can't be here."

The skin around her eyes turned red and puffy, her cheeks smeared with tears and stained with dark blotches. The pigtails all over her head stuck out chaotically, some pointing straight up, others drooping.

"This is Mommy's room," she declared. "Only Mommy and I can be here."

Chills ran down my spine. I glanced around, half-expecting to see the ghost of the dead woman hovering nearby. Then, an equally chilling suspicion rose in my mind. What if the poor girl wasn't well?

"Do you see your mother here?" I asked, trying to keep my voice as gentle as possible.

"Yeah. Don't you?" She pointed at the framed picture on the grass mound by the bed that served as a nightstand.

In the picture, a heavily pregnant Aldraian woman smiled broadly, her arms folded over her huge belly.

"Is that your mom?"

Ene nodded somberly.

This was the first time I'd seen an image of Xavran's late wife. She seemed happy, her smile flirty. I wondered if he was the one who took the picture and if that smile was meant for him. Stefan had said Xavran was madly in love with his late wife.

"Did your dad put it here?" I asked.

"No." Ene shook her head, making all her pigtails flop and wag. "I did. Grandma gave it to me."

"What was your mother's name?"

"Gelnall."

"It's pretty."

She sighed. "It is. I'm in there." Ene poked her finger at the woman's stomach. "My brothers and Illal too. All of us are together in this picture."

Except for Xavran. He wasn't there. Unless, of course, he took it. The picture must have been taken not long before the accident.

I rubbed my upper arms with my hands. "So, you come here when you're upset? Does it make you feel better?"

"Yes, it does." She stuck out her chin in challenge. "Because Mommy loved me. More than anyone does." There was a firm conviction in her voice, but when she lifted her gaze to me, she looked unsure. Questioning.

Was she expecting me to confirm that?

"Of course, she loved you," I said. "That's what mommies do. They love their children."

My words seem to pacify her a little. She nodded, staring at the grass on the ground in front of her. "Does your mom love you, too?"

"My mom... She's no longer alive," I said cautiously.

Ene gazed at me with interest. "Is she dead, like mine?"

Like mine.

The words were more accurate than she knew since my mother also died in a plane crash. I decided it was best not to mention that detail right now.

"Yes. She's been dead for six years."

"But did she love you when she was alive?"

I inhaled deeply.

"Well…" I knew what answer the little girl expected, but I detested lying to her. Even if it would be a white lie. "I'm sure she did," I started hesitantly. "In her own way, my mother probably loved Mara and me. Sadly, she didn't spend enough time with us for me to *feel* her love."

Ene tilted her head to the side, tugging at the pigtail over her right ear. "Did she work a lot, like my dad?"

"No. She didn't work, but she did a lot of other things outside of home."

"Like what?"

"Social things, like parties, galas, dinners, fundraisers…"

"What are those?" She squinted at me, wrinkling her nose in an adorable way.

"They are different forms of gatherings that some people think are important. And maybe they are…" I sensed she was waiting for me to say something positive. I desperately wanted to make her feel better. Sadly, there wasn't much positive I could offer from my relationship with my mother. "I liked helping her with those parties. As soon as I was old enough to be useful, I would tag along and do whatever she told me to do." That was my way to ensure my mother and I spent some time together. "I learned a lot. I can throw a kickass fundraiser in a flash if needed."

My upbeat voice made her smile, which was the point. Sadly, the smile was short-lived.

"My mother also bought me a lot of purple clothes," I said, not sure why.

"Purple? Do you like this color?"

"Not really. But it helped Mother to tell Mara and me apart, because she dressed Mara in pink."

"Your mom needed different color clothes to tell you apart?"

"Yeah..." That didn't sound very uplifting. I scrambled for something better to say. "But you know what, some of the nannies we had could tell us apart with no problems at all, regardless of what we wore."

"They could?"

"Yes. One nanny we had stayed with us for almost six years. Marissa." I smiled, remembering Marissa's warm hugs that always smelled like vanilla because of the body spray she used and the baking she loved to do. "She was kind and told the best goodnight stories. She always knew who was who, even when Mara and I tried to trick her on purpose."

Ene shifted a little closer. "Where is she now?"

"Well, Marissa was pretty old when she worked for us. She's long dead now."

"Oh." Ene's expression fell again.

Obviously, my cheering-up technique sucked.

I rubbed my forehead. "My point is that you don't really need to be related to people to feel close to them. Your family is kind of like a starter kit you get at birth. But it doesn't mean you can't adjust and add to it as you go. You meet all kinds of people out there. Some of them you may like more than anyone ever before. What I'm saying is... You can make your own family, Ene."

"So..." She appeared to be pondering my words. "Are you saying Marissa was your family?"

"Yes, I felt as close to her as a family would. Anyone you like can be your friend. Then, your best friends can be your closest family."

She bit her lip, staring at the grass for a moment. To my alarm, tears swelled in her light-gray eyes again.

"But what if they don't want to be my friends?"

Her voice came out shaky, and I forgot all about keeping the respectful distance. I plopped on the ground right next to her.

"Then they weren't meant to be your friends at all. Why waste time and energy on them? You know how many people are out there? Billions! You can't be friends with everyone. And you don't have to. It's the very few that matter. Choose your 'few' carefully."

She fell quiet, twisting a blade of grass between her fingers. Her pigtails swayed with a deep breath.

Sadness lingered in this desolate garden-room like a funeral shroud. Even the bright sky above didn't brighten it. I wished I could get her out of here, somehow.

"Hey, do you know what we can do?" I yanked my hair elastic off my ponytail. "I can show you all the fun and crazy ways in which women on Earth style their hair. Want to see that?"

"No. Don't touch my hair." She sulked again, shrinking back. "I want it to look like horns. Like Daddy's. I want to be as strong as he is, so I can punch everyone in their face when they laugh at me."

My optimism waned, and I struggled to regain some positivity.

"Well, your dad may be strong, but it doesn't mean he goes around punching people in their faces, does he?"

She nodded. "He punched Uncle Uttek at our birthday party two years ago."

"He did?" My jaw dropped. "Why?"

"Because Uncle Uttek agreed with Grandma when she said if it wasn't for Dad, Mom would still be alive. I guess Dad didn't want to punch Grandma, so he punched Uncle Uttek instead."

A lovely birthday party that must have been.

I feared I'd opened a can of worms that I really didn't want to sort through right now, especially with a kid.

"Okay, well... Let's braid *my* hair. I won't touch yours if you don't want me to. Come." I got up to my feet, eager to get out of this spooky place. "I'll show you all the hair care stuff I've brought from Earth. We can raid Mara's luggage too. I'm sure she has lots in all those bags that got delivered from the spaceport today."

Ene got up to follow me, and I released a long breath of relief. I honestly had no idea what I would've done had she said no again.

Chapter 13

Xavran

He was making a new batch of marinade in the kitchen, trying hard to focus on the ingredients instead of Susanna. It had been three days since she arrived, but her presence was just as unnerving to him as ever.

Dressed in a black skirt and a white blouse, she sat at the counter. Holding her tablet in her hands, she softly dictated into it, recording the recipe he was making. This was his mother's old recipe. He knew it by heart and had never bothered writing it down.

He wished Susanna was next to him, helping him with the spices. Or better yet, right in front of him, between him and the counter, so he could lean over her shoulder while she mixed and adjust her wrist when necessary, press into her backside, nuzzle her neck...

Heat surged through his chest, then rushed down to his groin.

Dammit.

He went rigid, focusing all his mental power on taming his lust once again. The measuring spoon slipped from his stiff fingers and clattered to the counter.

Susanna glanced up at him, her eyebrows raised in question.

"Clumsy me," he muttered.

He was leaving Diria for the frontier the day after tomorrow. It was about time, it seemed.

Stepping closer to the counter, he attempted to hide his raging erection behind it. It appeared to work, as she clearly didn't notice.

"You can't afford to be clumsy, Xavran," she teased. "You break things too easily."

She slid her finger along the long chip in the stone counter. The chip marked the spot where he'd dropped the cauldron yesterday. He'd lifted it when Susanna had leaned in to see the meat he had marinating there. Her neckline had shifted, revealing a sliver of the lacy breast harness underneath her blouse, and he'd let the cauldron fall.

That was all it took for him to lose control—a glimpse of her undergarment. He felt like he was a teenager again, with no control over his impulses. Clearly, being without a woman for this long had affected him more than he could have ever expected.

Of course, he couldn't tell her what had made him drop the cauldron. He'd told her he had accidentally stubbed his toe. Now, she thought him a clumsy oaf.

"What are you up to?" Mara walked into the kitchen unexpectedly.

Dressed in a tight white dress with a wide-brimmed hat on her head, she carried a leather bag on her forearm.

He'd barely exchanged a handful of words with his lawful spouse. Mara never sought his company. On the contrary, whenever he walked into a room, she immediately left.

Personally, it suited him just fine, but he had hoped she'd show more interest in his children.

Instead of getting married, he could have hired two or three nannies, but he decided to have a wife instead. A marriage seemed a more stable arrangement, and he wanted stability for his children, with some resemblance of a family. Nannies came and went, but he wanted his children to have someone who'd be there for them for years to come.

The marriage program was perfect for that. It'd allowed him to state his expectations in advance, hopefully avoiding any misunderstanding in the future. It seemed so simple. All he had to do was enter a list of requirements, like placing a mail order.

He wanted a mother for his children, not a lover for himself.

What he got...

What he got was a wife who clearly had no interest in his children and a nanny whom he could way too easily envision as his lover.

In fact, he had spent the past three nights *envisioning* Susanna in every position possible, despite his best efforts not to.

His cock jerked again, clearly ignoring his threats and warnings. Lust shot through him, hot and sweaty.

He gripped the spoon so hard, the wooden handle snapped.

Not again!

"Um..." Susanna carefully removed the broken pieces from his grip. "Maybe you should consider switching to metal cutlery?"

Mara sauntered closer, clearly displeased at being ignored.

"This looks like a lovely scene of domestic bliss," she said tersely.

She couldn't possibly be jealous. Mara didn't care about him. In fact, she often appeared to be pushing Susanna's company on him to avoid spending any time with him herself. She refused to go to the parent-teacher meeting with him yesterday, even after the teacher had explicitly requested her presence.

"I'm bored," she pouted.

He realized she wasn't jealous of *him*. Mara was envious of Susanna and him having something to do and spending time together.

"Is there really nothing to do around here?" Mara whined.

Susanna jerked her head impatiently. "There's plenty to do if you just look around. I'm busy every single day. There's no time to be bored."

"Yeah, well, *you* don't need much to be entertained. Simple minds and all that..." Mara waved a hand in the air.

Susanna glared at her sister, looking like she was ready to toss the broken spoon at her. She heaved a sigh instead, keeping her composure after all.

"So," Susanna said evenly. "Why doesn't your *superior* mind find you something better to do than coming in here and insulting the people who live under the same roof."

"There's no roof, remember?" Mara snorted, pointing her finger up at the open sky above them.

Susanna squared her shoulders. "Still better than losing one's head."

"Oh please." Mara rolled her eyes. "If you like it here so much, you should've come to Aldrai by yourself, without dragging me along. Just like I wanted you to do in the first place."

"And what would've happened to *you* if you stayed?" Giving her sister a pointed stare, Susanna made a cutting gesture at her throat with the edge of her hand.

Mara waved her off. "I would've been fine. I have enough connections in the city. I just happened to be scared that one night, and you took advantage of it."

Susanna shook her head, rolling her eyes skywards.

"What are you two talking about?" he interrupted. Somehow, he'd lost any understanding of their conversation about halfway through. Only one thing remained clear: the sisters were arguing.

"Nothing that would interest you." Mara stifled a yawn. "I'm going for a walk. You have fun cooking...or whatever it is you two are doing here." She produced a pair of sunglasses out of her purse and perched them on her nose.

"Make sure to stay within the town limits," he warned her.

"Or what? I'll get lost?"

"No, but there are a few things underground that may eat you if you leave the protection of the town borders." He kept his voice casual.

The desert monsters didn't make it that far into the terraformed territory often. His goal was to scare Mara just enough to make her remain within the protection of the town's ground shields. Not to terrify her out of her wits.

She gave him a suspicious look, obviously gauging whether he was joking or serious. He went to get another spoon, letting her guess.

When he returned to the counter, Mara was gone.

"What was your sister talking about?" he asked Susanna. "She didn't want to come to Aldrai?"

She set aside her tablet and chewed on her bottom lip while playing with the pieces of the broken spoon.

"Mara tried to talk me into switching places with her," she said finally.

"Why?" he asked, mostly out of curiosity. It made no difference to him whether Mara was here on Aldrai or back on Earth. "Why did she apply for the marriage program, then?"

"She wanted to come here at first, but then she changed her mind later. Since we look so alike, she tried to convince me to come instead of her, under her name."

That also didn't matter much. Either as his wife or his nanny, Susanna would be living in his home. Either way, he'd struggle to have a professional relationship with her while nursing an erection the size of an axe handle in his pants.

His children would have been better off, though. With Susanna as his wife, they would've had a stepmom who actually cared for them.

He'd watched Susanna with his children. He saw how much closer they'd gotten with her in just a few days. Even Ene, who had never been affectionate with strangers, had warmed up to Susanna, letting her brush and style her short hair every morning now.

"Why didn't you switch with Mara?" he asked.

"I didn't want to pretend to be someone else," she said, somewhat sheepishly. "I didn't want to lie."

A blush spread on her cheeks as she cast her eyes down. A sudden desire to grab her in his arms and kiss her face rushed over him.

What was he going to do with this woman?

Instead, he cleared his throat and said as calmly as he could, "I'm glad you didn't. I've had enough lies in my life."

She stared at him, as if waiting for him to elaborate. But what could he possibly tell her? After over a decade, some things from his past still hurt even to think about, let alone speak.

"Well." He lifted the new spoon. "Let's mix it then, shall we?"

For a while, they worked quietly. Everything felt comfortable in Susanna's presence, even the silence.

Then, Mara burst through the gate to the kitchen, marching in.

"Well, guess whom I met on my walk?" She paused, probably more for drama than actually expecting an answer. "An assistant from the mayor's office. He said there's a party in the town hall tomorrow night. Apparently, the entire town has been invited. The ambassador from the planet Tragul is the guest of honor! How come I didn't know about the invitation?" she demanded.

He stretched his neck. The easy feeling he'd enjoyed before her sudden arrival slipped away, replaced by tension in his shoulders. "I don't go to parties."

She scoffed. "Maybe you shouldn't be thinking only about yourself. How about *me*? I've been sitting here, dying of boredom. And you hide party invitations from me?"

He didn't hide anything. The open invitation could be easily viewed on the local network. But he didn't bring her attention to it, either. After years of ignoring the invites, it didn't even occur to him to consider this one.

"You can go." He shrugged.

"Oh, I will!" She stomped her foot. "You can bet your hard alien ass I will go and have fun. Anything is better than sitting here day after day."

"Mara, come on!" Susanna got off her seat. But her sister had stormed out, not sparing her a glance. "Sorry." She turned to him.

"No, she's right," he agreed. "She's been spending days just sitting in her room. It couldn't possibly be fun."

"But whose fault is that? There's plenty to do around here if she wanted to do anything other than party."

"I want her to be happy." He felt responsible for the wellbeing of both women he'd brought to Aldrai. After all, he'd taken them away from the only life they knew.

"Good luck with that," Susanna said under her breath. "Many men have tried making Mara happy. All failed miserably in the end."

No matter what, Mara was here because of him. Legally, she was his wife. He had to find a way to make her happy.

"You say she likes shopping. Maybe I should arrange a trip to Arqa for her to visit some stores. Would that please her?"

Susanna hiked up a shoulder. "It may. Temporarily."

And now he wondered what would make Susanna happy. The idea of pleasing *her* filled him with real excitement.

"Would you like to go to the party, too?" he found himself asking.

She tilted her head, considering his question. "It would be nice to meet the town people, wouldn't it?"

"Do you like dancing?" Maybe going to the party wouldn't be that bad after all. It'd be a good way to say goodbye before he left for work.

A spark of interest flashed in her eyes. "It depends. What kind of dancing? I took ballroom dance lessons for years. So, if it's anything like a waltz or foxtrot, I'm in. But what else do people at parties do here? Beside dancing?"

"Everything people on other planets do, I imagine. We dance, eat food, talk…"

The talking part was what he'd been trying to avoid all these years. But if Susanna wished to go, he would come along. Maybe it was time to get out and into the world a little.

"Sounds like fun. Can kids come, too?" Her voice lifted with excitement.

"Of course." He chuckled. "There's no way they'd let us leave them behind."

Chapter 14

Susanna

"How much longer?" Mara whined, picking her way on the cobblestone path with her stiletto sandals.

One would think she would've learned her lesson by now and switched to more practical footwear. Aldraians sure loved their cobblestones. Unlike in Xavran's home, the paths between the hedges of the Diria homes were laid with harder stones. Mara's heels clicked and slipped on them as all seven of us walked to the town hall.

"Why couldn't we just fly?" she complained.

Xavran stoically kept quiet.

"Because it's not that far." I held Illal's hand, keeping an eye on Ene, who skipped ahead of us with the boys.

As I had promised Illal, I hadn't spoken to anyone about the hair cutting incident. I felt like I had just started building trust with the children, and I didn't want to spoil that. But the situation worried me.

I watched Ene carefully when the kids came home from school every day. After our hair styling game, she'd asked me to braid her hair the next morning. I'd made her two French braids, then questioned Illal after school. Apparently, no one teased Ene that day. Some girls came up to take a closer look at her unusual hair arrangement. And one or two even asked if Ene's nanny could braid their hair that way too.

"Ugh, these stupid things!" Mara cursed under her breath as her heel slid off again, jerking her ankle.

"You're risking breaking your leg," I warned. "Take your shoes off, at least for now."

Xavran turned to face her.

"It's not that far now. I can carry you." He stepped closer, opening his arms with the clear intention of lifting her up.

"Oh no!" She backed away. "Don't you dare touch me." She quickly slid the sandals off her feet and marched ahead barefoot.

Personally, I saw nothing wrong with accepting his offer. The memory of how comforting his big arms felt around me the night I'd run, terrified of the fish in the tub, almost made me regret my choice of the sensible, flat-soled shoes I was wearing tonight.

Mara yanked down the skirt of her animal-print minidress. "I'll walk on my own, thank you very much."

"Suit yourself." He shrugged.

"Simply repulsive," she muttered under her breath, stomping ahead.

I snapped my gaze to his face, hoping he didn't hear that. By the way his jaw muscles flexed, I feared he had.

Illal let go of my hand, running to him. "Me, Daddy! Can you carry me?"

A corner of his mouth lifted in one of his half-smiles. "Sure."

I knew it was best for me not to stare at him as he bent over to pick up his daughter. I shouldn't be admiring how the thick ropes of muscles in his thighs pushed against the fabric of his pants. But there I was, watching his hard butt cheeks flex and trying to make out the outline of his tail between them.

"Me too!" Ivex bounced to Xavran.

His brother followed him. "And me!"

Xavran chuckled. "I only have two arms. So, two at a time."

He scooped Illal and Ivex up, fitting one kid on each arm.

I caught up with Ene, matching my step with hers.

"How about you?" I asked her. "Don't you want your dad to carry you, too?"

She rolled her eyes. "I have my own two feet, don't I? I can walk."

"All right then. Can I walk with you?"

She gave me a sideway glance but didn't move away. "Sure. It's a wide path. There's space for both of us."

A short while later, the lights of the town hall came up between the hedges in front of us. Upbeat music reached us.

"Party!" The kids rushed ahead, all four of them.

The rest of us reached the town hall a minute later.

There was no actual building, but a giant gazebo style roof stretched between at least a dozen trunks of live trees growing in no particular pattern.

The ground was covered with thick grass and a mesh of stone paths that intertwined artistically. Under the roof, strings of lights competed with the swarms of glowing insects in illuminating the space.

Aldraians of all ages mingled under the roof. Most congregated around the long tables laden with food.

A man hurried to us the moment we entered under the gazebo.

"Mara! I'm so glad you made it." He stretched his hand palm up, and she placed hers on top in the Aldraian greeting.

She tilted her head, smiling at him pleasantly. "I wouldn't miss this for the world. Thank you for the invitation."

I guessed the man must be the assistant from the mayor's office Mara had spoken about.

"The invitation was public. All of Diria are welcome. It's a town celebration." He turned to Xavran and me. "Welcome, Captain Rax and...Susanna, I believe? I'm Khezan, Assistant to the Mayor of Diria."

I gave him my hand. "Nice to meet you."

"I've heard about you from my sister, Yurie," he said, smiling. "Her children go to the same school as yours... I mean the captain's children. Not *yours*."

"Right." I remembered the name as that of one of the mothers I'd met at the kids' school. "Yurie is such a nice woman. She's been incredibly helpful with information. I have so much to learn, being in a new place and stuff."

"And who is that?" Mara murmured, pointing with her gaze at a person I recognized as a Ravil, from planet Tragul. "Is that the ambassador?"

Back on Earth, Mara had called Ravils handsome. And I certainly agreed with her on that. Tall and muscular, the man wasn't wearing a shirt. Short, golden-brown fur covered his entire body, shimmering in the lights. Sandy-blond hair curled around his ears and down his neck in thick waves like a lion's mane.

"Yes. That's Ambassador Zeigan Ussai from the country Ravi on planet Tragul," Khezan explained. "His country is recovering after a twenty-year-long war. He's the first ambassador sent to Aldrai in decades."

As if sensing the attention, the Ravil turned to us. His long tail with a tuft of fur on the end swayed behind him.

Mara's smile grew into a smolder at meeting his gaze. Ambassador Ussai took it as an invitation to head our way.

He pressed a hand to his chest with a deep bow as he approached. "I'm Ambassador Zeigan Ussai of Ravi."

"Captain Xavran Rax." Xavran returned the bow. His was rather jerky, compared to the ambassador's feline grace. "My wife, Mara. Her sister, Susanna Riley," he introduced us.

"It's an honor to meet you. What a surprise." The ambassador beamed at Mara and me. "I did not expect to find human women in Diria."

Mara flicked her hair over her shoulder. "Finding a high state official in this place is just as surprising."

He moved his gaze to me, then back to her again. The confused expression crossed his handsome face, typical for people seeing us for the first time.

"It's nice to meet you." I offered him my hand, palm up, and he covered it with his. "I'm Mara's twin sister," I explained. "We're identical twins. That's why we look so alike."

He kept staring. "It's phenomenal. Multiple births are a norm among Voranians and Aldraians, but I've never seen two people so perfectly alike. It's a good thing you're wearing different clothes." He chuckled, moving his other hand under mine to enclose it between his two. "There'd be no way of telling you apart otherwise."

"That's a good thing." I smiled, gliding the hand not trapped by the ambassador down the flared skirt of my black-and-white dress, the same one I wore on the day of our arrival. It was the dressiest thing I had for the occasion.

I was getting my first paycheck soon, and one of the moms I'd met through the kids' school had already offered to take me shopping in Ar-qa next weekend. I was looking forward to the trip. It'd be nice to have some casual clothes. My knits and polyester pieces had been fine for the cool weather in New York, but they didn't work well in the balmy climate of Aldrai.

The music slowed down a little.

The ambassador was still holding my hand. The top of his was covered with short fur. It seemed soft, with a pretty, golden sheen. Unable to hold back my curiosity, I placed my other hand on top of his, petting him slightly. It did feel soft.

His tail twitched my way. "Would you like to dance, Madam Riley?"

"Oh, sorry..." I jerked my hand away. As fascinating as meeting a new species was, stroking them like that was certainly inappropriate. "I—"

Xavran shouldered his way between the ambassador and me. "Susanna has already promised to dance with *me*."

Had I? I wasn't sure. But at the thought of dancing, a smile sprung to my lips.

Mara took the Ravil's hand from me. "I'd love to dance, Ambassador."

He moved his emerald-green eyes from me to her, his grin unwavering.

"Splendid." Placing his hands on her waist, he whisked her away to the music.

"Do you really want to dance?" I asked Xavran. Frankly, I couldn't imagine this man dancing. Some people just weren't built for that. "We can always just hang around the punch bowl, instead, or whatever they have here in place of that. It's a great way to meet new people."

"I don't want to meet any new people." He hugged me around my waist, drawing me closer. "I just want to dance with you."

"Oh!" I drew in a breath at finding myself in his arms so suddenly, then splayed my hands on his wide chest. "Well then, dance we shall."

Xavran took me around the open space in a slow circle, weaving between the other couples. I noticed the women had their hands wrapped around the men's horns on their shoulders while dancing. Maybe I should've done the same, but I liked touching his chest instead. As hard as his pectoral muscles were under his shirt, they still felt softer than the horns, warmer, too, making him more approachable somehow.

Mara's giggling reached me as the ambassador twirled her by us.

I followed them with my gaze for a few moments. "It's so neat to meet someone from yet another planet," I marveled out loud. "Ravils are fascinating. Is it a norm for them not to wear shirts? Or is it just the ambassador's way?"

Xavran frowned, not sparing the other man a glance. "Ravils never wear shirts."

"I suppose it's unnecessary since they have fur. It's warm here."

"They never cover their tails either." He shook his head disapprovingly.

"Oh, how shocking!" I gasped in fake horror.

He smirked. "But then again, other species' tails aren't nearly as indecent as those of Aldraians."

The images of the couple in a flower bed from the video I'd watched rose in my mind. The smile slid off my face as my cheeks heated.

"So I've heard." I averted my eyes from him, hoping he wouldn't notice my blush.

The music leaped faster, but Xavran's steps slowed. He moved his hands up my back, bringing us closer. With a slow twirl around one of the tree trunks that worked as support pillars for the roof, he swerved away from the lit space, taking me behind the hedge and out of view from the party.

In the shadows behind the hedge, he pressed my back to the tree trunk. His heart beat wildly under my hand on his chest.

One of his forearms pressed against the trunk above my head, he leaned over me.

"What are you doing to me, Susanna?" he growled. His eyes grew as dark as the night around us.

I could've asked him the same question. My heart thundered, beating frantically against my ribcage. The heat of his large, hard body pressed to mine felt invigorating.

Wishing to feel more of him, I slid my hands up his chest to his thick, corded neck. He sucked in a breath as I stroked his underjaw with my thumbs.

All this time I'd been struggling to keep a distance between us, when all I really wanted was to touch him. Everywhere.

Keeping his right hand above my head, he moved the other one up my side. He stopped it just under my breast.

"Tell me to get my hands off you," he whispered into my ear. "Because I'll do more if you don't."

I pressed my lips together, keeping my mouth shut.

He cupped my breast, finding my nipple with his thumb. Desire sparked hot in me. I released a breath with a soft moan.

"Tell me I repulse you, like your sister says," he demanded, bitterness seeping into his drawl. "Tell me I disgust you, to make it easier for me to leave you tomorrow."

Things would've been so much easier if I didn't feel for him what I was feeling. The wild, hot frenzy that swirled through my mind and body was not supposed to happen. The heat pulsing between my legs might be inappropriate. Inconvenient. But it was so wonderful.

I hadn't felt like that for a long time. In fact, I didn't remember ever feeling anything as intense with any other man ever.

I swallowed hard. "If I say that, I'd be lying, and I've had too many lies in my life already."

He took my face between his hands. "Say you'd hate it if I kissed you."

I stared straight into his eyes. "I'll say no such thing—"

He lowered his lips to mine. Words and thoughts deserted me, swept into a twister. Need coursed through my veins. I clung to his neck as he kissed me greedily, as a man starved. And maybe he was starved for physical contact, for affection, just like I was.

When he made a move to pull away, I gripped the horns on the side of his head and kissed him back.

"Don't go," rushed through my head.

I didn't want this to stop. He proved more intoxicating than wine, and I couldn't get enough of him. I craved more.

Gripping my backside, he pressed me tight to him, the hard ridge of his erection trapped between us.

Arousal zapped through me. I wanted to feel him inside me. If he were my intoxication, I wished to be drunk on him.

More.

Harder.

Faster...

My head was spinning. How did this man make me throw my caution to the wind?

Too fast...

All of this was happening way too soon.

I didn't need this, did I? I certainly wasn't searching for something like this. I didn't even know these feelings existed.

I didn't need a man right now, or another husband. Not that Xavran even could be my husband. Technically, he already had a wife. My sister.

Oh, that sounded really messed up.

Yanking back on his horns, I made him break the kiss.

"Susanna," he groaned. "I want you."

I shut my eyes for a moment, afraid to get lost in his again.

"Daddy!" Illal's voice rang from the other side of the hedge. "Dad!"

The world came crashing in, shattering our hot, sweaty bubble of lust. Xavran released me from his arms, and I shouldn't have disliked that as much as I did.

"We better go back," I mumbled, straightening my dress, then smoothing my hair.

"You go," he rasped.

Glancing down, I spotted the huge bulge tenting his pants.

He rubbed the back of his neck. "I'll...need a minute."

"Right, well..." I took a hesitant step away.

"Wait." He came after me, cupping my face. "This isn't over. Not at all. We'll need to talk."

We really should. *This*—whatever it was—needed to be sorted out.

"Okay." I nodded. "We will."

"Daddy!"

"I have to go." I dashed behind the hedge, escaping his intense gaze. I found Illal by one of the food tables. "What is it, Illal?"

"Where is Daddy?" she demanded.

"He is...um..." I bit my lip, becoming aware of how hot and tingling my lips were after Xavran's ravenous kiss. "Daddy must be here some-where. But can I help you instead?"

A calculating impression flickered in her bright orange eyes.

"Yeah. I want some *shohe*." She pointed at the huge cluster of small baby-blue fruit suspended under the roof of the gazebo.

Each elongated fruit glistened with crystalized syrup. *Shohe* was harvested in bunches, like giant grapes, but it was too dry and hard to eat fresh. Aldraians soaked it in sweet syrup for a few months. This was pretty much the only dessert available in Diria. Generally, Aldraians weren't into sweets, Illal being an obvious exception.

"Your dad would want you to eat something else first," I said. "Would you like some *cuqrel* stew? Or maybe a bit of *qhuiste* salad?"

Illal stomped her foot. "No. I want *shohe*."

"Oh, let the child have a treat." An Aldraian woman sauntered to us.

She seemed older. The color had bleached out of her hair over the years, making it lighter than her coral skin.

Illal immediately turned to her.

"Grandma! Can you get me that? Pleeeeease?" The girl sounded as sweet as *shohe* syrup.

"Of course, sweetie." The lady took a small wooden bowl and picked out a few fruits with a pair of tongs. "Here you go."

"Thanks." Grabbing her bounty, Illal ran to play with the other children under the gazebo.

The grandma sighed, watching her go. "These children have so little joy in life with that father of theirs." She offered me her hand. "I'm Inie. And you must be Xavran's new wife?" Pity filled her pale-pink eyes.

"No. I'm the nanny." I placed my hand on top of hers, briefly letting our palms touch. "Susanna."

"Oh, the nanny?" She glanced back at Mara, who was laughing in the company of the ambassador and the mayor's aid. A few more Aldraian men had joined them. "That must be the wife, then? Poor thing."

Mara looked anything but "poor," in any sense of that word. Dressed in one of her designer dresses and wearing a wide-brimmed hat, she held a tall glass with a colorful drink in her hand, laughing at something one of the men must've said.

"She has no idea what she got herself into," Inie sighed. "It would've been best for you to never have come here at all."

"Why is that?"

She pursed her lips, taking a pause before saying in a grave tone of voice, "Your new boss is a violent man."

"Xavran? Violent?" I'd heard others call him "gloomy" or "unsociable." This was the first time someone had ever referred to him as "violent." "He's been very nice, so far," I protested.

"So far..." Inie echoed, ominously. "Has he told you what happened to his first wife? My poor daughter, Gelnall?"

"No. But I heard it was an accident. I'm so sorry for your loss—"

"An accident!" She scoffed. "Then why does he refuse to speak about it? If it were an accident, he'd have nothing to lose by talking about it, wouldn't he?"

Losing one's wife in a tragic accident wouldn't be a pleasant topic to discuss with just anyone, I presumed, but said nothing.

Inie didn't appear to expect an answer, anyway, as she continued, "Why did he make sure the details of the 'accident' had been sealed off to the public?"

"He did that?"

"Oh yes, he did. But why? If he had nothing to hide?"

I had nothing to say to that. In a way, I understood her frustration. She had the right to know the circumstances of her daughter's death.

Inie leaned closer, speaking in a hushed voice, "The authorities said Gelnall was alone on that aircraft, but she couldn't have been."

I leaned in too, matching her tone of voice. "Why not?"

"Have you seen an Aldraian woman in the last stages of her pregnancy?"

"No."

"We can't fly. Physically. Our bellies grow so big, we can't even fit behind the control panel. Gelnall carried twelve fetuses. She couldn't be the one operating the aircraft that day."

"Are you saying..." I hated to admit it, but this sounded suspicious.

"Xavran was with her," she said with conviction.

"Do you think he was the one responsible for the crash?"

"I'm telling you, this was no accident. He's too good of a pilot to let that happen, especially on a nice sunny day like it was. Unless he *wanted* it to happen, of course."

I gasped, shocked by her revelations. "He crashed on purpose?"

"Exactly."

"But why?"

Inie heaved a breath. "Isn't it obvious?"

I shook my head, "No. Not at all. I've heard Xavran adored his wife."

"At the beginning, maybe. But it soon became clear what a horrible man he really was. He kept Gelnall isolated from me and the rest of her family. We never knew where she was. When I called, he'd make up excuses, not letting me speak to her. I wonder if she realized her mistake in marrying him and wanted to leave. Then, he decided to get rid of her rather than letting her go. And he succeeded."

She threw a glare behind me somewhere. I turned over my shoulder to find Xavran walking back under the canopy of the gazebo. When met with Inie's stare, his expression darkened.

"Murderer," Inie hissed under her breath. "Those poor children. My heart aches every time I think about them sharing a home with their mother's killer."

"But Xavran wouldn't do that," I protested. Everything inside me screamed it wasn't true. Though, logic told me I didn't really know him that well. "He couldn't have..."

Inie kept staring at Xavran, as if trying to incinerate him with her glare. "He hasn't shown any remorse for killing my daughter, not once."

"It simply can't be true. He would never deliberately put his kids in danger. He cares about them so much." I couldn't speak to Xavran's relationship with his wife, but I've seen him with his kids. I thought about how devastated he had looked at a mere mention of their birthday and how caring he had always been to his surviving children. "They are his whole life."

Inie shrugged. "Well, maybe he feels some guilt for killing their mother and siblings."

"It's just so... Horrible."

"It is. Imagine how I feel, seeing this criminal literally getting away with murder. My poor Gelnall has been dead for over a decade now, and her killer is still walking free."

Xavran squared his shoulders, heading our way in long, determined strides. My heart squeezed with worry. I sensed nothing good could come out of an encounter with his former mother-in-law.

The ground between him and us moved suddenly. The perfect pattern of the cobblestones cracked and broke.

"What's going on?" I spread my arms wide for balance. "Is it an earthquake?"

Color drained from Inie's face. She stared at the large mound that rose from the ground.

"We need to go home... Engage the shields... Home..." she kept saying rapidly, not moving an inch.

"Susanna!" Xavran shouted. "The children!"

He lunged our way, but the dirt jerked higher, throwing him backwards and off his feet.

Panic exploded around us. People screamed, rushing away from the mound.

The children!

I looked around wildly.

Illal was there, grabbing my hand.

"Daddy!" Ivex ran past me toward his dad, but the mound of dirt rose in his way.

"Ivex! Come here!" I got hold of his shoulder. "Where's your brother?"

The boy pointed at the nearby table. Xilvo climbed from under it, the bowl with *shohe* fruit in his hands.

"Come here, Xilvo." I waved at him.

We had to run, but where?

People rushed in every direction. The Ravil ambassador ushered Mara out from under the gazebo. I directed the children to follow them, but the ground kept rising all around us. The trench encircled the small group of people that included us, cutting all of us off from the exits.

Everyone seemed to try to stay as far from the churning soil as possible, and I did the same, stepping back.

"Stay close, guys," I said to the kids. "Where is Ene?"

I searched the chaos erupting all around us for her small figure.

Patches of grass, clumps of dirt, and loose path stones shot up into the air as if blasted out from an underground cannon.

"Watch out!" I drew the kids closer to me, trying to shield them with my body.

A cobblestone hit me on the shoulder. I ducked my head under my arm.

"Susanna!" Xavran's voice reached me through all the noise and shouting. "Don't move!"

Don't?

Did he want us to stay still? When everything around us was in motion? Even the hedges got uprooted. The chunks of their roots and branches shot up into the air, propelled by some invisible force.

What was happening?

"*Hogas* worm!" someone shouted.

The mound right in front of us grew even higher. A black, glossy dome rose out of it. It stretched upwards, narrowing into a thick column that towered over us.

The smooth end of it split open, then expanded, like a humongous umbrella. The inside of it was dark and glossy, like liquid ink, edged with circular rows of black, shiny teeth.

The monster hovered over us. The most nightmarish abomination I'd ever seen, either in dreams or reality.

Cold terror spread through me. My muscles vibrated with the urge to run.

But where?

The circle of the raised dirt surrounded us, moving closer, tightening around us.

"Don't move, Susanna!" Xavran yelled again, his voice thick with horror but also filled with determination.

He ripped the bracers from his forearms, revealing long, curved horns flattened from the sides, like blades.

Tossing the bracers away, he stomped his feet. Other men, outside of our "circle of doom," did the same, stomping and shouting, obviously trying to divert the attention of the terrifying creature away from us.

The thing didn't fall for it, though. Whatever this monster was, it had obviously set its sights on the few of us it had entrapped.

I wrapped my arms tightly around all three of the kids, willing my legs not to move, my feet rooted in place. Fear shook me, making my teeth chatter and my knees weak.

The giant umbrella swayed downwards toward us. A woman next to me whimpered, shrinking away from the creature.

As if having waited for that, the thing lunged for her. She leaped back, swerving out of its way. A man jumped forward, shielding the woman with his body. The edge of the "umbrella" mouth caught on one of the horns on the man's shoulder. With a hard yank, the creature freed itself, knocking the man off his feet and leaving a long smudge of black blood on his shoulder.

Aldraian men's bodies had considerably more protection than the women's. Without the man jumping to her defense, the woman would've been severely injured if not killed. As it happened, only the giant worm got hurt. So far.

The man helped the woman to her feet, but neither of them stayed up. The ground shifted right under our feet this time.

I cried out in shock, fighting to keep my balance.

The people outside of the circle still tried to make some noise. They upturned tables and threw things at the creature. All in vain.

Xavran cursed under his breath in frustration.

"Daddy!" Ene ran from the outside into the lit space under the roof.

I pressed a hand to my chest in relief at seeing her safe and sound. Thankfully, she was outside of the circle, free.

Ene stared at us, her eyes glistening with tears.

The giant worm dove for us. And Xavran launched at it from behind. Jumping up, he slammed both arms into the creature. The curved, narrow horns on the back of his forearms sank deep into the smooth, black body of the worm, leaving long slashes as he slid down.

The giant creature was at least ten feet in diameter. The wounds, as long and deep as they were, didn't do much to stop it, but Xavran definitely had its attention now.

The long column of the monster's body swayed. The "umbrella" pivoted, whipping around to face Xavran. Then, it dropped down, covering him whole.

"Daddy!" Ene screamed.

From the mess of the upturned dishes on the ground, she grabbed a cauldron, then threw it into the giant worm with all her might.

Terror struck me.

"Xavran!" I screamed. What if the worm disappeared back into the dirt it had come from, taking Xavran with it? "No!"

The sharp tips of his horns poked through the membrane of the "umbrella." They moved to the base, which was the worm's neck, then all the way across, spraying ink-black blood. The parts of the creature's terrible mouth fell apart.

Xavran climbed out from the gash.

He was covered in scratches from the worm's teeth. His red blood blended with the worm's black, painting his skin with gore. But he was alive.

The black column of the worm convulsed then collapsed to the ground, the creature's throat slashed from the inside.

"Daddy!" Ene ran to him. Ignoring the gore and the stench of the worm's steaming blood, she hugged him tightly.

Climbing over the piles of churned dirt, the rest of the children dashed to them. Xavran opened his arms for all of them.

My legs still shaking, I stepped closer. And he grabbed me, too, in the same wide sweep.

"Family hug," he rasped.

I leaned into it, spreading my arms around them as wide as I could. *Family.*

I'd never felt the meaning of that word as strongly as I did now.

Chapter 15

Susanna

"That was disgusting!" Mara sobbed, crying at the kitchen table when the rest of us finally made it home. "What was that thing?"

"*Hogas* worm," Xavran said, washing his face, neck, and arms in the stone sink. "A small one. Must be still a baby."

He put a new pair of rubber-like bracers on, concealing the lethal horns on his forearms.

"A *baby?*" she yelled, nearly choking on the word. "Why did no one tell me those ugly things existed? I would've never come here. Never. Ever!"

Xavran looked tired.

"The shields are up. We're safe now," he told her. He placed his hands on the shoulders of Ene and Ivex. Illal and Xilvo kept close too. "I'll take the children to bed."

He led them out of the kitchen.

With everyone gone, Mara directed the full force of her distress at me.

"I've had it with this place. Why would anyone want to live here? It's a nightmare! Why did you make me come here? How is being eaten alive any better than decapitation?"

"No one ate you. You're still alive," I pointed out.

"Thanks to Ambassador Zeigan. He saved my life. If it wasn't for him, I'd be dead."

"No, you wouldn't. Xavran killed the worm."

"Oh, please!" She rolled her eyes. "That doesn't make him a hero."

In my eyes, it totally did. But I felt too exhausted to argue.

"Come, Mara. Have a bath, get some sleep. I'll do the same." I just couldn't deal with her tonight.

I put my arm around her shoulders, leading her out of the kitchen.

"I swear I'm getting off this planet as soon as I can." She kept complaining on the way to her room. "No one deserves to live like this. It's barbaric. They don't even have one decent shop around here. And those things, popping out from the ground, like fucking daisies!" She shuddered.

"Calm down, Mara." I helped her out of her clothes and into the tub. "We're safe, now."

"Safe? We were supposed to be safe all along! That was a freaking country dance or something like it. A family event. It should've been as safe as could be."

"A shield failed, apparently." I repeated what we'd been told by the authorities when an enraged Xavran demanded an explanation back at the town hall. "It was scheduled for maintenance next month. Someone on the town council had tried to save money by spreading out its maintenance a bit too thin. They will have to re-adjust the schedule after this."

"Great!" She threw her hands up into the air, then dropped them back in the tub water with a splash. "They're not only painfully primitive around here but also grossly corrupt."

"It doesn't happen often. There hadn't been a *hogas* worm attack in Diria for over twenty years before tonight."

"Ha! Once in a lifetime event! Lucky me."

I stayed for another minute or two, making sure she'd calmed down enough to go straight to bed after her bath. As irritated as she was, I worried Mara might do something stupid, like make arrangements to go back to Earth or possibly request refuge on Tragul through her new friend, the ambassador. Knowing Mara, even the most outlandish scenario wasn't off the table for her.

But after lying in the tub for a few minutes, she seemed to have relaxed a little. I bid her good night, then shuffled to my bedroom. Afraid I'd fall asleep in the tub, as tired as I was, I took a quick shower instead.

Before going to bed, however, I threw on a bathrobe over my pajamas and headed out, intending to check on the children quickly. They had been through a lot tonight.

To be completely honest, I wished I could check on Xavran too. The medics had been called to the town hall. They had assessed his injuries and treated his cuts, but I was sure he'd been shaken by the whole ordeal more than anyone. I hoped it wouldn't keep him awake tonight, as he was going to work first thing tomorrow morning.

After I took the first turn, however, I ran straight into him.

"Oh..." I managed to stop just in time, without crashing into him. But he grabbed my shoulders and drew me close.

"Are you alright?"

"Me?" I asked, pressed to his bare chest. "How are *you* feeling?"

He'd bathed and changed into a pair of loose sleep pants.

"I'm glad." He sounded calm. But as he heaved a long breath, a shudder ran through his large body. "Glad that it ended the way it did."

He was right. It could've been much worse. He could've lost his entire family tonight. And I... I could've lost him. The image of the worm nearly swallowing Xavran would stay burned into my memory forever.

"I'm glad it all ended the way it did too." I wound my arms around his middle, leaning into the warmth and safety radiating from him.

Best hug ever.

"How are the kids?" I asked, not letting go of him.

"They're well. I'm so proud of them. Ivex is disappointed that he didn't get to throw anything at the worm like Ene did." His wide chest vibrated with a chuckle. "They decided to sleep in one room tonight."

"I understand them way too well," I blurted out. "I wouldn't want to be alone tonight, either."

Tonight would be great to spend with a family. Except that I only had Mara. And she would kick me out in a flash if I tried to climb into bed with her.

Xavran's breathing hitched.

"Susanna," he said softly. "You don't need to be alone. I'll stay with you. If you want."

"Stay," I breathed out, without taking any time to think. I just wished for him to keep holding me.

That one word was all he needed. His one arm around my shoulders, he walked me back into my room. After closing the gate, he turned me to face him.

I wrapped my arms around his neck, and he easily lifted me off the ground.

"Susanna," he breathed out my name like a prayer.

I circled his waist with my legs, and he kissed me, carrying me to bed. Wrapping my hands around his horns, I kept him where I wanted him. His kisses proved to be even more addictive than his hugs.

He placed me on the mattress and climbed over me, covering my face with hot, urgent kisses.

Heat spread through me from his touch. Desire raged, stronger than ever. Suddenly, I wanted him more than the air I breathed.

Such a loss of control was...unnerving.

He yanked at the belt of my robe, untying the knot, and I grabbed his hand, stopping him.

"Xavran, please," I begged. "Slow down."

All of this was happening incredibly fast. My feelings for him made my head spin, leaving me no time to absorb and adjust. I didn't come to Aldrai in search of a man. I'd just lost a husband. I wasn't ready for anything else so soon.

It felt as if I'd just crawled out of a car wreck and was already speeding down a highway on the way to what very well could be another disaster.

"It's just way too fast," I pleaded.

He pressed his forehead to my shoulder. "I'm afraid I can't go slow with you. It's like a frenzy that only taking you will calm."

I stroked his back, my fingers trailing up and down the raised bumps over his vertebrae.

"I don't think I can handle a frenzy, Xavran. It's too much, too soon, and too...scary."

He rolled off me onto his side. "I don't want to scare you. But it is rather intimidating, isn't it? The moment I met you, my feelings for you have been uncontrollable. Like a wildfire."

That was exactly how being with him felt to me: wild, hot, and out of control.

I'd promised myself to be honest, so I told him the truth. "I don't want whatever it is between us to burn out too quickly, leaving us with nothing but ashes. I care about you, but maybe..." I rose on my elbow to see his face better. "Maybe, we should take it slow. To see if something *real* is possible between us. What do you think?"

Xavran could never be just a fling. I'd never met anyone like him, and that wasn't because he came from another planet. I'd seen the courage and integrity in him that I'd never seen in any other man.

I didn't just want him, I admired him. He was someone worth getting to know. He was worth more. I could only hope he felt I was worth more too.

"What do you think?" I asked again, holding my breath in anticipation of his answer.

I'd never put myself out there like that before. But the idea of playing games made me sick to my stomach. The only thing I could do was to say it as it was.

The night was dark. Even the glowing insects had gone to sleep by now, shutting off their tiny golden lights. Only a handful of them still flickered faintly in the canopies of the trees above us, framed by the starry sky above.

Xavran's eyes glistened in the darkness, unreadable like pools of black ink. "You want more than one night with me?"

I shook my head. "Nights are easy. I want to see how well you and I will keep handling the stress and worries of the *days*. And maybe sometime in the future, the two of us will decide to spend all our nights and days together."

I searched his face, trying to guess his reaction. We hadn't spoken about any of this before. Was I being too straightforward? Would he have preferred games to this kind of blunt honesty? I was sure many people would.

"Would that be something you want?" I asked tentatively.

He lifted his hand to my face, then gently moved away the strand of my hair that had fallen over my forehead.

"Taking it slow will be hard." A corner of his mouth lifted, curving it into a crooked grin. "In the past decade, I thought I'd become a master of celibacy. But then you came along, and... Well, suddenly, all I can think of is sex. Every day, I try and fail not to imagine you naked. In my bed, on the grass, on the kitchen counter... With your legs spread open, and my tongue—"

I slammed my hand over his mouth. "This is the *opposite* of 'taking it slow.'"

He chuckled, removing my hand from his face, then placed a gentle kiss in the middle of my palm.

"All I'm saying is that it'll be *hard*." He placed an emphasis on the last word, arching a brow ridge. "But I will master patience."

"Really? You would?" I was afraid to believe he understood me and relieved that he did, at the same time.

He tied the belt of my bathrobe back for me. "I feel like I've waited for you all my life, Susanna. I don't mind taking my time now that you're here."

My heart seemed to melt at his words, leaving me speechless.

He placed a kiss on the corner of my mouth. It was gentle and sweet—different from the wild frenzy of before but just as wonderful.

"It's hard to trust again, isn't it?" he asked with understanding.

I sighed. "Oh, you have no idea."

"I think I do."

He placed his head back on the pillow, and I curled up against his side. The tension drained from me. My muscles relaxed.

"Will you stay, anyway?" I murmured. "Just to sleep?"

He placed an arm over me, drawing me closer. "I'm not going anywhere. Not until tomorrow, at least."

The morning seemed way too close now. Then, he'd leave.

I sighed, breathing in his warm, masculine scent.

"How is Mara?" he asked abruptly. "She seemed really upset."

"She is *upset,* alright." That was too mild a word to describe my sister's freaking out. Livid, angry, furious—all would've suited better.

"She doesn't like it here," he stated.

Sadly, Mara never even tried to hide her dislike of Xavran or his home.

"I'm sorry she makes it way too obvious."

"No need to apologize for her," he assured me. "I'm afraid I don't care enough about her opinion to feel offended. But I never meant to hold anyone against their will. Our contract stipulates one year, but it can be dissolved earlier if both parties agree to it."

I shifted back. "You want to divorce her?"

"I don't want her to be unhappy. If she wants to go back home, I'll never hold her here."

"But she can't go back." The confession poured out of me. "Neither of us can. If we do, we'll be killed."

He tensed. "Killed?"

I drew in a deep breath. "It's a long story."

"Tell me," he demanded.

I hesitated. "I don't want to trouble you with our problems..."

He jerked his head impatiently. "Susanna, if your life is at stake, is not just *your* problem. I need to know who is threatening you so I can protect you from them."

God, that was so good to hear, to know that someone cared whether I was dead or alive.

"You're already protecting me, Xavran. Thank you for opening your home to us. Sorry for not being open with you about this before."

"Who wants to kill you?" he insisted.

"Bad guys." A wave of former fear washed over me. My lip trembled, and I bit it down. "Very, very bad guys."

"Why? What did you do?"

I drew in another long breath, then released it slowly. "I married the wrong man, Xavran. Mara introduced us. He was handsome and charming when we met. I fell in love quickly. We were married for less than a year, and I thought we had a great marriage. He apparently thought otherwise."

The muscles in his jaw moved. "Did he hurt you?"

"Not physically." Though, learning about Tom's betrayal had felt worse than a punch in the gut. "Apparently, he had an affair with a woman from work. Together, they ran an investment fraud scheme, combined with a money laundering operation for a criminal organization. After getting their hands on as much money as they could, they ran away. Mara's fiancé Jim was also involved."

"They need to be held accountable."

I nodded. "The criminals already took care of that. They found both my husband and Mara's fiancé and..." I swallowed hard, closing my eyes, the image of the bloodied cardboard box as clear as ever in my mind. "They killed them both. They've threatened to kill Mara and me, too, unless we find and return the money Tom and Jim stole from them. As if we would know where the money is. Knowing Tom, most of it was probably spent on fancy cars and diamond watches. I recently learned he had a gambling problem too. So... There is no money. Only the bad guys don't want to hear that."

"Why don't your authorities act on that?"

"They are acting. There's an ongoing investigation. But apparently, it's not that easy, I've been told. We're dealing with organized criminals." I sighed again. "Catching them and bringing them to justice will take time. Until then, the authorities approved for us to go to Aldrai."

He hugged me again. "You're safe here."

"I know." That was a wonderful feeling to have. In that sense, Xavran turned out to be simply godsent to Mara and me.

"You both will stay," he said.

"Thank you."

"But I can't dissolve the marriage agreement, then. Mara's legal status on Aldrai is as my wife. If she's no longer married to me, she'd be sent back to Earth immediately."

Their marriage didn't bother me. I knew it was as fake as could be, simply a formality.

"Then let's just leave things the way they are for now," I said, snuggling closer. "You're leaving anyway tomorrow." That came out with more wistfulness than I'd intended.

"I'll call every day," he promised.

"I hope you will." I slid my hand up his chest, past the horns on his shoulder, and around his neck. "I'll be waiting for your calls."

I rested my head on the inside of his bicep.

Like every time before, the peace I'd craved descended upon me in his arms.

FOR ONCE, I SLEPT SO deeply, I didn't wake up until my alarm went off.

Xavran wasn't in my bed the next morning.

I climbed from under the covers, ripping off my bathrobe in a hurry. If I changed quickly, maybe I could still catch Xavran before he left.

My communication disc pinged from the night table. Its screen lit up with swirls of blobs—the written characters of the Aldraian language.

"Incoming message from Captain Xavran Rax," the mechanical voice of the device announced.

Then, Xavran's deep drawl sounded.

"You slept so peacefully, I didn't have the heart to wake you up, even to say goodbye. I'm on my way to the crozan. We'll do a video call as soon as I arrive."

I rushed to the night table to grab the device. It wasn't a live call, though. The message had been recorded and programmed to play after my alarm went off.

"I'm already missing you, Susanna." A smile filtered into his voice, softening it. *"Do you know how adorable you look in your sleep?"*

I pressed the device to my chest, giddy with a shimmering swirl of emotions rising in my chest.

For someone who had begged to take it slow, I was falling for this man way too fast.

Chapter 16

Susanna

"Daddy! Daddy is calling!" Illal burst into the kitchen where I was making dinner.

She carried her communication device in her outstretched hands. Plopping the device on the table, she hit a blob on the screen. A 3D hologram of Xavran's figure appeared over it.

It had been two weeks since he'd left. And he'd been calling almost every day, unless sandstorms made communication impossible.

"Hi Dad!" The other three children ran in, then climbed on the chairs around the table.

I remained behind the counter, kneading the dough I was about to bake into rolls. Despite all my advancements in the kitchen, the dough recipe was too complicated for me to even attempt to make from scratch. Xavran had made it in advance, separated it into the batches of appropriate size, and frozen them for me to use while he was gone.

My hands kept pressing and squeezing as my attention was glued to the man on the screen.

Xavran was sitting in a chair, one ankle crossed over a knee. Dressed in dusty coveralls the color of terracotta, he appeared to have just come in from working outside.

He grinned. "How are you doing today, guys?"

"My tree sapling measured the tallest in the school garden today!" Xilvo declared proudly.

Ivex scoffed. "Mine is soooo going to beat it in a day or two."

"Maybe it will, maybe it won't." Xilvo made a face at his brother. "Mine is still growing too."

Illal rolled her eyes with a long-suffering look on her face.

"I won the pollination contest," she bragged to her dad. "My *osa* bush has the most fruit out of the entire school, even though it didn't have the most flowers. Do you know what pollinators I've selected?"

"Oh boy," I muttered under my breath, bracing myself for her long list of pollinators.

"No." Xavran laughed. "But I'm sure you'll tell me."

That was the only invitation Illal needed to list all twenty-three species of bugs she'd used for her project. I knew there were exactly twenty-three because she'd already named them all for me on the flight home from school and made me count them with her.

The kids jostled for space closer to the device with the image of their smiling father. Even Ene seemed to be in a good mood. She fetched from her room the picture she painted in school that day to show it to Xavran.

From my hiding spot out of the camera view, I watched him, taking in every familiar line of his face and noting all the new ones.

He looked tired. From our conversations during his calls, I'd learned his workdays started early and often stretched late into the night. Being the captain of the crew didn't shield Xavran from getting his hands dirty. Some days, he appeared in the hologram dressed in the white and gray uniform of an officer. Other days, like today, he'd be wearing the work coveralls, which meant he'd been working down in the dirt and grease of the bowls of the giant machinery that *crozan* was.

"Where's Susanna?" Xavran's question snapped me out of my ogling him.

"I'm here." I wiped my hands on the kitchen towel and stepped into the view of the camera.

His smile changed, his expression smoldering.

"There you are," he murmured. The rumble of his voice resonated inside me. "I missed you."

Oh, I missed him too. Every night before going to bed, I imagined his arms around me. That had become my one true happy place, and I desperately wished for more of his hugs.

The children glanced from the screen to me as I just stood there, silent and smiling.

"It's nice to see you again," was all I really could say in their presence.

"How have you been?" he asked in the same low, rumbling voice of his that rolled over me with another swell of heat.

"Good," I cleared my throat. "I've been good. Thank you."

He didn't ask about Mara. Just as she never asked about him, either. She wasn't at home, anyway. She went on a trip to Arqa three days ago. It had been the third time in two weeks she'd gone to the capital city. I didn't mind. She seemed in a much better mood after those trips.

"Bye, Dad!" Xilvo jumped off the chair, obviously growing bored with the conversation.

Ivex hopped off too. "I'll race you to your room!"

"We're leaving for your swimming lessons in forty minutes!" I yelled after them as all four ran out of the kitchen.

"You know I dream about you every night," Xavran's voice sounded from behind me.

I whipped around to face his hologram.

"You do?"

Normally, we spoke about his work, or the kids, or how my day went. However, Xavran always managed to slip something sweet and sexy into our conversation when we were alone.

He leaned back in his chair. "Do you ever think about me?"

Every. Freaking. Minute.

"Sometimes." I stepped closer to the table, clasping my hands in front of me.

He roamed his gaze over my body with the hunger in his eyes I'd never seen in any other man before him.

"Take me to your room," he suddenly demanded.

"Um… I'm making buns… For dinner. To go with the stew."

"The *vehnun* buns?"

"Yes. From the dough you had in the freezer."

"Put them in the grill on the lowest setting. They'll be done by the time you come back from swimming."

That was my plan all along. Except that seeing that smolder of his had made all my plans flutter out of my head.

I did as he said, putting the tray with the rolls onto the grill, covering it with the lid, and adjusting the setting to low.

Then I grabbed the device from the table. His hologram ended up at my eye level. Xavran leaned closer into the camera. The 3D effect of the image was so realistic, it appeared I could touch his face if I reached out.

His dark eyes stared into mine. "Being away from you is torture, Susanna. Let me tell you what you and I did in my dream last night—"

"Xavran, no!" I slapped my hand over his mouth. It went through the image, breaking it into white glowing dots for a few seconds. "Oops, sorry. It's just that the kids may be in earshot, you know?"

He grinned, leaning back in his chair. "Take me to your room, then."

"All right."

Holding the device in my hands, I hurried to my bedroom. With no roof or real walls, the space offered a little more privacy than the kitchen only because of its size and location. The garden-rooms in Xavran's home were large and spread out.

"Get on the bed," he ordered in a tone that allowed no room for arguments.

Not that I wanted to argue, anyway. Tingles of anticipation rushed through me as I climbed onto the bed and placed the device in front of me.

"Now, lower the privacy shield." He tipped his chin at the small control panel attached to one of the tree trunks that served as bed posts.

I pressed a button. The energy field descended over my bed in a dome. It was clear, almost invisible, except for a few pale, iridescent tendrils swirling through its surface every now and then. The shields descended automatically in case of rain or any other detectable threat from the sky. But they could also be lowered and adjusted manually if one so wished.

"Make it opaque," Xavran instructed.

I slid a finger along a dial on the control panel. The air around me turned milky white, like a solid dome, enclosing me and the bed in a bubble that was completely sound and waterproof.

Xavran yanked at the closure of his neckline. The top of his sleeveless coveralls opened in the front, and he drew in a heavy breath as if struggling for air.

My gaze immediately went to the sliver of his bare chest visible in the opening. I caught myself wishing I could lick it.

"Show me." His voice came out low and deep.

"Show you what?" I blinked innocently.

"Everything that I wish I could touch but can't. Open your shirt for me. Please." With the last word, his tone slid from commanding into pleading, filled with need.

I bit my lip, hiding a smile. So much for taking it slow. Just two weeks apart, and we could barely make it without each other. If it wasn't for the physical distance between us, I would've jumped on him myself right then and there.

"Show me," he begged.

I brought my hand up to the front of my shirt and opened the top
button. I did it slowly because I needed some time to steady my breathing, but also because watching his gaze burn with need as he followed
my every move was simply mesmerizing.

I opened another button, then another. Then I slid my hand inside
my bra. My fingers brushed by the hard pebble of my nipple, sending a
charge of arousal through me.

It'd been so long since a man made love to me. In the past months,
I hadn't even felt like touching myself, either wrecked by worries and
fear or overwhelmed while adjusting to my new life.

I met Xavran's eyes in the hologram, and the spark of desire inside
me burst into flames, spurred on by his heated gaze.

He licked his lips, flicking his gaze to my hand. I fondled my breast
still covered by the material of the shirt. All he could see would be the
movement of the fabric, yet he didn't look away.

"More," he demanded in a raspy half-whisper. "Let me see more of
you."

With my other hand, I slid my shirt aside, then took the bra strap off my shoulder, tugging down the cup. My breast was now concealed only by my hand. I parted my fingers, letting the tip of my breast slip out between them. Then I pressed my fingers together, squeezing the nipple.

A swirl of arousal rushed through my belly down to my core. I tossed back my head, releasing a moan.

Cursing under his breath, Xavran yanked his coveralls open all the way. Whipping out his massive erection, he fisted it with a groan. His chiseled abs flexed as he inhaled slowly.

His heavy stare landed on my face again. "Take off your shirt. And the harness."

The harness.

I smiled. That was the word for the undergarment that Aldraian women wore on their torsos. With them having considerably more breasts than humans, that piece of their wardrobe looked very different from our bra.

I "unharnessed" my two breasts, setting them free for his viewing pleasure.

"Nice," he growled, looking extremely pleased. "Now tell me about all the ways you like being pleasured."

Oh, God... His words had a stronger effect on me than my own touch, right now. The smile slipped off my face under his intense stare. Need pulsed through me.

"I... I'm afraid I can't *tell* you that. You'll have to come home and figure it out for yourself."

I squeezed my breasts harder, pinching my nipples. But it wasn't enough. I wanted Xavran's large, calloused hands on my skin instead of my own.

His gaze roamed over my body, from my face to my chest, then down to my thighs, concealed by my skirt.

"Will you let me, Susanna? Will you let me touch you like that when I see you again?"

"Oh yes... Please." I couldn't hold back anymore. Slipping a hand under my skirt, I pressed it between my legs.

"Yesss," he hissed, stroking himself. "Will you let me touch and kiss your breasts? When I get home in a week, will you let me suck on your nipples? Lick your sex? Will you let me inside you?"

I breathed hard, heat spreading through me in all the places he'd mentioned.

"Let me see where your hand is now," he demanded.

I jerked my hand out from under my dress. But the throbbing heat between my legs demanded attention.

"Lift your skirt. Take off your underpants. Now." He pumped his hand harder along his length. It glistened with moisture.

"Show me," I asked in turn. "Show me what's in *your* hand, first."

Slowly, he unclenched his fist, revealing his magnificent dick to me in all its glory. He would give the guy in that sex-in-the-giant-flower video a run for his money. Honestly, Xavran could be a porn star himself. Lucky for me, this show was for my eyes only.

I leaned closer to the device, to get a better look.

"Those bumps... They leak when you press them?"

He circled one of the raised bumps on his shaft with his finger.

"It's to ease my entry into your passage." He pressed on one, allowing the clear liquid to escape. It coated the tip of his finger. He groaned, sucking in a breath through his teeth.

"Does it hurt when you do that?" I asked with sympathy.

"Normally, no. But I want you so much right now, everything hurts." He released a tortured sound, fisting his massive dick again.

I imagined him shoving that thick, slick thing inside me. Heat throbbed stronger between my legs. Obviously, my body was all for the idea of that invasion. I couldn't help a needy whimper.

"Oh, I think I know exactly how you feel." I squirmed, slipping my hand back under my skirt.

Lust flared hot in his black eyes.

"Show me where I will enter you." He circled his length with his fingers, thrusting his hips into his hand. When compressed, his bumps released more of the clear gel. I imagined them tugging at my opening as he slid inside me; his natural lubricant would make the glide nice and easy, despite his impressive size. I imagined stretching around him, wider and wider as he pushed deeper.

"Oh God..." I yanked up my skirt and shoved my panties down my legs.

"Open wider for me," he growled from the hologram.

I sat back against the cushions and opened my legs, placing a foot on each side of the device.

"Beautiful," he growled with approval. "Now put a finger inside you. Show me how far you can take me."

I slipped a finger in, stroking myself from the inside. It was a poor substitute to Xavran's girth. I moved it in circles, stretching myself.

"Perfect, just like that..." He leaned back in his chair, sliding his hand up and down his length, his stare buried between my legs.

I slipped a second finger in, then circled the swollen bud of my clit, both fingers slick and slippery with my arousal.

"Oh, Xavran, this feels so good," I moaned, lying back into the pile of pillows.

"Rub it harder now," he rasped. "I want you to come with me."

He was so right. I needed more.

I pressed harder, rubbing faster. My eyelids fluttered closed as pleasure ebbed and swelled through my body.

Xavran's ragged breathing synced with mine as he pumped his hand harder too.

Orgasm teased me. So close.

"Come for me." Xavran's deep half-whisper served as a trigger.

I gasped as an orgasm erupted through me.

His growls grew into a roar.

Intense pleasure rolled through me, and I let it take me.

My body trembled. I rolled to the side, pressing my legs together. If his words and stare did this to me, I could only imagine what his touch could do.

"I wish you were here." I voiced my heart's deepest desire out loud.

I felt apprehensive about seeing his reaction when I opened my eyes.

He had cleaned and tucked himself back in. But his coveralls remained open, exposing his chest and abs.

"You have no idea how much I wish to be there to hold you right now," he said. Longing shone in his eyes, making me feel all warm and fuzzy inside.

"Come back soon," I pleaded.

He groaned with frustration. "I can't wait that long. I can't wait until my shift is over."

"Just another week."

He shook his head. "It's too long." Leaning forward, he placed his elbows on his knees. "Why don't you come here, instead?"

I sat up, fixing my bra. "Is that allowed?"

"Family visits are within the rules."

"But I'm not your family, not even on paper."

"I'll make an exception for you." He grinned. "I'm the captain. I can do that."

I arranged my skirt around my legs, taking a moment to think.

"But who will stay with the children?" Mara was useless for that. I couldn't even go shopping to Arqa on the weekend as I'd planned because I didn't feel comfortable leaving her with the kids even for a few hours. Instead, I'd made a quick trip to the city during the week while the kids were in school, just to buy myself some more comfortable clothes.

"Bring them with you," he said. "The last time they were on a *crozan*, they were too small to remember much."

"But what about their school?"

"You can come in a few days, after school is done for the week. Stay here for the weekend, then all of us could go home together."

That way, I'd get to see him only four days from now, instead of seven.

Oh, it was so tempting.

"I—"

"*Susanna!!!!*" My name in English suddenly bounced across the hologram screen, followed by an obscene number of exclamation signs.

"*Where the fuck are you?????*" An even greater number of question marks.

"Mara!" Of course, who *else* could it be? "I'd better go."

I grabbed the device from the bed.

"Say 'I'll see you soon,'" he insisted.

"I'll see you soon," I repeated with a smile.

His expression brightened. "I'll make all the necessary arrangements for your trip."

"Okay." My smile grew wider. I would've given anything to be able to kiss him right now. "Thank you."

We got disconnected. Xavran's image dispersed into the air, leaving Mara's words pulsing on the screen of the device.

I glanced at them with concern. This could be an emergency. However, knowing my sister, the emergency could be something as trivial as her misplacing a shoe.

I hit the button on the control panel to get rid of the protective shield over my bed.

Mara burst into my room without knocking.

I barely managed to scramble out of bed to face her.

"You're home?"

"Duh." She spread her arms. "The question is, where the hell were you? Shouldn't you be in the kitchen at this hour or something?"

I rubbed my neck. "What happened? What do you need me for?"

"Here." She shoved her device my way. "The school principal is calling me."

"Why?" I took it from her, placing mine under my arm.

"How am I supposed to know?"

"Pick it up and ask?"

"What? Why would I do that? What if she asks me something about the kids?"

True. Talking to Mara about them would be useless.

She glanced at the screen in my hands. "Great. She hung up already. Now you'll have to call her back."

"I will." I handed the device back to her. "How was your trip?"

"Fine." She moved her attention to the bed behind me. "Why are you in bed? It's not even dinnertime."

I glanced over my shoulder at my rumpled bed, my panties lying discarded on the covers.

This wasn't a situation of Xavran and me sneaking around on Mara. She'd made no secret of having zero feelings for him, and I'd been open with her from the beginning about how I felt about him.

Still, I felt the need to explain.

"I..." I took my device from under my arm. "I had a call with Xavran."

"In bed?" She arched one perfectly groomed eyebrow.

I nodded. "Yes."

She slid her gaze down my front. I had straightened my bra and shirt, but my buttons remained opened to my waist.

Understanding spread on her face. "Ooh... Are you two finally fucking?"

I cleared my throat, shoving a strand of my hair behind my ear.

"Well, not in the direct sense of that word. Not yet, anyway."

She glanced at the device in my hand. "Starting with online sex first? Can't blame you. It couldn't be easy with that one. It must take a while to get used to the idea of him touching you." She made a face.

"Come on, Mara. He's not even remotely repulsive." Everything about Xavran's appearance was nothing but pure hotness to me, lately.

She rolled her eyes, a shudder running across her shoulders. "I really don't get what anyone can see in *that*. But whatever rocks your boat, sister."

"Right." I stopped arguing.

At the end of the day, it didn't matter. I found Xavran insanely attractive, and I didn't care what the rest of the world thought about him.

I buttoned up my shirt. "How was your trip?"

"Wonderful." Her expression lit up, then fell again as she plopped her butt on my bed. "Sadly, Zeigan is leaving for Tragul today."

It took me a moment to remember the name.

"Are you talking about the Ravil Ambassador Zeigan Ussai? You saw him in the city?"

She gave me a look as if I'd said something completely stupid. "Why do you think I keep going to Arqa?"

"To shop?"

"Well, that too." She nodded. "And to go to the restaurants. And the parties. Life has definitely been more exciting since Zeigan came along." She giggled. "Honestly, Susanna, if you want good sex, don't bother with fugly Aldraians. Get yourself a Ravil."

"So, you've been...seeing Ambassador Ussai all this time?"

"*Seeing.*" She nodded again. "And fucking."

"Are you dating?"

"Dating? That's not what I said. He's cute. The sex is great. That tail...." She bit her lip with a guttural moan. "He really knows how to use all his appendages, if you know what I mean."

"Why don't you want to get serious with him, then?"

I didn't recall Mara ever truly falling for any man. She'd been so good at not letting her heart get involved, it'd made me wonder whether she even had a heart. But Ambassador Ussai met some of Mara's most important requirements—he held a position of power, which probably meant he had money too. Him being handsome and good in bed obviously didn't hurt, either.

She winced at my question.

"He invited me to come to Tragul with him."

"But you don't want to go?"

"God, no! His country is still recovering from that war they had..." She waved her hand in the air. "It's not fun there. He lives in...in like a log cabin in the jungle somewhere." Her features crumpled with disgust. "It's just sooo not me."

It certainly didn't sound like it was.

"Well, I guess it's a good thing that he's gone, then."

"Yeah." She sighed. "I've had the worst luck with men. And now I'm stuck here again, with you and those little brats. Oh, that reminds me. One of them wants to know where her bathing suit is."

"Who? Ene or Illal?" I put my communication device on the grass mound by my bed.

Mara shrugged. "How am I supposed to know? It's the one with the hair. She was looking for you in the kitchen when I got home." She got up from my bed and headed to the exit. "I'm so tired. I need a bath."

I followed her out. "Just to let you know, the kids and I are leaving soon. We have swimming lessons."

"Whatever. Just don't forget to call the school principal. I don't want her to hound me with her calls."

Chapter 17

Susanna

"**P**lease take your seat, Madam Rax." The principal, a stately woman with slate-gray hair and skin, gestured at the chair in front of her desk.

Mara heaved a long-suffering sigh. Smoothing the pencil skirt of her cream-white dress, she lowered herself into the chair and crossed her legs at the ankles, like the lady our mother had taught us to be.

"I'm glad you found the time to come here today." The principal took her seat behind her desk. "It has been extremely difficult for me to arrange for meetings with your husband."

"Dad's busy," Illal blurted out.

She and Ene sat by the hedge that circled the principal's garden office. Exactly opposite from them, by the other hedge, another girl their age dangled her feet, sitting in a chair. That was Kessra, Ene's arch-nemesis, as far as I was concerned.

Kessra's mom sat in front of the principal's desk, at arms-length from Mara. Since there was no third chair next to the adults, I took a seat next to Ene.

"I know your father is busy, Illal," the principal replied evenly. "Being the captain of a *crozan* is a rewarding but a very demanding career." She turned to Mara. "I'm glad the children have another parent now."

"Of course." Mara shifted in her seat, looking rather uncomfortable.

"I would like to discuss Ene's behavior with you, Madam Rax," the principal continued. "It has been escalating lately, and we could use your help."

I sat up straight, shocked to hear that. "Her behavior? Escalating? What do you mean?"

Ene had been rather agreeable at home. I hadn't seen her cry, and she participated in all the family activities with visible joy.

The principal smoothed down the hair above her ear, even though her neat high ponytail required no adjustments.

"Yes. We have concerns, Madam..." She moved her gaze from Mara to me, then back again, as if searching for differences between us.

As always, the only visible differences were our clothes. Unlike Mara's elegant dress and high heels, I was wearing flat shoes, a loose shirt, and a pair of knee-length shorts. The clothes were new, made from a lighter and more breathable material than anything I'd brought here from Earth. The flowy cut of the shirt allowed for either one or three pairs of breasts without requiring any alterations.

"I beg your pardon, I don't know your name," the principal confessed.

She had seen me on many occasions. I'd visited the school daily and participated in many family events with the kids. I'd never talked to her, though. The principal must've been mistaking me for Mara all that time.

"I'm Susanna." I gave her a nod.

Mara sighed again, rubbing her forehead.

"The nanny," she clarified impatiently.

"Oh, the nanny. Of course." The principal ran her hand over her hair again. "Anyway. I wanted to talk about Ene—"

"What about her?" I felt defensive.

The principal flinched at my voice but didn't glance my way, not allowing herself to be distracted, I guess.

Kessra's mom turned to me, however.

"She's been terrorizing my daughter," she stated flatly.

"She...what?" My mouth fell open.

Ene's shoulders dropped. Illal placed a hand on her knee, and Ene grabbed onto it.

The principal nodded.

"Just this past week, there have been two incidents of unacceptable behavior. One, she spilled Kessra's paints all over her dress—"

"A brand-new dress we just got her a month ago." Kessra's mom added tersely.

"It wasn't her fault!" Illal jumped to her feet. "Kessra was bugging her while she was drawing. Then Kessra and Tazeal painted over Ene's picture and ruined it."

"Illal, please sit down," the principal said in a calm, even voice. She turned to Mara. "It may be best for the children to leave for now."

Mara glanced at me over her shoulder.

"I don't think they should leave," I said. "Illal is Ene's classmate and a witness. The least we could do is hear her out."

"Kessra has been mean to Ene for ages!" Illal blurted out. "And now that lots of other girls want to be Ene's friends, she's jealous."

The girl's mom huffed with indignation, making Illal falter under her glare. "My daughter would never—"

"Wouldn't she?" I couldn't sit back any longer. "Who cut Ene's hair?"

"Kessra did." Illal plopped back in her seat, her sister getting hold of her hand again right away.

"Are you aware of that incident?" I demanded from the principal. "How are things like that even allowed to happen in your school? We got no calls about that at all."

The principal pursed her lips. "I was trying to get a hold of Captain Rax. Unsuccessfully. That incident has been discussed with both girls."

"Then you just swept it under the carpet after that, didn't you?"

Looking uneasy, she glanced at the kids. "Girls, why don't you go to the play area? Find your brothers?"

All three girls climbed off their chairs and filed out of the room, one by one.

"My daughter—" Kessra's mom started again.

But I was too wound up already to let her finish whatever excuses she wished to conjure. I interrupted her by raising my hand.

"I may not know much about child psychology or...well, children in general." I scratched my shoulder, searching for the most accurate way to put my thoughts into words. "But you should have a good conversation with your daughter. She's obviously unhappy about something in her life, and she chose to pick on my girl to make herself feel better. It's not Ene's job to serve as the punching bag for Kessra's moods. This bullying will have to stop."

The principal blinked at me in confusion, then turned to Mara. "I would prefer to discuss this matter with the *parents* of the students. Madam Rax, what do you think?"

Mara waved her off, looking bored. "Whatever Susanna said. Now, if we're done here, I hope you'll excuse me, but I have a previous engagement." She got up.

Her "previous engagement" of course would be watching movies and chatting online with the few acquaintances she'd made in Arqa. But I wasn't the one to set her straight in front of the principal.

"Oh...Well. Um..." The principal switched from staring at her to blinking at me again.

I lifted a finger, calling for everyone's attention.

"I will most definitely speak about this to Captain Rax, but I am the children's primary caregiver in his absence. And if I hear about another bully attack on Ene by *your* daughter..." I pointed the finger at Kessra's mom, "...on *your* school property..." I swung my accusing finger the principal's way.

Mara strolled to me.

"Yeah, yeah, there will be hell to pay. They get it." She grabbed me with her arm around my middle. "Let's go. I'm expecting a message at home. It was nice meeting you, Madam Principal."

With the sweetest smile at both women, she dragged me out.

"Don't you care?" I fumed on the way to the play area to pick up the kids. "Ene has been bullied for God knows how long. The poor kid. She's been keeping it all to herself all this time. If it wasn't for Illal, I wouldn't even know—"

"So?" Mara shrugged a shoulder.

I stopped in my tracks. "You have to agree, it's unacceptable."

She didn't look concerned, not even a bit. "Whatever doesn't kill you makes you stronger, right?"

"Not in this case."

"*Especially* in this case," she said with emphasis. "That's how one grows thick skin. School is preparation for life in the real world, is it not? And the real world is full of bullies. What that girl needs to learn is that she'll always be a victim unless she becomes a bully herself."

"No way! Is that what you really think?"

"Haven't you learned anything in this life, Susanna? You and I were born into the same family and raised by the same parents. Aside from your poor taste in clothes, we are very much the same. You know that in this life, all that matters is the size of your bank account, and to grow that, one needs to be ruthless. Look at our parents or at your own husband."

"All of them are dead," I pointed out.

"Only because they all made a mistake. Tom and Jim made the stupid mistake of getting caught. Before that, they actually had a smart plan."

"Smart? Are you calling their scheme to defraud people of money *smart?*"

"It worked, didn't it?" She crossed her arms over her chest, cocking a hip. "We were the stupid ones, Susanna, for not seeing what was coming to us, for letting them do things behind our backs."

I blew out a breath. "In that one thing, you're right. We are very much alike. We both suck at judging men's character."

"Well, just don't make the same mistake again."

I snapped my gaze to hers. "What do you mean?"

"Don't trust the alien. Do you know what people say about him?"

I realized she was talking about Xavran. "What?"

"That he killed his wife."

"But that's not true." I shook my head.

"How can you be so sure? How well do you really know him?"

I didn't reply. I'd known Tom for much longer than I had Xavran and still got blindsided when I discovered what kind of man Tom turned out to be at the end.

Mara leaned closer to me and whispered in my ear excitedly, "Don't worry. I'm just waiting for confirmation. From the last message I got from Jason, it looked like they were getting really close to arresting Bolshoy and his posse. We can go home soon."

Chapter 18

Susanna

"Look, look!" Xilvo elbowed his way closer to the window of the large aircraft that we took to fly to the frontier. "There's Dad's *crozan*!"

Xavran didn't want us to travel such a long distance in his small family aircraft. Instead, he'd arranged for tickets on the cargo airship that delivered supplies to his *crozan*. We had the entire passenger lounge to ourselves here, which made for a very comfortable trip.

"Are you talking about his truck?" Mara stepped to the window too.

She'd come with us after deciding that it couldn't be any worse than sitting in the "garden patch" of Xavran's home all by herself.

"Where's his tractor?" She pressed her forehead to the window, staring at the ground below.

"You're looking at it, silly!" Xilvo laughed.

He pointed at the huge piece of machinery in the desert below the airship.

I knew *crozans* were huge, but even after watching a few videos about them, I wasn't prepared for how enormous they were in real life. It was the size of a large apartment complex that sprawled for a few city blocks.

"What? That *whole* thing?" Mara pointed at the brown-red body of the machinery. "I thought that was a town!"

From this distance, the *crozan* appeared to crawl along the vast desert, but I'd read their speed could match that of our cars on the highway.

To the right of it lay the reddish sand of the Aldraian desert. The crests of wind-swept dunes appeared to smoke from the tendrils of sand curling around them.

To the left and directly behind the giant machine, the ground was a much darker shade of brown. The dirt appeared heavier there too. Instead of the dunes, it'd been combed into neat rows by the *crozan.*

"My dad is turning the desert into a garden," Ene announced proudly.

Mara arched an eyebrow. "That dirt doesn't look much like a garden to me."

"It will be. In ten to twenty years," Ivex said.

Illal stirred eagerly. "And in another fifty years or so, people will be living here. Kids may be playing right in this very spot."

"Fifty years!" Mara gasped.

"It takes time to change the world," Xilvo observed with a wisdom beyond his years. "That's what my teacher says."

"Dad works on the very edge of the desert," Ivex explained. "His *crozan* does the very first step of terraforming, but there are many more."

"Like what?" Mara appeared genuinely interested.

"After Dad's *crozan,*" the boy said, "they need to modify the climate in the area. Or else the dry desert would just take over again."

"So, they introduce microorganisms to the soil," Xilvo chimed in. "And a whole bunch of bugs. They also bring the groundwater up, for irritation—"

"*Irrigation,*" Illal corrected, rolling her eyes at her brother.

"That's what I said."

"No, you dummy. You said *irritation.* Which is the definition of what you're making me feel right now."

To my ear, the two words appeared almost identical. In Aldraian, they seemed to be even closer in pronunciation than in English.

"All right, all right," I stepped into the role of a peacekeeper, which I often had to play with these four. "All of you are very smart. It's nice to see you're paying attention in school. Thank you for filling Mara in on the Aldraian process of terraforming. Now, we need to get back in our seats and buckle in. We're going to be landing very soon."

"THIS THING IS HUGE," Mara muttered under her breath, setting her designer heels on the landing deck of the *crozan*. "Bigger than a cruise ship."

"Much bigger," I agreed, glancing around the top deck where the cargo aircraft had landed.

The air felt dry and hot here, despite the strong breeze blowing over the deck. The midday sun seemed to hang right over our heads, blasting down heat.

A trickle of sweat quickly formed along my spine under my yellow sundress. For once, I envied Mara for wearing a high-brimmed hat and a pair of huge sunglasses with her outfit of white slacks and a sleeveless blouse.

"Listen, is the alien in charge of this *entire* thing?" she enquired. "He's the captain. Does it mean he's the head guy here?"

I opened my mouth to remind her once again that "the alien" had a name and that he wasn't an alien on his own planet.

However, I was interrupted by a group of Aldraians who climbed the stairs to the landing deck and headed our way.

My heart skidded and flipped when I spotted Xavran among them.

"Daddy!" Ivex took off first.

"Dad!" The other three kids ran after the boy to their father.

Dressed in a white uniform with elegant gray accents, he looked rather dashing. Though, he'd long become the most handsome man in the Universe for me, regardless of what he wore.

He hugged his children all at once. I wished so badly to be in the middle of that pile of hugs and happy giggles, with his arms around all of us. Afraid that joining them might be deemed inappropriate, I held back.

His gaze crossed with mine, and his face split with a wide smile.

"Susanna," he said my name in that deep, low voice of his, making me weak in the knees.

Flanked by two kids on each side, he strolled to me.

It took all I had not to run into his arms. Instead, I just smiled back at him, willing my feet to remain planted in the metal of the deck.

"Well, we made it," I said, spreading my arms.

"Xavran!" Mara rushed by me. Wedging a hip between him and Ivex, she got hold of Xavran's arm. "It's nice to see you, honey. This place is amazing! Tell me, how many people are on this...um, ship of yours?"

He blinked, looking utterly bewildered by the sudden attention from his "wife." I was shocked by the fact that she actually remembered his name.

A man from the group who came with Xavran stepped forward.

"Our core crew consists of seven hundred and eighty people, Madam," the man said. "But we also house a few hundred of the crew's family members and visitors on any given day."

"It's very impressive," Mara cooed approvingly.

"Susanna, Mara, this is First Officer Qhax," Xavran introduced the man. "He is my Second-in-Command."

First Officer Qhax beamed at us. "Nice to meet you—"

Mara offered him a hand before I could even blink. "I'm the wife. She's the nanny. So..." She gestured around. "This place is huge. What do you do for fun?"

Xavran tried to free his arm discreetly, but she dug her nails into his bicep, not giving him an inch.

First Officer Qhax looked pleased by her interest. "Oh, you can only see a very small part of our empire from here, Madam Rax. The *crozan* is a small city, entirely self-contained. We have several gardens here, a gym with a running track, a dance hall, a swimming pool with slides—"

"A swimming pool!" The kids bounced with excitement. "Can we go swimming? Please, Susanna?"

I sure could use a nice cool dip. Sticky sweat plastered my dress to my back under the burning sun. Besides, I had no desire to watch Mara publicly claim her wife status all of a sudden.

"You can go." Mara waved us away.

"Susanna." Xavran turned after me and the children. "Wait."

"Come on." Gripping his arm, Mara placed her other hand in the crook of the elbow of First Officer Qhax. "Why don't you give me a tour, boys?" she murmured. "Then, you can show me our bedroom, Xavran."

"WHY IS MY STUFF HERE?" Mara stomped her foot.

"On the captain's orders, I suppose." I folded my arms across my chest, standing in front of her in our two-bedroom suite.

The rooms on the *crozan* were real, with proper walls and ceilings, though every surface inside was painted with luscious green landscapes and white puffy clouds.

To Mara's displeasure, Xavran hadn't taken her on a private tour of the *crozan*. He and his Second-in-Command had just shown us how to find the swimming pool, then taken us to our rooms before both were called away to deal with some technical issue I didn't even pretend to understand.

The kids' suite was located between Xavran's and ours. All three were on one of the upper levels of this huge machine.

"But I'm his wife!" Mara raged. "I'm supposed to be staying with my husband."

I gasped dramatically, clutching the imaginary pearls on my neck. "What? I can't believe it. Is Mara Takolsky considering sharing a room with the *ugly alien truck driver?*"

"Oh, stop mocking me." She waved me off with a snarl. "Fine, I'll admit it. I might've misjudged him. A little. So what if he's ugly?" She strolled across the room. "It can still be romantic between us. It's like Beauty and the Beast. The Beast will finally get his Beauty."

I snorted, rolling my eyes.

"And what makes you think 'the Beast' would want to have anything to do with 'the Beauty,' especially after the way she's been treating him?"

"Don't worry, I'll make it up to him." She sounded completely unconcerned. "One night with me, and he'll forget everything, including his own name." She surveyed the pile of her bags and suitcases in the middle of the living area of the suite. "I just need to get someone to move my things. The captain's suite is so much nicer than this one."

She looked determined, but I wasn't worried about her seducing Xavran. He wouldn't go for it, anyway.

Or would he?

I had no real claim on him. After all, she was his lawfully wedded wife, whether I liked it or not.

"Mara..." I took a step her way, clasping my hands together tightly.

"What?" She glanced up from the pile of her stuff. "If it's about you sleeping with my husband, then don't worry about it. I forgive you."

"Thanks," I replied, sarcastically. "It's very generous of you, though we haven't really slept together yet."

"Then what's the matter?" She shrugged impatiently.

"I think... I... Well, I really care about Xavran. And I believe he likes me too. It's not just about sex between us."

"So?" Obviously, our feelings didn't mean much to her.

"He is not one of those men you were seeing in New York. I don't want you using him."

"Oh, is that what this is about?" She squinted at me. "You don't want me to get all the attention as the captain's wife. You heard what First Officer Qhax told me. There are only a few hundred of these...um, vehicles in the entire Universe. It's a tremendous honor to operate one of these. It takes years to become the captain of one, and it pays a lot of money. This alien is rich."

Money and power had always been Mara's aphrodisiacs. Whatever repulsion she'd held for Xavran disappeared instantly the moment she realized her "farmer" husband who didn't even have a "farm" was indeed a highly esteemed captain of an extremely sophisticated piece of equipment with hundreds of people under his command.

The "alien" she was talking about, however, had been playing a major role in *my* dreams lately. I'd already grown to think of him as *my* Xavran.

"He is not just some rich dude, Mara. You can't take advantage of him." I heaved a sigh. "He deserves better."

"Better? And who do you think is better than me? You?" She slid a mocking glance down my figure. "Sweetie, you couldn't hold on to a man even if your life depended on it. It's not your fault, of course. I'm just a better version of you, in every way. When men have a choice, they prefer me."

Having self-confidence was admirable. However, what Mara had was arrogance that clearly bordered on egotism.

I shook my head. "You're delirious. Really."

"Am I?" She jerked her chin up. "You've never been anything but my substitute. Tom started dating you only after I'd turned him down. And he came back to me, the moment I let him—" She bit her lip, stopping herself, but she'd already said enough.

Understanding sliced through me, cutting painfully sharp.

"What do you mean 'he came back?' When?" Old suspicions I'd never wished to believe rose to the surface, marring my past like black ink spreading through water. "What did you and Tom do behind my back, Mara?"

Shifting her eyes to the side, she rested her hands on her hips.

"Tom asked me to marry him first. I said no."

"You declined his marriage proposal, but then allowed him to 'come back?'" I put air quotes around these two words with my fingers. "Why?" I demanded. I needed to hear it from her. "Did you sleep with Tom even after our wedding?"

She rolled her eyes to the ceiling, making me wish I could slap her. And maybe I should have. She certainly deserved it.

"What could I do? Tom never stopped wanting me," she said. "It's like I said, Susanna, you've always been just a substitute—someone who looked like me. The next best thing."

Why did her words hurt so much?

I'd long learned what kind of man Tom was. Nothing should be a surprise now.

Then I realized the reason.

It wasn't about Tom or any other man. It was about Mara and my relationship with her. It had always been shaky, but now it was simply no longer possible.

Tom had turned out to be an asshole. But when I'd married him, I loved him. Mara knew that. Yet she still betrayed me, behind my back. It felt like I had just lost my sister, the last of my family.

"Why are you upset?" she asked casually. "I slept with your husband, you slept with mine. We're even, now."

Did she really think it was the same?

"Mara..." My voice broke, and I swallowed a painful lump in my throat. "I didn't break your heart by falling for Xavran. Not even close. But you've just broken mine."

She huffed. "Oh, you're just being overly dramatic."

I fisted my hands to stop them from trembling. It didn't help much as my entire body was shaking now.

"I want you out of my life," I said quietly, even as inside I felt like screaming. "And stay away from Xavran."

She raised her head in challenge. "Why would I? For all intents and purposes, we're married."

I shook my head. "You can't do it now. It's not fair."

"Why not? I can and I will." She propped her hands on her hips. "He is my husband, and I wish to keep him." She shrugged. "For now, anyway."

"You listen to me." I pointed a finger at her. "You can't use him for whatever plans you may have brewing in your head. I won't let him become one of those men you've tossed aside once they'd served their purpose—"

"You have absolutely no right to tell me what to do."

That was true. Her marriage to Xavran might be fake, but I had no part of it, whatsoever. I had no legal right to do anything.

I felt helpless.

"You don't care about Xavran," I said, "not even a tiny bit. You never wanted him, not until you came here."

"It doesn't matter what I wanted *before*," she retorted. "I want him *now*. He's my husband. So, *you're* the one who has to stay away."

"No, Mara, please don't use him," I begged. "You'll hurt him..."

"Susanna!" Someone pounded on the door of our suite, Illal, by the sound of it. "We're ready!"

Xilvo shoved the door open, running in. "Let's go swimming!"

My heart still thundered wildly in my chest. Anger and frustration coursed through me.

I held my sister's stare. "Mara, please don't do anything you may regret."

A self-assured smile spread across her face. "I don't regret anything I do. Ever."

Chapter 19

Xavran

She was so close.

A swarm of flutter bugs swirled in his belly as he finished adjusting the *khuts* in one of the dispensing shafts.

Ever since he'd met her, Susanna had been in his thoughts incessantly. And by now, the woman had become an essential part of his existence. He'd caught himself talking to her in his mind, discussing his day and wondering what her answers would be.

"How are you doing there, Captain?" His Second-in-Command peeked into the wide shaft.

"Almost done." He fixed the lever in the new position.

His crew included several skilled technicians and mechanics, but the higher officers weren't afraid to get their hands dirty, too, if required. He and First Officer Qhax had calculated that the new setting would allow this part of the machinery to operate with more efficiency. He had to set it himself, precisely to the parameters they had determined.

He inspected his work. "Looks good. I'm ready to get out." Climbing out of the shaft, he turned to Qhax. "Try it now."

The first officer adjusted a dial on the control panel. One of the hundreds of conveyor belts jerked slightly, gradually increasing its speed. The clumps of minerals on it fell apart from the vibration of the movement. The fine powder was then fed into the dirt and folded into the red sand of the desert floor outside, along with fertile organic matter.

"So far, so good." Qhax nodded.

"Let's give the new setting a couple of days. We'll evaluate the results then."

"Great. I'll take it from here, Captain." Qhax winked at Xavran. "I'm sure you have better things to do now that your wife is here."

His *wife.*

In his first marriage, that word was often associated with trouble, worries, and shame.

He'd hoped to feel nothing at all for his second wife, and it'd worked. In terms of emotions, Mara turned out to be exactly the spouse he'd been looking for. His second marriage was supposed to be just that—practical, unemotional, and convenient.

If it wasn't for Susanna.

She'd turned all his plans upside down. In contrast to his carefully arranged marriage of convenience, she'd brought a whole storm of inconveniences. She was responsible for the chaos in his head and his body.

Yet he wouldn't have it any other way.

She had become the mother he wanted for his children, but she also became so much for him. The anticipation of holding her in his arms added bounce to his step as he exited the dispensing room into the scorching hot air of the open lower deck.

A gust of wind blasted him with sand. A storm was coming from the desert. They were frequent here.

He raised the wide, soft collar of his coveralls to shield his face from another blast of sand, then glanced up to the landing deck that loomed high above.

The cargo airship must be finishing unloading and would depart soon. Enough time remained for it to leave safely before the storm would hit full force and make air travel in the area impossible.

The wind almost ripped the door handle out of his hands when he opened it. He stopped in the main control room to make sure the *crozan* was ready to weather the storm. All the windows had been shuttered, the open areas covered. Everyone was inside, except for the few crew members preparing the cargo airship for take-off.

For once, he didn't mind staying inside during the storm. Today, he'd be weathering it with his family. Maybe he'd get a chance to take Susanna aside long enough to steal a kiss or two. Their video sessions had been wonderful, but they'd only whetted his appetite for her, making him wish for more.

Entering his suite, he opened the front of his coveralls. Sand sifted to the floor from the folds of the fabric. He'd worn his dress uniform to greet his family earlier but had to change into his work clothes before climbing down the dispensing shaft.

He wondered if Susanna would mind him getting her dirty, then smirked to himself at the thought of getting 'dirty' with her.

Soft humming and splashing came from the bathroom.

He wasn't alone.

Toeing his shoes off, he padded barefoot toward the sound.

Someone was in his bathroom, sitting in the tub. He recognized the blond head leaning on the edge of the tub, the hair tied into a knot on the very top to keep them dry.

"Susanna!" Excitement burst through him.

"Oh..." She turned, looking a little surprised and so tantalizingly naked.

She didn't wait for him to come and find her. She found him herself.

What a lucky man he was.

He rushed to her. "You've no idea how much I missed you."

"Oh," she exclaimed again as he sat on the edge of the tub at her side. She met his eyes, staring into them for a moment. "You really care about—" she blinked, "about me."

He grinned. "I thought I've made it clear. On numerous occasions."

She blew out a breath, then smiled, the familiar pair of dimples gracing her cheekbones.

"Well, I hope you don't mind then that I invaded your space? It is a gorgeous suite you have here."

Itching to touch her, he moved a lock of damp hair from her face. "Not at all. Do you know how long I've dreamed about having you in my space?"

"Aw, you're so sweet." She rose from the tub, climbing into his lap and drenching his clothes in the process.

He didn't mind that, either.

"Come here," she murmured, pressing herself to him. Her skin felt refreshingly cool against his bare chest in the opening of his coveralls. "Let's get you out of this." She yanked on the closures on his shoulders. "How does it work?"

Aldraian male clothing had no sleeves and was held at the shoulders by clasps. It was the most convenient style for the men of his species. The clusters of thick, short horns on their shoulders and hard bumps over their elbows made wearing sleeves impractical if not impossible.

"Let me..." He clicked the clasps open.

The top part of the coveralls dropped to his waist, stopped by his belt from falling any further. Dust rose in the air, sand shaking down to the floor.

"What a mess." She wrinkled her nose, then gave him a sultry look. "Maybe you'll join me in the tub? I'll make sure it'll be the best bath you've ever had."

There certainly was enough space in the tub for both of them.

She took his head between her hands, leaning closer. Her eyelids dropped seductively. Her lips parted in invitation. This was the expression of a willing woman, yet something held him back.

Something was missing.

The warmth of affection he'd grown to love seeing in Susanna's eyes wasn't there. Passion used to burn so brightly in her blue eyes before, he'd seen it clearly even in the hologram image of the communication device.

Now, her eyes were...empty.

"What's the matter?" She leaned back with a pout.

"Mara..." he exhaled.

The sound of his voice overlapped with the gasp coming from the door.

Susanna—*his* Susanna in her yellow summer dress—stood in the entrance to the bathroom.

Pleasure burst through him at the sight of her. Dread chilled him next as her slim eyebrows knotted into a frown.

He jumped to his feet. "Susanna!"

Mara slid from his lap, plopping back into the bath with a splash and a cry of protest.

Susanna bit her lip, fisting her hands at her sides.

"That's enough," she said, her voice firm and determined. Turning on her heel, she rushed out of the suite.

He couldn't let her go. He simply could not lose this woman.

"Susanna! Wait!" He stomped after her.

With every step she took away from him, his chest squeezed tighter, making it harder and harder to breathe. She'd become a part of every aspect of his life, the glue that held his existence together. Without her, he'd be nothing but a pile of ruins, going through the motions without a spark.

He had to do everything it took to keep her. Everything.

He rushed through the covered hallway to her suite.

A huge suitcase was standing by the door. Huffing and puffing, Susanna was dragging another one from the suite.

Was she leaving?

Leaving him?

His heart all but stopped, sending a body-shuddering chill down his spine.

"Susanna. Please."

She glanced up at him. "Care to help? This thing is heavy."

"Please, don't."

The sight of her, as angry as she was, took his breath away. That was the problem—he simply couldn't breathe without this woman anymore.

He had to keep her. At all costs.

"Don't go." He sank to his knees.

She inhaled sharply as he leaned his forehead to her belly. The curve of his front horn fit neatly between her breasts.

"You can't leave," he said fervently. "Not now. Not ever. You're a part of our lives now. I can't imagine my home without you. How am I supposed to rip you out of my heart if you *are* my heart? You can't—"

"Xavran..." She slid her hands down his side horns to cup his cheeks, then tilted his head back, peering into his eyes. "Why would I leave? When next to you is the only place I want to be?"

The dimples appeared on her cheeks with a smile. But it was the deep affection in her eyes that made her expression magical to him. No woman had ever looked like that at him.

She stroked the sharp ridges of his cheekbones with her thumbs. "I'm not going anywhere. I know my sister way too well to be angry with *you*."

He climbed to his feet. Still afraid to let go of her, he kept his hands on her waist.

"These aren't my suitcases. I'm not leaving," she said. Her expression hardened when she glanced behind him. "Mara is."

He turned to find her sister strolling their way. Wrapped in one of his towels, her clothes under her arm, she sauntered past them and into the suite.

"You missed your chance, buddy," she tossed over her shoulder to him.

For some unfathomable reason, Mara obviously believed she was better than him, better than her sister too. Ironically, she'd made it as far as his lap only because he'd been so eager to see Susanna. For one stupid moment, he'd actually believed that Mara could be her.

To him, a barrelful of Maras would never be worth Susanna's little finger.

"She's wrong." He smiled at the woman in his arms. "I haven't missed it. I'm holding on to my one real chance at happiness with everything I have. And I'm not letting her go."

Chapter 20

Susanna

A strong wind pushed me against the railing of the landing deck on the top level of the *crozan*. Hot blasts of air showered me with sand. I hid my mouth and nose in the shawl wrapped around my shoulders, shielding myself from the approaching storm the best I could.

Everyone on the *crozan* had taken cover below. Only the crew of the cargo aircraft were finishing the final preparations for their takeoff. One of them loaded the numerous suitcases of my sister into the now empty cargo bay.

Mara marched by me toward the ramp for boarding.

"Came to gloat?" she sneered at me. "Or to make sure I left?"

I wouldn't put it past her to stow away on the *crozan* somewhere if it served her purpose. But that wasn't why I came to see her off.

Whether I liked it or not, Mara was my closest family—the only one I had left. With her leaving, it felt like the last connection to my home world and my past life was breaking.

"I just wanted to say goodbye."

"Well, goodbye then." She pinched her lips. "Have a nice life because I'm not staying on this stupid planet much longer. And I'm sure as hell never coming back."

"Where are you planning to go?"

"Back to Earth, of course, where things actually make sense. Unlike here."

Despite everything, worry for her tugged inside me. "It's not safe for you back home."

"It will be. They'll arrest those thugs any day now." She headed up the ramp. "Well, good luck with your alien. Make sure to turn the lights off when you bang him. It's not like your 'beast' would ever turn into a Prince Charming."

My blood boiled anew. She just couldn't refrain from shooting insults, even as we might be saying goodbyes for a very long time.

Why did I even bother?

I pressed my back to the railing, watching the airship take off. The wind blasted its sides with sand, polishing the hull to a shine. In a few minutes, the aircraft's bulky shape shrank into the distance before going out of sight completely.

The sand clouds grew thicker, obstructing the sun from view at times.

"Susanna!" Xavran yelled through the wind.

He climbed the stairs to the landing deck. Fighting his way through the grasping winds, he made his way to me and wrapped his arm around my shoulders. "Time to go. It's not safe here during the storm."

"Yeah, it's way too windy." Letting go of the railing, I gripped his arm.

"Not just that. High winds unearth nasty creatures from the desert sand," he said, leading me back to the stairs.

"What creatures?"

My question drowned in the howls of the wind and a weird clacking noise. Dark shapes emerged from the clouds, their massive wings spinning sand into swirls.

Xavran's body stiffened against mine. He let go of me.

"Run!" He shoved me toward the stairs.

The alarm in his voice spurred me into action without questioning it. I sprinted across the landing deck. Half-blinded by the storm, I found my way by touch, making it to the top step. I grabbed on to the railing, then I heard a strangled sound behind me.

"Xavran?" Hiding from the wind behind my shawl, I turned around.

A whole flock of flying creatures descended upon the deck. They looked like a cross between a bird, a bat, and an insect. Each was as large as an ostrich, covered in rusty-brown feathers. Their nearly transparent leathery wings were as wide as the sales on a boat.

One of them grabbed Xavran by the horns, yanking him back so hard it knocked him off his feet. The jolt seemed hard enough to break a person's neck.

Horror speared through me.

"Xavran!" I screamed into the wind.

The flying creature flapped its giant wings, taking Xavran over the side railing and off the *crozan*.

"No!" I lunged after it.

The taut leather of a wing brushed over my head, and I grabbed on to it. I wasn't sure what I was thinking at that moment, only that I couldn't let that thing carry Xavran away.

With another flap of its wings, the flying animal swept me off the deck and into the swirling storm beyond.

Dust and sand blinded me. Hurled through the air, I clung to the creature's wing. It moved it once, twice...losing momentum with every flap.

As strong as this flying monster was, carrying Xavran in its claws and staying airborne with me dangling from its wing proved too much for it. Its one wing drooped weakly, while it still flapped with the other. The motion sent us all into a tailspin.

Flung in a circle, I no longer knew where was up or down. I hit something hard with my shoulder. Sand sprayed out in the shape of a fan.

An angry clicking sounded right above me. The creature hopped on the ground, dragging me behind, as I held its wing in a death grip.

Where was Xavran?

Since the creature had landed on both its feet, it must've dropped him somewhere. I really hoped it hadn't eaten him while still in the air.

The thing turned around, snapping its sharp mandibles menacingly. It was obviously trying to determine what trapped its wing, causing the crash.

I forced my fingers to uncurl, releasing the creature.

It flapped its wings and lunged for me.

Something long and glossy propelled through the storm. It looked like a black leather rope with a long spike on the end. It speared through the flying creature, pinning it to the ground. Dark blood poured from the wound on its chest.

What was that?

I crawled on all fours away from the dead monster. My shawl caught in the shoulder strap of my sundress, dragging behind me.

"Xavran!" I called against the sand that surrounded me from all sides.

The cloud to the left of me seemed exceptionally dense, as if the darkness itself had solidified there. Unsure whether I should move toward it or away from it, I held still.

The ground shook. The sand between me and the dark wall rose like a swell, the smell of freshly turned dirt reached me.

That was the *crozan!*

The giant machine was just a few dozen feet away from me. Thankfully, it wasn't moving in my direction. It was passing me by.

I had to find Xavran.

What if the flying predator had dropped him into the path of the moving *crozan*? He could be crushed by his own machine.

Panic exploded through me.

"Xavran!" I screamed.

The wind tore his name to shreds the moment it left my lips.

Crawling on my hands and knees along the giant moving vehicle, I searched the ground. Blinded by the wind, I had to trust my sense of touch more than my sight.

My hand landed on something cool and flexible, like a piece of tarp or plastic. I picked it up before realizing it was the wing of the flying thing. The *dead* flying thing. I was back where I started, lost in the darkness of the storm.

A huge head of another creature appeared from behind the dead body. This one was coal black, with two mandibles, sharp and long like swords.

"Oh no..." I froze as the creature's unblinking round eyes focused on me.

The black, leathery "rope" with the spiked tip rose from behind the monster and curved above its head. The spike was aimed at me.

Fear gripped my throat, and I ran. I tripped and fell, only to scramble back up in the desperate dash for my life.

The "rope" shot forward over the creature's head. I lurched sideways. The spike sank into the sand, missing me by barely an inch.

Horror froze my limbs. Any moment now, the monster would yank back its tail—or whatever the hell that "rope" was—and whip it at me again.

Instead of a hard yank, however, the long appendage just shook limply. The spike inched out of the sand, then tilted over.

I ventured a glance over my shoulder.

The creature had climbed over its winged victim. This monster had a long, hard-plated body with several dozen skinny legs along each side.

It had nearly doubled over, curling the end part of its body over its head to attack me with its long, flexible tail with the spike.

It was motionless now. Its thin legs dug into the sand. Then, it tipped over on its side, still curled into a hoop, like a giant, spiked tire. A wave of sand rose from its impact with the ground and showered over me.

I whimpered, gathering my arms and legs under me.

"Susanna!" the familiar voice tore through the wind.

I plopped back on the ground, afraid to believe my eyes as Xavran appeared from the thick sand clouds churning around us. He rushed around the dead monster to me.

His armguards were off. A milky-white liquid was dripping from the sharp horns on his forearms. Judging by the sudden demise of the last monster, I assumed this was the creature's blood on his arms.

"Susanna!" He dropped to his knees and grabbed my shoulders. "Are you hurt? Wounded anywhere? Did the *pheiza* get to you?"

I understood he must be talking about one of the dead creatures.

"No. I'm fine. Neither of them hurt me..." Gripping the horns on his shoulders, I leaned into his chest. "It's so, so good to see you, Xavran. You have no idea..."

Relief spread warm and thick through me, making me feel light-headed. He wasn't lying crushed under the *crozan*. The winged thing hadn't snapped his neck. And no other deadly desert creature got him...

Fear receded, and I sobbed into his chest.

"There, there." He buried his face into my hair, soothingly stroking my back. "It's all good now. I've got you."

He's got me.

When I was in his arms, nothing scared me. Not the storm, not the nightmarish creatures, not the mafia back home. With Xavran by my side, I could deal with anything.

I drew in a deep breath, wrestling my panic under control. We had to figure out what to do next. "We fell off the *crozan*. We need to make them stop and pick us up."

The machine was so enormous, it was still moving past us, its dark mass visible through the veil of the storm. We just needed to get the attention of the crew somehow.

He kept stroking my hair, shielding me from the wind. "The *crozan* never stops. Even if someone heard us, which is impossible in this weather, they would not be able to stop it for us."

Panic lanced through me again.

"They can't just leave us behind. What are we going to do?"

"Right now, we have to find shelter. When the *crozan* has passed by, we'll be in the open."

He shifted me to his side, peering through the storm at the dead creatures.

He was right. The massive shape of the moving *crozan* was shielding us from some of the wind. I could only imagine what it would be like once its protection was gone.

"Come." Xavran dragged me through the raging wind toward the dead centipede. "Get in here." He directed me inside the circle formed by its body.

Once I sat down next to the creature's arched back, Xavran freed my shawl from the shoulder strap of my dress. He then tied the corners of the shawl to the long skinny legs of the monster. They stuck above us like the spikes of an umbrella. Stretching my shawl over them, Xavran created a semblance of a roof.

The wind kept blasting ferociously, but it was much calmer inside our makeshift shelter.

"Better?" Xavran sat next to me, and I leaned against him.

"Yes. Thank you." I exhaled a shaky breath.

Everything was better with him by my side, even the brutal sandstorm in the most hostile part of the planet.

Chapter 21

Susanna

"What are we going to do?" I asked Xavran.

The wind howled like a wild beast outside of our macabre shelter made from the carcass of the dead creature.

"There's not much to do during a storm in the desert but wait until it's over." He stretched his long legs in front of him, leaning back against the centipede.

I remained sitting upright. My back felt stiff. But I preferred that to getting too close to the corpse.

"How long will it take?"

"At least a couple of hours. But most likely all night. Sandstorms in these parts like to take their time."

The prospect of sitting here all night sounded dreadful. But going out there right now would be stupid—if not outright suicidal—with all those nasty creatures roaming the desert.

"The frontier is a horrible place," I determined.

"It sure isn't a walk in a garden." He chuckled. "But this is how all Aldrai used to look in the not-so-distant past. My ancestors survived in the desert for hundreds of thousands of years."

"I can't imagine how." I was getting thirsty. The sand seemed to have made its way everywhere on my body. I wouldn't be surprised if it were found in my bloodstream too.

It was hot like in an oven, even as the sun was no longer visible at all.

"There are ways to make this survivable," Xavran assured me. "Lean against the *pheiza*."

I shook my head. "No way. I'm not touching that."

"Trust me." He splayed his hand on the hard plating of the dead creature's back. "It's cooler here."

"Cooler?" I touched the glossy plates too. They indeed felt colder than the air around us, like a tiled floor in a basement on a hot day.

"Instead of generating heat, a *pheiza's* body converts energy into cold, allowing it to stay outside even on the most scorching days. Its body will take at least a few hours to warm up to the same temperature as the air around us. My ancestors used to hunt them for that and for their blood."

"What did they use the blood for?"

"*Pheiza's* legs are basically hollow, save for one muscle, thin like a thread." He rose to his knees. Using one of the sharp narrow horns on his right forearm, he chopped off a leg of the dead creature. Milky blood dripped from the cut. "See?" He showed me the leg. It looked like a thick drinking straw filled with watered-down milk. "Have some."

"Um... You mean to drink?" I cringed inside.

"It's cool and refreshing," he assured me. His expression remained open and genuine. He wasn't kidding. "You must be thirsty."

"Not enough to drink a dead bug's blood." I shook my head resolutely.

"Suit yourself. But it tastes the best when it's cold." He took a sip, like sipping a cocktail from a straw. Emptying the leg, he tossed it aside.

As Xavran took his place by the creature's back again, I touched its hard plates once more. They really felt like ceramic tiles. Maybe I could pretend I was relaxing against a tiled shower wall or something?

Shifting back, I tentatively leaned against the *pheiza*. It didn't feel too bad if I didn't think about my back support having been a ruthless predator that had been trying to kill me just a little while ago.

"Well, it's...okay."

I would've loved to lean against Xavran's arm too. I wouldn't even mind the gore of the *pheiza's* blood on his forearm horns from killing the creature. It had mostly been rubbed off by the sand, anyway. But all the horns and bumps on his shoulders and elbows seemed to be designed specifically to deter any close contact.

As if reading my mind, he lifted his arm.

"Come here," he invited me under it.

I wasn't going to make him ask twice. Crawling closer, I cuddled against his chest. He was all bumps, horns, and hard places on the outside, but his chest, belly, and the inside of his arms had no horns and no hard plating. It was the most comfortable place to be. I almost didn't mind being tossed off the *crozan*. Almost.

My thoughts rushed back to that giant piece of machinery and what we'd left on it.

"I hope the children are okay."

His chest rose with a deep breath. "They're safe on my *crozan*. The crew will take care of them until we return."

His calm voice was reassuring.

"How do we get back?"

By the time the storm was over, the *crozan* might be hundreds of miles away. Even if we headed after it now, we'd never catch up.

"Once the crew realize we're missing, they'll search for us," Xavran replied. "In the worst-case scenario, another *crozan* will be coming here two weeks from now. It's doing the next step in the terraforming process after mine."

"Two weeks!" I gasped.

He rubbed my arm soothingly.

"Hopefully, the weather will be nice enough then for us to get their attention."

Two weeks of surviving on dead bugs and their blood and trying not to become their food while hunting them. I sighed, not looking forward to that.

"I suppose it could've been worse," I said. "At least we're alive and uninjured."

That *was* a very good thing.

We fell silent. I thought back to the start of the storm and the attack of the giant flying animals, then even further back to saying goodbye to Mara.

"Will the cargo airship be okay in this storm?" I asked.

"Yes," he assured me. "It took off in time to avoid the worst. Your sister will be fine."

"Good."

He shifted uneasily.

"Susanna. I want you to know I never had any feelings for your sister. I never thought about my marriage to her as anything more than a formality on paper, which I clearly stated in the contract before she and I were even matched. All I wanted in a wife was a partner to help me with the family."

I tilted my head back, trying to see his face in the darkness.

"I never doubted that," I said.

He cupped my cheek. "I made a huge mistake. I married the wrong sister."

I didn't blame him for that, either. He'd never had the chance to make a choice *before* he met us. I was just grateful that he and I got a chance to meet at all.

"Mara never laid any claim on me before," he continued. "I refuse to believe my feelings for you have been in any way dishonest."

Was this about Mara trying to "claim" him in the bathroom? Did he feel guilty about what she did?

"Earlier today, for a few unfortunate moments, I mistook her for you," he said. "She knew that. I called her by your name, and she didn't correct me. If I've misled her somehow—"

"Xavran," I wasn't going to let guilt over Mara's actions rack him. "The only reason Mara got naked and climbed into your tub was because First Officer Qhax told her how important your job was and how much it paid. It had nothing to do with you. She never cared about you as a person, either before or after that."

He exhaled a laugh. "Oh, I've been well aware of her lack of feelings. Her sudden...interest in me back on the landing deck was rather shocking."

He had looked genuinely perplexed back then.

"Well, like I said, the explanation is simple. Money and power would make Mara interested in just about anyone. Trust me, it had nothing to do with what you did or what you said. Don't beat yourself up over it."

He remained silent for a moment. I pressed my cheek to his chest, drawing with my finger little circles on the material of his coveralls.

"I don't think Mara will want to stay in Diria now," he said. "She never liked it there, anyway. But I'll pay for any accommodation she finds suitable in Arqa for as long as she needs."

"That's really nice of you. I suspect she may want to go back to Earth, though."

He made a surprised sound. "But you said it's not safe for the two of you to return home."

"Well, apparently the bad guys are about to be caught. She wants to go back after that happens."

"Are you considering going back, too?" he asked with concern.

No one waited for me back home. All my hopes for the future lay here, on Aldrai. But we hadn't exactly spoken about my staying after the year was up.

"Well, I still have some time left of my employment contract with you..." I said tentatively.

"And you've been doing such a great job that I've been thinking about extending it," he teased with a smile in his voice.

"You have?" I matched his tone. "For how long are you thinking of extending it?"

He flexed his arm around my shoulders, holding me tight. "Indefinitely."

"I may consider that." I snuggled closer into his side.

"But I want to propose some changes to the terms of our agreement."

"Like what?"

He shifted to make us both a little more comfortable. "For one, you won't have your own bedroom anymore. You'll be moving into mine. Permanently."

"Will you take my paycheck away, too?"

"Yes. And I'll extend your working hours. From now on, I'll expect you to be available for me at night too."

"That sounds like an outrageous exploitation." I huffed dramatically, faking indignation. "Hard to believe anyone would fall for that."

He smiled. "Isn't that what they say? That the job of a wife and a mother is the most demanding one of all?"

True. Inside, I felt giddy with excitement at the "changes to the agreement" he'd proposed. On the outside, I kept a stern expression, however.

"I'll hire as many helpers as you need," he offered. "To make sure you have time to relax."

"Will I be getting any compensation at all?"

"Yes." His voice turned serious. "You'll get my unconditional love and affection. My full support in everything you do. My undying devotion until the end of our days and beyond. And my heart...if you want it."

That was exactly what I wanted—to spend the rest of my life with this man, to become a part of his family, and to grow old together, side by side with him, surrounded by our children.

I wrapped my arms around him and buried my face in his chest, afraid that if I said a word, all the wonderful feelings that bubbled in my chest right now would overflow with tears.

"I'll think about it," I finally mumbled into his chest.

"I'll wait," he exhaled, kissing my hair, "for as long as it takes."

I thought about our life together so far. There had been challenges I'd never thought I'd be able to handle before. It still felt like I was failing sometimes.

"I've never thought I could be any good at looking after four children," I confessed. My thoughts went back to my visit to the principal's office. "There's something I really need to talk to you about. The kids' principal wants to speak with you. She said she'd been trying to get a hold of you."

"What happened?" His voice dropped with worry. "She never left a message."

"Hm. I wonder why?" I asked, a bit puzzled.

He rubbed the back of his neck. "I don't think she really wants to see me. The last time I went to her office, she told me a boy was mean to Illal, and...well, I might have lost my temper. A little."

"I can't say I did much better. Just to warn you, she may complain about my behavior at our meeting with her." I heaved a breath. "To be honest, I often feel over my head with the kids. I've ordered a few books on Aldraian child psychology and development. I feel like I need to learn so much."

"The learning never stops," he agreed. "I've had children for eleven years now, and there're always situations when I just don't know what to do."

I sat up, turning his way, though that didn't help me see him any better in the darkness. "Ene has had some troubles with another girl in school. I knew about that for some time, but I promised Illal not to tell anyone. I didn't want to break the promise, but maybe I should have."

"What happened? How is Ene?"

"Better now. But I think she could use some help. Maybe we could get someone, a professional counselor or someone like that, to help her deal with her mother's...with the loss of her mother."

"Is that really the problem?" he sounded doubtful. "Ene has never met her mother. She wouldn't even remember her."

"That doesn't mean she is not affected by her loss." I laced my fingers together. "You know she goes into your wife's old room?"

He shifted to sit straighter. "What for?"

"To cry when she's sad or feels alone. I'd rather she came to you. Or to me. Or to anyone who is alive and can actually listen and help her. Instead, she cries to a picture."

He released a breath. "I didn't know that."

"It's heart-breaking."

"How often does she do it?"

"Not often. In fact, she hadn't gone in there for weeks now, which is a good thing, I hope. Still, we should talk to someone. And...maybe it's time to do something else with that room?" I asked carefully. "What do you think?"

"I should never have kept it for this long." Deep remorse filtered into his voice. "It's just that... I couldn't bring myself to go in there. I pushed off having to deal with it. But you're right, it's time to get rid of it."

His voice lifted a bit at the end, and I ventured to ask.

"Why do you have that room in the first place, Xavran?" Married couples slept together on Aldrai, just like they did on Earth. Yet it appeared Xavran and his late wife had separate bedrooms. "What happened between you and your wife?"

Chapter 22

Susanna

For a few heartbeats, Xavran remained silent. But if I was going to share my life with him, I really needed to know the answers to my questions, so I pressed on.

"How did your first wife die, Xavran? Please tell me the truth."

He fisted his hands in his lap.

"Gelnall died in a crash. The aircraft she traveled in fell into the lake, right behind my home."

"People say you were somehow responsible," I said softly.

He leaned forward, his dark eyes glistening in the night. "Do you believe that?"

"No. I wouldn't be here if I did." The more I got to know him, the less sense the rumors made. Xavran wouldn't deliberately hurt anyone. He would never put his family in danger. I'd seen him fight the monstrous worm, ready to die for his children. "I just want to understand what happened."

"I was the first at the crash scene, so that much is true," he said. "I was fishing on Diria Lake. I saw the aircraft coming in. I witnessed the crash. I dove to get them and managed to pull them both into my boat."

"Both? Who was with her?"

He frowned, staring straight ahead of him. It looked like my questions had opened a wound, and I kept silent, afraid to poke it too much.

Once opened, however, it brought the need to let it all out, as he spoke again.

"I could've killed him right then and there." He rubbed his forehead, his voice hollow. "But she was hurt. And I had to save her. That was the priority, not my anger." He drew in a long breath and released it with a tremor running through his entire body. "It was too late. Only four children survived. She and the rest were gone."

I took his hand between both of mine.

"I'm so sorry, Xavran." I expected tears in his eyes, but when he turned to me, there was only anger shining dangerously bright.

"I asked her to wait until the babies were born. I begged her. But she just couldn't help it." He drew in a breath. "Maybe I shouldn't blame her as much as I do. I read recently that it could be a condition. Something to do with the way her brain worked. An addiction of sorts."

"What kind of addiction?"

"Gelnall had a secret she kept from everyone, even her parents. The asshole who crashed the aircraft wasn't the only one. She had many men. An awful lot of them."

"And you knew about them?"

"Not at the beginning. When we first met, she told me she wasn't seeing anyone else, and maybe she wasn't, though I've doubted that since. I learned she was meeting a man in Arqa shortly after we found out she was pregnant, a month or two after our wedding." He ran a hand over his left horn. "Pregnancy is a rare thing for Aldraians. I was elated when it happened for us so quickly. I believed Gelnall was happy, too, but family life wasn't for her. She got bored quickly. For a while, I blamed myself for failing to make my wife happy. Now, I believe she wouldn't have been happy with any one man. She craved excitement, and she found it in having affairs."

"Yet you stayed together. Why?"

He stretched his neck, rubbing his nape. "I was furious when I found out she'd lied to me about her trips to Arqa. I asked for a divorce, but she wouldn't give it to me."

"Why not? You said she was bored. She didn't like being married."

"I was surprised by that, too, at first," he said. "But that was the nature of Gelnall's addiction. She didn't want to be free. She needed the thrill of sneaking around, of inventing lies, and risking being caught. All of that excited her, making her feel alive."

"Did you hope she'd change?"

He shook his head. "If I ever did, that hope died quickly. Gelnall didn't believe she had to change. If there were any treatments, she refused to even talk about getting help. Once my initial shock and hurt had passed, I decided to stay with her."

"Why?"

"She was pregnant."

"Right."

"I promised to stay with her until the children were born," he continued. "In exchange, I asked her to help me take care of her, to be careful. Despite all our medical advancements, the last month of pregnancy is never easy. She carried twelve fetuses in her belly. The doctors told her to relax, rest a lot, and avoid any strenuous activities. Instead, she took a trip with one of her lovers."

"Was that where they went *that* day?" I held my breath, waiting for his answer.

He nodded again. "They were returning from the trip when she went into labor, right there in the aircraft. The man she was with claimed he turned off the auto-pilot system by mistake. Maybe he did. Maybe he was hand-flying all along. Either way, he panicked and made a mistake. They crashed."

He went quiet. I could only imagine what was going through his head as he recalled that day.

"You never told anyone she wasn't alone," I said.

"The authorities know. Her lover got lucky. He only had a few bruises when I pulled him out of the water. Should've let him drown," he spat through his teeth. "But he gave his statement to the investigators, which cleared me from their suspicions."

"They never made those statements public, though."

"I asked them not to," he confessed.

"Why?"

He rubbed his chest. "When I found out about Gelnall's...um, life choices, she begged me not to tell anyone. I ended up lying for her, covering up her absences, because she was terrified what people would think if they knew the truth, especially her parents. They thought she was perfect in every way. They still think so."

"You allowed her parents to think you were her murderer? Do you realize that you've been protecting her reputation at the expense of yours?"

He jerked his head, his horns scraping against the hard plates of the *pheiza*.

"The authorities cleared me. Most people in Diria don't dare accuse me to my face, and I don't care what they say behind my back."

"Meanwhile, everyone believes Gelnall was a saint."

"Susanna." He took my hands in his, staring at me intently. "I'd love to keep it that way. Everything I told you right now was said in confidence."

"You don't have to worry about me," I assured him. "But have *you* considered eventually telling the truth about all of that? Maybe to Gelnall's parents, at least?"

He scoffed. "Her parents would never believe me. They would accuse me of lying, only fueling more rumors. I don't want my children to hear whatever nasty things may be said about their mother after that."

I didn't argue with that. After all, he knew those people much better than I did. Things might change with time, and he might reconsider his decision in the future.

"I'll just have to warn you," I said. "I'll have a hard time not snapping at your ex-mother-in-law if she tells me I fell for a dangerous man."

"So, you *fell* for me?" His voice lifted.

I shook my head with a smile. "Is that all you got from what I've just said?"

He shifted closer. "No, but that part struck me as the most exciting." He circled me with his arms, pulling me into his lap. "You are my heart, Susanna."

I cupped his face, leaning my forehead against his. "I really, really care about you, Xavran."

He roamed his hands up and down my back. "You've taken over my thoughts completely. At night, I dream about you. During the day, I think about you constantly. I haven't felt such a fierce desire for anyone before. But it's so much more than that. I feel at peace, knowing you're in my home with my children. I trust you. In my mind, I talk to you about everything that has happened to me during the day. You are in every aspect of my life now, even when you aren't physically there."

I placed a kiss on the corner of his mouth.

"You've given me more than any man has before. You've given me purpose." That was true. In his home, I felt needed. He made me feel appreciated more than I had ever been in my entire life.

As for the desire...

"I've never wanted a man in my life more than I want you," I whispered into his ear.

I wished to do now everything we'd done through the hologram of the communication device before. When I rocked my hips, however, the sand covering his pants grated against my inner thighs.

"The sand is everywhere." I bit my lip in frustration. "It won't work."

I thought about his self-lubricating bumps. If sand stuck to them, sex would really hurt both him and me.

He exhaled a humorless laugh. "Of all the things that may keep you from me, I've never thought of the sand." He kissed my neck, kneading my backside. "We have to keep our clothes on, then."

I couldn't take my hands off him. I caressed the back of his neck as he kissed the side of mine. "It's best not to touch then, either."

He slid his hands up my sides to cup my breasts.

"Who said anything about *not* touching?" he growled. "I've been dreaming about caressing, stroking, and fondling every part of your body. Everything you've shown me on the screen, I need to touch for myself now." Finding my nipples through my bra and dress, he rubbed and pinched them, turning them hard in an instant. "These are just as sensitive through all these layers," he murmured approvingly.

Desire sparked in my body. Pressure throbbed between my legs. Straddling his thighs, I pressed my core against his hardening length through his pants and my panties.

He groaned, bucking his hips.

"No," he rasped. Sliding his hand between us, he replaced his dick with his hand.

Somewhere in my mind clouded by lust, I understood that if we were to spend two weeks in the desert with no water to wash up, he would prefer not to come into his pants.

Then, all thoughts left me as he curled his finger, rubbing at my most sensitive spot through my panties.

"Oh, yesss..." I gripped the horns on his shoulders, riding his hand.

With his other hand, he massaged my breast, pinching the tip between his thumb and his finger, just like I had done on camera before. The sensation was even more intense now, when it was his large hand caressing my body instead of my own.

Everything fell away, even the howls of the storm above us. Climax teased me, flickering on the tips of his fingers.

I arched my back, pressing my chest into his touch and rubbing my core against his hand, harder and faster.

"Oh, God, yes... Xavran, I'm..."

Orgasm crested, blinding me with pleasure. Gripping his shoulder horns, I pressed my forehead to the side of his neck, riding the waves. He stroked me gently, sending ripples of aftershock through my body, then held me in his arms.

"You're even better in person than on screen," I finally managed, catching my breath.

He chuckled.

"Wait until I finally have the chance to get you out of these clothes."

Chapter 23

Susanna

Listening to the storm raging above us, I curled against Xavran's wide chest and must've dozed off.

The quiet woke me up. And the heat. My dress was drenched in sweat where my body was pressed to Xavran's. He appeared to be asleep. Quietly, trying not to disturb him, I crawled off him.

It was still dark, but the storm had finally died out. One side of our shelter had collapsed, ripping my shawl. Sand piled up against the dead *pheiza*, spilling inside. My mouth was so dry, drinking the bug's blood no longer seemed impossible.

I climbed up the pile of sand and out of the shelter. There was no trace of the *crozan*. It had moved ahead and out of sight.

Aldrai had no moons. It was pitch dark out here. Only the crests of the sand dunes glowed faintly. Some of the lights moved, proving they belonged to the desert creatures that scurried around.

Without the moonlight, many species on this planet had developed the ability to illuminate their own way at night by emitting a glow similar to the deep-water fish back on Earth.

If I remembered correctly, night was also the busiest time in the desert—the time to hunt. I was not looking forward to any more encounters with the local predators. The memories of the last two still made me shudder.

"Susanna," Xavran called softly, climbing up the sand pile next to me. "Be careful, my heart."

"Have you ever been alone in the desert at night?" I asked.

He nodded. "A few times."

"Why?"

"Some of it was part of my survival training before I even took this job. A few times happened later. The last time I ended up stranded overnight, I had to follow one of my crew members. He fell through a dispenser chute and was hurt. I had to jump off the *crozan* and stay with him until help arrived."

"Did anything attack you while you waited for the rescue?"

"Once." He didn't elaborate, and I decided against asking for details. It was spooky enough out here without scary stories.

A light separated from the glow in the distance, moving in our direction.

"What is that?" I grabbed Xavran's arm. "A giant spider? A killer firefly? What glows like that and can kill us?"

"A lot of things." He raised his other arm, getting ready to strike the approaching menace.

Never before had I wished so much to have something hard and sharp growing from my body, too, to have a built-it weapon for protection. Honestly, why was the human body so soft and exposed? We had no sharp fangs, no long claws, not even a nice hard shell to hide in.

I really, really could use a shell to hide in right now.

The light smoothly moved closer. It wasn't just a glow, but a ray, directed at the ground. It moved in a zig-zag pattern, side to side.

"*Captain Xavran Rax. Madam Susanna Riley,*" a mechanical voice said, repeating our names over and over.

"That's a search and rescue drone." Xavran exhaled with relief. "Here!" He stood taller, waving both arms in the air.

The ray jerked our way, shining straight at us. Momentarily blinded by it, I shielded my eyes with my arm.

"It's us." Closing his eyes from the light, Xavran lifted his face into the ray for identification. "Send the signal. We've been found."

"Signal sent," the device droned. *"It will take approximately twenty-two minutes for the rescue aircraft to arrive. Are you injured? Do you require any first-aid items or medicine? Do you need sustenance?"*

Xavran glanced at me. I shook my head, only asking, "Water?"

A compartment opened on the side of the disc-shaped drone. "Two bottles of water."

I grabbed one, nearly emptying it all in a few hungry, hurried gulps. Cool water sliding down my throat was the best thing I'd ever tasted in my entire life.

"Feeling better?" Xavran asked, watching me with a smile.

I moaned, finally taking the bottle away from my mouth.

"You have no idea how glad I am that I don't have to drink the dead bug's blood, after all."

"I WANT TO SEE THE CHILDREN," Xavran demanded the moment we made it back to the *crozan*.

We'd been examined by a medic on the rescue aircraft. We'd also gotten a chance to wash the sand from our hands and faces and to clean the bug's blood off Xavran's forearm horns. But we were still wearing the same dusty clothes.

Sand sifted from my hair onto my shoulders with every step I took. I badly needed a bath. But I also wanted to make sure that the kids were alright.

A crew member gestured down the hallway. "The children are in their suite. They're asleep now, but we have a drone watching over them."

Xavran took off toward the kids' room. I hurried alongside him.

The suite wasn't entirely dark. Soft flickering lights under the ceiling imitated the glow of the flying insects from Xavran's garden home. The kids' bedrooms were on the opposite sides of the common area.

The doors to both were open. A red, glossy drone noiselessly hovered between the doors.

Xavran tiptoed to the room on the right.

"Daddy?" a sleepy voice called. "You're back!" Ene sat in her bed, rubbing her eyes.

"Shh." Xavran rushed to her. "You'll wake up your sister."

Ene hugged his neck.

"I'm not sleeping," Illal's little voice sounded from her bed nearby. She made a move to get out of bed, but Xavran came to her next, giving her a hug too. "I knew you'd be fine, Daddy. I told everyone you'd be alright."

"No. You cried," her sister set her straight. "It was Xilvo who said Dad knew what to do in the desert, that he'd be fine, and that he'd look after Susanna."

Illal just smiled. "Whatever." She stretched her arms to me for a hug next. "Xilvo said that, but I knew it too. I knew you'd be fine, Susanna." She hugged me tightly. "Because Daddy would take care of you. He's great at that."

"He sure is." I smiled. "He saved me from a giant bug."

"A giant bug?" Xilvo ran from the boys' bedroom across the living area. "Which one was it? Did you kill it, Dad?"

"Are you awake, too?" Xavran frowned but caught the boy in his arms for a cuddle when he ran to him.

"Ivex isn't sleeping, either." Xilvo giggled. "He's just slow getting out of bed."

The second boy was already running our way. He crashed into my side at full speed, wrapping his arms around my middle. "You're back!"

Xavran laughed.

"Well, if you're all up, how about a family hug?" He wrapped his arms around Ivex and me. The other three kids joined us, plastering themselves to us from all sides.

I smiled, feeling all warm and gooey inside. "It feels so good to be back, you guys."

"We need to have a celebration," Illal declared.

Xavran raised an eyebrow ridge. "A celebration?"

"Ooh, yes! A party!" The boys jumped around us.

"What for?" Xavran shook his head.

"Well, we have a few reasons. We made it back from the desert in one piece." I counted off on my fingers. "You're coming home next week..."

"Mara is gone," Ene added, matching my tone of voice while sticking out a finger.

"Um..." I glanced at her. "Is that really a cause for celebration?"

Ene blanched, but Illal nodded. "Yeah, I couldn't stand her whining about how terrible Diria was."

"Diria is nice." Ivex shrugged. "Mara just doesn't like the same things we do."

The kids had been paying attention all along, it seemed.

"A party it is then," Xavran conceded.

Ene furrowed her forehead, pressing her lips together. "Except that no one would come."

"Oh, right." Illal nodded. "Kessra is having a party next week too."

"We can have ours the week after," I suggested. "Maybe the weekend before your dad goes back to work?" I glanced at Xavran.

"I'm planning to change my schedule a bit," he announced. "I've decided to share the job with another captain."

"What does that mean?" I asked.

He grinned at me. "That means I'd work for only half a month, then be at home for the other half. That'll give me more time to spend with the children." He leaned my way, lowering his voice a bit. "And *you.*"

His face was so close to mine, it was all I could do not to steal a kiss from him. I refrained only for the sake of the children.

"That's wonderful." I smiled at him. "You see, guys, we can have the party the week after Kessra's. Your father will still be home."

The excitement appeared to have evaporated from the girls, though.

"What's the matter?" I asked.

Illal made a long face. "Kessra's parties are the best. No one will want to come to ours after hers."

"Nonsense! There can never be too many parties." I propped my hands on my hips. "Besides, who said hers are the best?"

"Everyone," the boys drawled in unison.

I sat on the bed, getting down to their eye level. "Listen. I promise we'll have a party like no one in Diria has ever seen before. Everyone will come because no one will want to miss it."

"Really?"

I smiled with confidence.

"I may not have many talents. I can't put an outfit together as brilliantly as Mara or make the cauldron dinner as delicious as your father, but there is one thing I'm really, really good at. I can throw a fantastic party. You'll see. It'll be truly out of this world."

Chapter 24

Susanna

"Tired?" Xavran asked me when we'd finally calmed down the kids enough to put them back in their beds.

"A little." I stifled a yawn.

I was exhausted, but not enough to fall asleep right away. A part of me—the very horny part—really wished to give Xavran the chance to get me out of my clothes as he'd wished for back in the desert.

"Let's get you to bed then." He wrapped an arm around my shoulders, turning left.

"My room is that way." I pointed right.

"But your bed is *this* way." He gestured to the left, in the direction of the captain's suite. "I'm not letting you out of my sight anymore."

"Do you have more than one bed in your bedroom?" I teased, allowing him to lead me toward his suite.

"No. But the one I have is big enough for two."

"I'm too filthy for a bed." I shook my skirt, sending a shower of sand to the floor.

"Then I'll give you a bath. Though, I hope it won't make you any less *filthy* in all the ways that matter."

I couldn't hold back a giggle as we entered his suite. "You are determined to get me out of these clothes, I see."

"I've never made a secret out of that. I've liked you naked from the very first time I saw you without your clothes. You looked gorgeous, naked and dripping wet. I've been dreaming about that ever since."

I giggled again, thinking back to me running from the fish in the tub the very first night I came to Aldrai.

In the bathroom, he unbuttoned my sundress, then slid the straps off my shoulders, taking the bra straps with them. Slowly, as if savoring the moment, he freed my breasts from the bra cups.

He sat on the edge of the tub, then drew me closer between his legs.

"Something I've been dying to do." He dragged his tongue over my nipple, then sucked it into his mouth. A rumble resonated through his chest as he rolled the hardened bud between his teeth.

"Ohh..." I exhaled, pressing my breast into his mouth.

Desire flickered and burned, banishing the tiredness completely. Need for him flared through me anew. I slid my hand between us, finding his hardness through his clothes.

"I want you, Xavran," I rubbed him through his pants.

With a low groan, he yanked my bra and the dress down to my waist. A shower of sand spilled to the floor from my clothes.

"Oh no!" I slapped a hand over my mouth, unsure whether to laugh or feel mortified.

"Bath," he growled, shoving all my clothes, including the underwear, down my hips and legs.

Lifting me over the edge, he deposited me into the tub. The inside of it was laid with stone tiles, giving the tub the look and feel of the carved rock basins we had in Xavran's home.

I lay back, stretching in the warm water.

Not taking his eyes off me, Xavran opened the closures at his shoulders, then yanked his coverall down his body and stepped out of his boots.

The pile of sand from our clothes on the floor grew bigger.

"It looks like we brought half of the desert back with us," I chuckled.

He didn't smile, tossing his clothes aside.

I managed to catch but a glimpse of his strong, muscled thighs, with his long, thick erection bobbing in the front, before he raised his leg and stepped into the tub with me. I sat upright, and he got down on his knees, straddling my legs.

He took a jar from the stand nearby. "I don't have the soap that women use to wash their hair, but this should work."

He scooped some of the pearly white paste from the jar, lathered it between his palms, then gently massaged it into my hair.

"Let's rinse it off." Holding my head, he lowered me backwards into the water, washing the suds out of my hair.

Only my face remained above the water, my head submerged past my ears. He lowered his head to kiss me. I gasped, afraid to go under, and hooked my arms around his neck.

He chuckled against my lips. "I won't let you go."

"Promise?"

"Promise." He kissed me.

I ran my hands down his torso, feeling every hard ridge and rise of his strong body.

Sand still clung to both of us.

"Let me..." I took some of the paste from the jar, then lathered him with it, from the tips of his horns down to his waist, as the rest of him remained under the water.

I tried to rinse him off by splashing over his chest, but he just laughed.

"It's easier *this* way." Grabbing me around my waist, he flipped us over, sinking completely under, including his face.

I lay on his chest. His erection pressing against my stomach.

Taking hold of the horns on the side of his head, I lifted his face out of the water. He opened his eyes, dark as the Aldraian night in the desert. They were deep, still a bit mysterious, but the look in them wasn't intimidating, not at all. Warm and beckoning, it drew me in.

"My turn," I whispered, lowering my mouth to his.

The fragrance of the soap rose from the tub. Weariness drained from me as my muscles relaxed. Arousal swirled through every cell of my body.

Not breaking the kiss, Xavran leaned back against the edge of the tub. His hands traveled down my back, a finger slipping between my legs. When he moved his hands up my sides, I realized that wasn't a finger caressing me, but his tail. The tip of it twirled around my opening, slipping in and out.

With a soft gasp, I sat back.

Xavran flashed me a cheeky smile. "Should I put it away?"

I rocked my hips against the tail. It flicked the throbbing bud above my opening, spiking my arousal.

"No..." I panted. "Keep it... Please."

The tail wiggled its way back. Needing more contact, I pressed my core to the ridge of his erection.

"Susanna..." he groaned, arching his back to rub himself against me.

I rocked on my bent knees, water splashing around us and out of the tub. He sat up, the tip of his hard length pressing against me.

"I need you," he rasped.

I wiggled my hips, easing his sizable girth inside me. The spongy bumps along his length tugged at my opening with a delicious sensation spreading through me.

"So good," I moaned, gripping the horns on his shoulders.

Tossing his head back, he groaned, sliding deeper. Eased by the slick liquid produced by the bumps, his thick shaft stretched me in a most delightful way. I rose, then sank back down on my knees, enjoying the tight slide of him inside me.

His tail slipped further back, caressing up and down between my butt cheeks.

"More?" he asked, with that crooked half-smile of his.

"What do you mean by *more?*" I exhaled, still waiting for my body to fully adjust around the massive dick buried inside me. I couldn't possibly take anything bigger than that.

He twirled the tip of his tail around my back opening.

"Ooh," I murmured in understanding.

The images from the sex video I'd watched rose in my mind. Aldraian tails made double-play possible with just one man for a partner.

I moved my hips from side to side, shifting back a little to meet his tail.

"Well, come in then." I bit my lip, trying not to squirm too much as the tip inched inside me through the orifice I'd only ever used once or twice during sex before.

"How does it feel?" Xavran asked, stalling the progress of his tail. He appeared to hold his breath.

"How sensitive are Aldraian tails?" I asked in turn.

He blew out a breath, only to still his breathing again. "Very... Very sensitive."

"Good." I smiled, rocking my hips into him again, to shove both of his appendages deeper inside me.

I felt so incredibly full. Excitement coursed through me, heating my blood with desire. This was like fulfilling a fantasy I never knew I had.

"Susanna," he roared, gripping my sides. "I..."

I couldn't reply. Pleasure spread through me, hot and thick, robbing me of words and thoughts as he pumped into me from both ends. I arched my back, making our bodies connect at just the right angle for me.

Pressure built between my legs until it exploded into the blinding fireworks of an orgasm. It rocked through me with an intensity I'd never experienced before.

I pressed my forehead to his, riding the waves of my climax. With another hard thrust, he came, too, pumping his release into me.

Draped over him, I was catching my breath as he leaned back into the water again. A wide, satisfied smile spread across his face—an expression of utter bliss.

"Was this the best sex you've had in the past decade?" I teased.

"It was the best in my life, my heart," he replied. "The best in my entire life."

Chapter 25

Susanna

Two weeks later.

"Ready?" Xavran poked his head into our bedroom in his home in Diria.

"Yes." I smoothed my hands down my paisley-print maxi dress.

Its loose fit not only kept me cool in the warm weather on Aldrai, it also hadn't required any alteration when I bought it. All tight-fitting clothes for women on Aldrai had three pairs of darts, tailored to accommodate six pairs of breasts, which left me with four useless bumps in the front. When buying ready-to-wear clothing, I always looked for something loose and flowy for that reason.

"Come." Xavran took my hand. "Arkrel and Yurie are here with their children already."

Arkrel and Yurie were the mothers of some of the kid's friends from school. I got along really well with both women. The three of us had recently gone on a shopping trip to Arqa, and I'd been to Arkrel's home for a "girls' night in" when their husbands and Xavran took all our children on a fishing trip one afternoon.

"All right, let's do it." I smiled, letting him lead me down the pathway from our bedroom to the common area of our garden-home.

Xavran had expanded this space by merging it with Gelnall's old room. The children and I had helped him with moving the hedges, rearranging the paths, and seeding the grass. It looked large and airy now, though still a bit short on flowers.

Garlands of hand-painted paper flowers decorated the hedges, instead. The kids had been working on those for days. Their schoolmates had helped them too.

All the extra space allowed us to set up almost every possible yard game I could remember from Earth. From the horseshoe pitching, to ladder toss, to beanbags—they all were here, mixed in with the Aldraian games for the kids to play.

Xilvo and Ivex were running around, explaining the game rules to anyone who cared to listen.

Poles decorated with flowers held up strings with kids' drawings. Almost every person in the kid's school had contributed their art for our decoration.

Arkrel beelined to Xavran and me. "So, what are we celebrating?"

I shrugged. "Do we need a reason?"

Yurie came by, chewing on my version of pigs-in-a-blanket that I'd managed to re-create with local sausage and some modifications to Xavran's bread dough. "These are so good! You've got to give me the recipe."

"Of course we need a reason for the party," Arkrel insisted.

"A spring party?" I suggested uncertainly. Without any clearly defined seasons on Aldrai, it was hard to celebrate any of them.

"What holidays do you have back on Earth at this time of the year?" Xavran prompted. "Maybe we could celebrate one of them?"

"Right, well... I need to see. Do you have your communications device on you?"

He produced the small disk from his pants pocket, and I verified the calendar from back home. It didn't perfectly align with the Aldraian, but the two were close enough.

"Well, the closest holiday is Mother's Day. It's celebrated this week in North America," I said.

Ene and Illal were running by. Both stopped at my words abruptly.

"Mother's Day?" Ene tilted her head.

"How do you celebrate that?" Illal wondered.

"Usually, by getting together for brunch or dinner. But a party like this would be very appropriate, too," I assured them. "People hug their mothers and wish them a happy Mother's Day. When I was little, I remember I also made a necklace from painted macaroni for my mother once."

My nanny Marissa and I had spent a whole day first painting the dry macaroni, then waiting for them to dry. I was so excited to give it to my mother during the formal Mother's Day brunch she was hosting. After the brunch, however, I found the necklace in the garbage bin in the kitchen.

I was too little to realize that painted macaroni wouldn't go well with my mother's designer clothes and fine jewelry. I cried that day and never made her anything ever again. But as I got older, I realized that the best part of that day had been painting the macaroni with Marissa, no matter what my mother did with the necklace afterwards.

"Well, that's what we're celebrating, then." Ene shrugged, then hugged me unexpectedly. "Happy Mother's Day, Susanna."

"Happy Mother's Day!" Illal joined her.

"Oh!" I gasped, momentarily lost for words.

Xavran leaned to my ear. "Ene told me you spoke to her about choosing your own family. I guess they've made their choice."

"Hey!" Illal ran to a group of children by the snack table. "It's a Mother's Day party. You're supposed to hug your mothers and wish them a happy Mother's Day!"

Arkrel laughed as all eleven of her children rushed to hug her. "Well... If that's how traditions are shared between the worlds, I don't mind it one bit."

Soft humming of the engines of landing aircraft announced the arrival of more guests. I spotted Inie, Xavran's ex-mother-in-law. Xilvo ran to me with a hug, then turned to see his grandmother enter the room.

"Ene invited her," he said. "We decided to give her another chance to be our grandma. But only if she doesn't yell at our dad."

"Hey, Susanna, Xavran!" Stefan waved to us from the entrance. He walked toward us, supporting his wife Esstal under her elbow. A giant two-tier baby stroller hovered next to them.

"Thank you for inviting us," Esstal said after our greetings.

Dressed in a long, loose dress, she had it tied with bright belts around her torso three times, under each pair of breasts.

"How are the babies?" I cooed, leaning over the stroller where their two-week old infants lay in two rows. A tube tipped with a nipple descended from a large bottle on top of the stroller, allowing each baby to feed whenever they wished. "They're so precious."

"They've been pretty good. Calm and happy." Esstal arched her back, rubbing her side. "But they eat all the time." She laughed. "I'm either nursing or pumping all day."

A woman walked in at that moment, accompanied by at least a dozen little boys and one girl who held a square of paper in her hands. I recognized Kessra and her mother from the meeting at the principal's office.

"Kessra is here," Illal whispered under her breath.

Ene squared her shoulders.

I took her hand. "This is our home and our party, Ene," I reminded her. "We are nice to our guests, and we expect them to treat us the same. Right?"

She nodded. "But if they don't behave, they'll have to leave."

"Absolutely. But can we give everyone a chance first?" I asked.

Ene drew in a breath. "Fine."

Letting go of my hand, she followed Illal to greet Kessra and her brothers.

"Here." Kessra thrust the paper she was holding into Ene's hands. "I painted this for your decorations." She gestured at the strings with pictures above our heads.

"Thanks." Ene took the picture and gave it to Xavran. "Can you hang it up, Daddy?"

Illal took Kessra's hand. "Do you want to try some *fruit punch?* It's a drink. It's pink. Susanna made it. It's pretty sweet, but if you add some ice to it, it's not so bad."

"Sure." Kessra nodded, and they all headed to the food tables.

Arkrel and Yurie followed them, possibly for more pigs-in-a-blanket. Xilvo dragged Stefan and Esstal away to show them the games.

For a moment, Xavran and I happened to be left alone.

"Girls..." Xavran shook his head, watching Ene pour a glass of fruit punch for Kessra. "I'll never understand them. One day they fight, the next day, they're best friends."

"It goes for all kids, I believe." I might be new to this job, but if I had learned anything about children so far, it was that every day brought something new—sometimes scary, often unpredictable, but also exciting.

Xavran's communication device lit up in my hand. A message swirled in a circle on its round screen.

"Here," I handed it to him. The written language of Aldrai remained a complete mystery to me.

He stared at the screen for a second or two. "It's from the Liaison Committee."

"What do they want?"

"Mara has submitted the application to dissolve our marriage."

A hint of regret still tugged at my heart at the sound of my sister's name. I wished things had been different between us. "She did?"

"They say she wants to go back to Earth. All she needs is my signature for her travel papers to be approved." His brow ridges moved close together in a frown. "Is it safe for her to return?"

Mara had been living in a hotel in Arqa for the past two weeks. Xavran had been paying her expenses, but we'd had no communication from her. I only knew how she was doing through the Liaison Committee.

"I guess they must've finally arrested the bad guys," I said. "I'll send her a message to make sure." Though, I doubted Mara would reply to my messages, at least not until she needed something from me again. So far, she'd ignored the two I'd sent.

Xavran gave me a look. "You're not interested in going back to Earth, though, are you?"

I smiled, having no desire to play games. "No, Xavran. I'm quite happy where I am. Right here."

He wrapped his arm around my shoulders, drawing me into his side.

"I'm happy when you are right here too."

I lifted my face to his, and he placed a kiss on my smiling mouth.

"So, are you going to be officially single, then?" I asked.

"As soon as I reply to this message." He tapped the screen of the device, selecting a few language characters to send his reply.

"Signed and sent. I no longer have a wife, not even on paper." He shoved the device back into his pocket, then turned me in his arms to face him. "Though the position is not exactly vacant. It's reserved for you."

"For how long?"

"For as long as you need. You promised to think about it," he reminded me.

For all intents and purposes, we already were a couple. We shared a home, a bed, and all the responsibilities of raising a family. The only reason for us to make it official would be to define my immigration status on Aldrai.

"Well, we did want to take it slow." I smiled.

He laughed. "Slow? With you? Not a chance!" He grabbed me into a bear hug, kissing me so hard, I forgot about everything around me for a moment.

"I've made mistakes," he said, breaking the kiss. "More mistakes than I care to count. But I've never been so sure in my life about anything as I am about us. I love you, my heart. I'll wait for you forever if you so wish. Because there can never be anyone else for me but you."

Being with Xavran felt like I had finally arrived in a safe harbor after a long, turbulent journey. He was my destination, my purpose in life.

"I love you, Xavran. I'll marry you in a heartbeat. Fast or slow doesn't matter anymore, as long as I'm with you."

Epilogue

Xavran

A year later.

"What do you think?" he asked, moving his arm in a sweeping gesture across the field of *khulmis* flowers. They were in full bloom this time of year.

He and Susanna had just exited the forest trail after swimming in a waterfall nearby. It'd been nearly a year since Susanna became his wife and made him the happiest male in the Universe. He'd planned this trip for a while now. The children were at an overnight camp with their class this week, and he'd gotten some time to spend alone with Susanna.

"Wow!" she gasped, her eyes opening wide in wonder. Just the reaction he'd been hoping for. "This is even more impressive than in pictures and videos, Xavran."

This place was truly magical. He couldn't wait to spend the night here with her.

"That pink flower to the side of the field is all ours for the night." He gestured at the round blossom with several layers of petals, like a frilly skirt. It was supported by a wide stem with a ladder running along it.

"The pink one? My favorite color." Susanna clapped her hands in excitement.

It warmed his heart to see her happy. Of course, he knew her favorite color was pink. Of course, he specifically requested a flower of that color when booking this trip. He hoped it would make her happy.

He just never could predict exactly how much it would thrill him to see her excited.

He hugged her shoulders, drawing her into his side as they walked toward the flower through the soft grass covering the ground.

"They say the fragrance of *khulmis* flowers helps to get the best sleep ever," he murmured, kissing her hair.

"I don't think you'll let me get much sleep," she quipped, making him laugh.

True, he most definitely planned to keep her up for a good part of the night.

As they entered the field, rainbow flies rose into the air. Their multicolored wings were as big as the *khulmis* flower petals. It appeared as if some of the blossoms came to life, fluttering up into the sky.

"Oh, Xavran, just look at that!" Susanna swirled around, taking in the beautiful sight. "This is like a fairy tale. We're surrounded by flowers, above and below!"

Floral scents filled the air. The view was truly spectacular. But he couldn't keep his eyes off his wife.

Her golden hair, still damp after their swim in the waterfalls, swirled around her face, caught in the breeze stirred by the rainbow flies' wings. Her cheeks were tinted pink after the hike, her eyes shining with delight. She was the most beautiful woman he'd ever seen. And the best part was that she belonged to him. *His* woman. Body and soul.

Susanna was not just his wife. She had become his best friend, his confidante, his lover, and his partner. The trust between them was absolute and their connection unbreakable.

When they reached the stem of the flower, he took the bag with provisions off his shoulder. "Are you hungry?"

She gave him a playful smile. "Nope. Not for food, anyway."

"Perfect." He grinned, hanging the bag on the hook on the ladder under the flower.

"I want to see what it's like inside." She started climbing the ladder.

Her hips swayed as she moved her legs up the rungs. He stared, mesmerized.

"Are you coming?" Her teasing voice reached him.

He blinked. He really could *come* just by looking at her.

She reached the top and slid between the petals inside the flower.

"Ooh, it's so soft!" He heard her delighted giggle.

Scaling the ladder in a flash, he joined her inside. The soft, round middle of the flower was covered by a smooth, silky sheet. Several pillows and folded blankets lay in a neat pile on one side.

The sun had tipped to the horizon already. The innermost layer of the petals had lifted enough to shield them from view of any passersby, provided there even were any in this secluded spot.

They took their shoes off and hung them on the stem outside.

"It's warm. And comfy." Susanna bounced on the cushy middle of the blossom. Her expression turned flirty. "Too warm." She lifted her arms up and slid her white frilly top over her head.

He hadn't bothered putting his shirt back on after the swim. Now, he wished his pants were off too. They grew uncomfortably tight around his hips as both his tail and his cock jumped to attention at the sight of Susanna taking the rest of her clothes off.

She got down on her hands and knees, then crawled to him. His chest vibrated with a growl as he stared at her, her breasts swaying under her, her hips rocking side to side.

"Stop growling and come get me, darling," she murmured seductively.

He caught her in his arms, then rolled her onto her back. Blood rushed to his groin. The need burned through him, making his cock throb. His nodules leaked the slick without even being touched yet.

He pried her legs open with his knee.

"Yes..." She breathed out, rubbing herself against his thigh.

He shifted down her body, fitting his head between her legs. She moaned when he slid his tongue between her folds, hot and slick and ready for him.

"I want to do it to you, too…" she demanded, pivoting under him.

He rose on his knees for her to slide under him, her head under his crotch.

"Take these off." She unfastened his pants and yanked them down his legs, freeing his straining cock.

He sucked in a breath through his teeth as she flicked her wet, pink tongue over the bulbous tip.

"You're killing me, woman…" He gripped her thighs, putting his mouth on her.

"Killing?" She dragged her tongue along his length, making his hips jerk with a charge of pleasure rushing through his entire body. "*This* part of you looks very much alive." She wrapped her lips around him, sucking the tip in.

He growled against her slick, tender flesh, making her gasp and moan. She took him deeper into her mouth, letting her teeth graze the spongy nodules on his shaft. When suppressed, they sent a hot wave of pleasure through his belly and down his inner thighs.

He lapped at her as she sucked him. The firmer she wrapped her lips around him and the faster she moved, the harder he took her with his mouth. He twirled his tongue inside her, sweeping it around her inner walls. Stretching his tongue out as far as he could, he felt the spot inside her that made her whimper and moan against his cock.

His legs shook. His ball sack tightened, ready to spill. She quivered around his tongue, ready to let go, too, he sensed.

He yanked his head up, breaking the contact. "I want to come inside you."

She groaned in protest, lifting her hips up in search of his tongue. Grabbing his side horns, she yanked his head back to her.

He bent his head, refusing to give her control. The curved base of his front horn connected with her heated core.

"Please…" She rubbed herself against his horn.

His wife was in such a desperate need for him. Lust raged in him, shaking him to the core.

"I've got to fuck you," he gritted through his teeth.

He flipped her on her stomach, then fitted himself behind her. Grabbing her ass with his hands, he propped his cock at her entrance.

He loved this view. Susanna with her chest on the sheet, her backside raised up in the air for him. Human women produced their own lubrication when aroused. His wife wanted him so badly, the evidence of her arousal dripped down her thighs.

She was so wet, he slipped inside smoothly. His girth fit snugly, stretching her for him.

"Oh, yesss…" She reached between her legs to touch herself, but he swatted her hand away.

"Mine," he bit out, finding with his tail the spot she wished to rub. Leaning over her back, he grazed her shoulder with his teeth. "Is this what you tried to do, my heart?" He circled the bud of her clit with the tip of his tail. "Is this how you wanted to play with it?"

Her moans were her only answer.

He drew back a little then slammed into her again. She gripped the sheets with her hands, lifting her torso just enough for him to cup one of her breasts. She grabbed the other one herself, pinching and pulling the tip. He rubbed her clit, pumping harder.

Her breathing halted, then a loud shuddering moan tore from her chest. Her inner muscles tightened around him, spurring his climax too.

He roared in ecstasy, pumping his release into her, the aftershocks of her orgasm blending with his.

Warm bliss descended on him, making him weak in his knees. Holding her with one arm around her middle, he crashed to his side.

She panted, gripping his hand with both of hers. "This was...by far...so much more intense than in that video I made you watch, remember?"

He chuckled into her mussed hair. "Videos never do this place justice." And nothing could ever compare to sex with his wife.

Stroking her arm in a soothing gesture, he noticed a red scratch on her skin.

"Is this from one of my horns?" he asked, appalled with himself.

Humans were so soft and vulnerable. How could he be such a savage in his lust-filled frenzy?

She glanced at the scratch and shrugged. "Possibly."

"I'm so sorry." He leaned to kiss the injury.

"Don't be." She placed a kiss on the tip of his left horn. "I'm sure you have a few fresh scratches from my nails too. And has that bite mark on your ass healed yet? Remember the one I left there last time?"

She had gone into a lust frenzy herself, in a most delightful way. The thought of the *last time* brought a new spark of excitement.

"I don't know." He smiled. "It's not like I can see it there."

"I should inspect it for you," she murmured, reaching back to cup his butt cheek.

Her touch resonated through him with a new wave of desire. The thought of her teeth, lips, and tongue anywhere on his body sent a rush of excitement through his body again. His cock jerked, pressed to her backside. As if on its own, his tail moved towards her.

"Xavran?" She sounded rather serious this time.

"What is it, my love?"

"Do you ever think about having more children? In the future sometime?"

"More?" His excitement spiked. He couldn't contain a smile when she turned her head to look at him over her shoulder.

"I've always wanted a baby..."

"It wouldn't be just one with me, you know that." Aldraian-human unions resulted in fewer fetuses per pregnancy, but it would still be anywhere between four to six.

"I know. It's a bit intimidating, but..."

He slipped his tail between her legs.

"Just say the word," he murmured in her ear.

The tip of his tail twitched, finding what he was looking for. She was hot and slick inside. He swirled his tail, stroking the inner walls of her channel.

With a brief, needy sound, she pressed her legs together, trapping his tail between them.

"Are you...ready again?" she asked breathlessly.

Holding her from behind, he cupped her breast.

"I'm always ready for you, my heart." He kept moving his tail inside her while kneading her breast. "I've warned you, I'm keeping you up tonight. We may as well start working on more babies..."

She exhaled a soft giggle. "That's not how it works. With my pill...Oh!"

He prodded her with his cock from behind, and she arched her back, pressing her bottom to him.

"We'll practice then." He grinned, parting her legs to gain better access.

Her body relaxed against his, willing and ready. "I love you, Xavran. So much."

"I love you, too, my heart. You're it for me. My one and only."

Susanna

"THERE THEY ARE!" I pointed at the familiar figures of our children running to us across the school grounds.

Xilvo was ahead of everyone, with Ivex close on his heels. I hadn't even realized how much I missed them all during our trip with Xavran. I couldn't hold back, taking off towards them.

"Hi, Mom!" Xilvo crashed into me, nearly knocking me off my feet before catching me in a hug.

"Yay! You're back!" Ivex slammed into me from the other side, his arms wrapping tight around me.

"Easy," Xavran laughed, catching our girls in a hug. "Don't hurt your mother, boys!"

The kids had been getting so big. After yet another growth spurt recently, the boys were almost taller than me now. Their horns were quickly catching up with their dad's impressive crown.

"How was camp?" I asked after all the hugs and kisses.

"Great!" Ene beamed at us. "We went swimming."

"And we had to sleep in a shelter," Xilvo exclaimed excitedly. "With a roof!"

"Yep," Illal confirmed. "A real roof made of wood and leaves. They have no energy shields in the forest, so they have to make roofs to hide from the rain.

"No energy shields? Talk about roughing it." I laughed. At least, there was no danger of any giant worms bursting through the ground that far into the terraformed territory.

Ene took her bag off her shoulder. "And we did lots of crafts."

Xilvo dropped his bag too. "We made this for you!" He yanked something out of the bag.

"Me too!" Ivex dug into his bag as well.

"For me?" I took a string of long, colorful beads from Xilvo.

"It's a necklace." Ene gestured for me to lean closer, then placed a string of her own around my neck.

Illal did the same, followed by the boys. Soon, I had four strings of colorful painted cylinders cascading down my chest.

"We don't have *macaroni*," Ene explained. "So, we dried up some *ustor* stems, cut them up and painted them."

"Oh…" I clutched the strings of handmade beads in my hands, my heart filling with so much emotion, I feared it'd burst.

"It's been a year since our Mother's Day party, right?" Illal said.

"We figured yesterday was Mother's Day again," Xilvo explained.

Had it been a year? Already? Time had flown by so fast. Aldrai had become my true home. All my friends and family were here. Except for Mara. She remained on Earth. From what I'd heard, Jason never proposed to her, and she was still in search of a perfect man who, I feared, didn't exist.

Ene slid her finger down the colorful beads in my hands. "Since you were away, we couldn't give these to you."

"But now we can!" Ivex grinned, his smile sliding a bit sideways, just like his dad's.

I wasn't going to tell them that Mother's Day was celebrated on a Sunday and fell on a different date each year. It didn't matter right now. What mattered was that I had four amazing children, and they made their version of macaroni necklaces for me.

"I…" Love filled me to the rim—warm, effervescent, and wonderful. My heart felt so full, it overflowed with tears.

"Oh no, she's crying," Illal gasped.

"Great job, you guys." Ivex huffed. "We made Mom upset. On Mother's Day."

"But how?" Xilvo scratched behind his right horn. "What did we do?"

"Shh," Ene hushed them. "This could be good. She cries when she's happy too. Remember when we gave her flowers for her birthday?"

Illal perked up. "Right! And when Ene invited her to school to speak about the job of being a mother on Career Day, remember? Mom cried then too."

"Oh, stop it…" I waved both hands in front of my face, trying to collect myself. A new bout of tears threatened to erupt from thinking about that day when Ene, the last of the four, had finally called me 'Mom.' I sniffled. "Just… give me a minute."

"Come here, my heart." Xavran wrapped me into his big, strong arms. "Tell me you're happy or else I'll have to find whatever made you upset and fix it."

"Oh, I am happy, darling." I sniffled again, wiping my tears with my arm. Kids giggled, joining us in the 'family hug.' "I'm so, so happy to have all of you in my life."

More in My Holiday Tails

My Pumpkin

Cassy

"I want this one!" I threw myself onto the biggest pumpkin at the stand. It was so huge, the farmer had it on the ground, not in the wagon with the rest of them.

Mom tapped my shoulder. "Cassy, baby, it won't even fit into our apartment."

She smiled apologetically at the man selling the pumpkins at the farmer's market in our part of the city. But I refused to let go. This was the biggest pumpkin I'd ever seen in the ten years of my life. My arms didn't even come close to wrapping all the way around it.

I wanted it.

"I'll keep it in my room." I'd have to shove my bed all the way to the wall to make space for this thing, but it'd be totally worth it.

"Cassidy," mom's voice gained that stern note it always did when she called me by my full name. "We're not getting that one. We can't even lift it. How are we going to carry it back to our building? Choose another one."

The farmer grinned at me, gesturing at the wagon piled high with bright orange pumpkins. "I've got a whole wagon-full of them. See? Surely, you'll find one you like in here."

I briefly considered stomping my feet and maybe whining a little. It rarely helped me get my way. But if we were in public, Mom would give in sometimes just to keep me quiet.

By the look of her, however, it was unlikely to happen today. Mom had her arms crossed over her chest. Her dark-brown eyes narrowed. And her lips were pinched into that unimpressed expression she had when I acted up.

"Fine." I gave up and climbed off the giant pumpkin, then shuffled over to the wagon filled with the smaller, far less impressive ones.

They were okay. Some were perfectly round, others had funny squished or elongated shapes. None looked good enough after that giant one, though.

Something twinkled deep inside the pile. An orange glow shone from the darkness between the orbs.

"Ooh, what's that?" Straining my barely there arm muscles, I rolled aside a couple of pumpkins to find the one that was glowing.

This one was small, even smaller than most. It'd easily fit into my room. I wouldn't even have to move the furniture around to accommodate it. It'd fit on my bookshelf. Or even on the windowsill.

"How about this one?" I presented it to my mom.

"I don't think it's a pumpkin, hun." She took it from me and turned it over in her hands.

The glow stopped when she took it. But I still liked it. It was smooth and just a little brighter orange than the rest.

"I want to get this one," I insisted.

Mom seemed doubtful.

"It looks plastic. You won't be able to carve it." She turned to the farmer. "What is it, actually?"

He rubbed the back of his neck.

"Not sure. I've no idea how it got there. Is it yours, Linda?" he asked the vendor to his left, a plump woman in a gorgeous sweater with black cats printed on it. She was selling home-made Halloween decorations.

"Nope." She shook her head. "It can't be one of mine. You must've brought it from the farm. It was buried all the way in your wagon."

If no one was selling it, then I found it. And finders were keepers, right? I wrapped my arms tightly around my new pumpkin.

Mom hesitated. "Maybe it's someone's toy? A kid lost it? We should take it to the lost-and-found."

"But it's not lost. It's mine," I protested.

The pumpkin glowed softly again. When I pressed it to my chest, I felt it pulse warmly. I smiled, already imagining it in my room. I didn't even need to put a candle inside it because it shone all on its own.

"Well, Linda may be right." The farmer scratched his chin. "It might've come from the farm with us. Though, I've no idea how it got to the farm, either."

"I want to buy it," I had to remind the grownups of the task at hand. Mom and I came here to buy a pumpkin for Halloween. And I'd chosen one.

Mom looked around. "Well, if it doesn't belong to anyone..."

"It belongs to me," I said resolutely. "Finders keepers."

The farmer laughed.

"That's fine. Just keep it." He waved his hand.

"How much is it?" Mom opened her purse.

The man shrugged. "I don't even know what to charge. It clearly didn't grow on my farm. Just take it."

Happy I got what I wanted after all, I left them to figure out the details between themselves. Hugging my pumpkin to my chest, I skipped to the stand nearby that sold skewers of whimsically decorated marshmallows. Mom always got me one of those when we came to the farmer's market right before Halloween. I loved coming here.

It was the best day ever.

A year later.

I OPENED THE DOOR TO our apartment and hung my school bag on the hook by the door.

It was quiet. The apartment was empty. Mom worked long shifts at the hospital as a nurse. She wasn't coming home until much later that night. Dad wouldn't be back until the day after tomorrow. He worked as a pilot and was often gone for several days at a time.

When I was smaller, they'd tried to schedule their work shifts so that one of them was always home with me. Occasionally, when their schedules had overlapped despite their best efforts, they had hired our elderly neighbor to look after me.

Now that I was bigger and didn't need a babysitter, they didn't mind having their work shifts overlap. That way, we had more time to spend as a family when they both got days off at the same time.

I skipped down the hallway toward the kitchen to make myself a snack when a loud crash came from inside of the apartment. I froze.

Did we have an intruder? I backed up to the front door.

In case of an emergency, I had two options: either call nine-one-one or run downstairs and get the doorman, Mister Riley. Depending on the kind of emergency, of course, which wasn't always that easy to figure out, as I'd learned.

My face warmed up at the embarrassing memory of me running downstairs in my pajamas last spring because Mom and Dad weren't home and there was a funny noise coming from the bathroom. The noise as it had turned out was made by a bee caught in the shower curtain, not by a scary robot from outer space like I'd convinced myself to believe. Dad had laughed his head off when Mister Riley had told him that story. And Mom had told me that it was a good idea to think first about what an emergency meant.

"Sometimes," she'd said, "it wouldn't hurt to investigate a little on your own instead of panicking right away."

I stopped with my back to the front door, without opening it to run outside, and listened for the noise again.

No other suspicious sounds came. Maybe this wasn't an emergency, after all? What if something just fell off my desk, like a book or a toy? I'd look really stupid if I ran to Mister Riley again.

Mom was right, I had to *investigate*.

The noise appeared to have come from my bedroom. It was the first room up the hallway after the kitchen. I made a quick detour to the kitchen to grab a rolling pin just in case there *was* an intruder waiting for me in my room.

Holding the rolling pin in front of me, I padded to my bedroom door. Not a sound came from behind the door. I leaned closer and pressed my ear to it. Still, all seemed quiet. Maybe there hadn't been a noise at all, and I'd just imagined it?

Unless the intruder knew I was in the apartment and was waiting for me, very quietly.

I took a few deep breaths before placing a hand on the door handle and turning it. Holding the rolling pin ready, I cracked the door open.

My bed with the pink and orange bedspread came into view. Mom and I had cleaned my room just a day ago, so there weren't any piles of clothes or toys on the floor for an intruder to hide in.

The door to my closet was open, as it should be. I always had it open—less chance for closet monsters to sneak up on me undetected.

Thankfully, both the room and the closet looked empty and monster-free. The only place for the intruder to hide would be under my bed. But Mom stored boxes with my winter clothes under there. So, the intruder would have to be really short and skinny to fit into the space between the boxes.

Clutching the rolling pin in both hands, I entered the room, keeping an eye on the bed. The bright orange pieces of my pumpkin on the floor caught my eye, and I forgot all about the intruder.

"Oh no!" I tossed the rolling pin onto the bed and crouched by the broken pieces under the window.

This was my pumpkin, the one I'd gotten at the farmer's market last year. I'd kept it on my windowsill ever since. It was my favorite nightlight. Its soft pulsing glow made me feel safe at night, even when Mom and Dad weren't home. And when I felt sad, I liked to cuddle with it. It always made me feel warm and fuzzy inside when I hugged it.

Now, it was broken. Three large chunks of the orange shell lay on the carpet. The outer side was smooth and glossy. The inside—the part I'd never seen before—happened to be white and soft, like a squishy marshmallow.

I picked up two of the pieces and tried to fit them together.

"Maybe Daddy can glue it back together?" I muttered under my breath.

Something scratched under the bed. The sound sent me up to my feet again. Grabbing the rolling pin, I jumped onto the bed.

"Who's there?" I tried to make my voice sound deep and scary. "Get out!"

There really wasn't that much space under my bed. The last time I'd crawled under there myself was to get a baseball that had rolled under there by accident. It happened months ago, and it'd been a tight fit between the boxes, even for me.

I adjusted my hands on the rolling pin. The fact that the intruder couldn't be much bigger than me felt encouraging.

A tapping sound came from under the bed. It moved from one end to the other and sounded very much like tiny footsteps. If it was an intruder, it would be the size of...a garden gnome? No one higher than that could actually *walk* under my bed. I leaned over the edge, feeling more confused than scared now.

Something orange crawled from under the bed. It looked round. Its color was the same bright shade as my pumpkin. Only instead of glossy and smooth, the thing was...fluffy.

"Hey," I called from the bed.

The thing turned around and blinked its long chocolate-brown eyelashes at me. It had two eyes—one blue, one green—with lighter dots pulsing inside them. Two pointy furry ears stood up. It also had a black button nose, four short paws, and two, yes *two*, tails that were so fluffy, they looked like two fuzzy pompoms attached to his chubby bum.

The creature looked like a toy. But it was most definitely alive.

"You're so stinking cute!" I squeaked, tossing aside the rolling pin.

The creature had clearly come from my pumpkin. Though, I wasn't entirely sure how that could've happened. I didn't really care, either. The thing was so fluffy, I just wanted to grab, pet, and squeeze it.

"Come here, you... Whatever the heck you are." I picked it up.

It snorted but didn't protest much. Its orange fur had some white in it, I discovered, upon a closer inspection. It was thicker around its neck, like a wide fur collar. Its feet were black, as if it was wearing socks. And it had the softest white belly I'd ever seen.

I scratched behind its ears, and the animal nuzzled into my elbow.

"You look like a puppy," I said uncertainly. "I'd never had a puppy before. I hope Mom will let me keep you."

Because I really, really wanted to keep him. Or *her*. Or *it*... Whatever it was.

Holding my new puppy in one arm, I grabbed my tablet and typed into the search bar *"kinds of dogs."* I had to figure out what kind I got. It wasn't always easy to tell with puppies, I'd heard.

"I think you might be a corgi," I determined after some research. The orange and white colors of my new dog fit that breed. As did the cute little face. "You're a bit fluffier than them. And shorter. And you have two tails. And black paws... Well, maybe you're not entirely a corgi. Maybe you're a mix with something else." Not that it really mattered, anyway. It was the cutest puppy I'd ever seen, and I loved it already.

Next, I researched what in our kitchen I could feed to the puppy since we didn't have any dog food in the house. The puppy refused to eat a raw egg but seemed happy with the ham and cheese sandwich I made for myself and then shared with it.

"I never had a pet," I told it. "But I always wanted one."

At night, I made a bed for the puppy in one of the drawers of the dresser in my room. Then I brushed my teeth and turned off the lights to go to bed.

My room looked different without the soft, warm glow of the pumpkin I'd gotten used to in the past year. The streetlights didn't have the same color. Their light was bluish and cold, making me think of ghosts or spaceships with aliens. The sound of traffic on the street below my window also kept me awake for some reason. Normally, I was used to it and even found it soothing. But not tonight.

A tiny squealing noise came from the dresser drawer.

"You can't sleep either?" I climbed off the bed and picked up the puppy. "Well, I guess you can sleep with me tonight."

I climbed back under the covers. The puppy was warm and fluffy. Its little heart thudded softly against my chest when I pressed its small, round body to me.

"Just for tonight, though, okay? Mom is not going to like it if she sees you in my bed…" I yawned, feeling comfy and warm. "I think I'll call you Pumpkin," I mumbled, drifting off to sleep.

"CASSY? WHAT IS THIS?" Mom stood in the kitchen, still wearing her scrubs.

When she'd come home after a long, late shift, she often was too tired to change. She'd just crash on the couch for a few hours. In the morning, she'd wake up to have breakfast with me and to take a shower.

After I'd leave for school, she'd go to her bedroom to sleep, often until I came home in the afternoon.

That morning, I'd made us some bacon and scrambled eggs while she'd slept on the couch. It was her favorite breakfast. I hoped it'd put her in a good mood before she saw Pumpkin. But she hadn't even taken a bite before the silly puppy waddled out of my bedroom.

"I'm asking what this is?" She pointed at the round, fluffy thing.

I blew out a breath, hanging my head. "A puppy. I think."

Come to think of it, the creature didn't really look that much like a dog, more like a stuffed toy, or a cartoon character, or something.

"A puppy?" Mom stared at it. "Cassidy, where did you get a dog?"

She used my full name again. It was not a good sign.

I nervously tugged at one of my two dozen braids. "Well, funny thing... But I think it came from my pumpkin. The one I had on my window, remember? I came home from school yesterday, and the pumpkin was broken, and—"

She stopped my rambling by lifting a hand, then headed to the coffeemaker.

"I swear, Mom," I insisted. "The pumpkin must've hatched or something..."

"Right. And my head is about to crack open, too." She rubbed her forehead before starting the coffeemaker, then stared at Pumpkin, her hands on her hips. "He can't stay."

The puppy looked up at her, blinking innocently, then plopped down, sitting with his butt on my foot.

"But where else can he go?" I asked. Somehow, Pumpkin was now a "he."

Mom blew a lock of her chestnut hair away from her face. Her hair was wavy, not nearly as curly as mine. I got Dad's hair and skin color. But I had Mom's brown eyes. Dad's were much darker than hers or mine, almost black.

"The puppy has to go back to where he came from, Cassy," she said firmly. "He must belong to someone in the building. He probably wandered off into the hallway and snuck into our apartment when you opened the door. He's likely the one who knocked your pumpkin off the window, too, and broke it. He's trouble. We need to return him as soon as possible."

"But *where?*" I protested. "There are no missing dog posters in the building. No one is looking for him. He has nowhere else to go."

Mom leaned with her hip against the counter as the coffeemaker sputtered and brewed. "We'll have to speak with Mister Riley to see if someone is looking for a lost puppy."

"But if no one is, can we keep him?" I wouldn't give up hope.

She pursed her lips in that unimpressed expression of hers. Except that she also looked tired. Very tired. Long shifts at the hospital were hard.

"Cassy, we can't look after it," she said in a much softer voice.

Hope sparked brighter in me.

"But I can! I'll walk him first thing in the morning, before school. Then, I'll walk him again after school. And you know what? Pumpkin knows how to use the toilet, anyway."

"What are you talking about?" She got a cup from the cabinet and filled it with coffee. She always drank it black—no cream, no sugar.

"Yes, he does. He peed on the bathroom floor this morning. I cleaned it up with the toilet paper and flushed it. Then he climbed onto the seat and pooped into the toilet." I chatted, piling a plate high with bacon and eggs for her. She needed to eat. She always seemed to be in a better mood when she wasn't hungry.

"Thanks, baby." Mom took a fork I gave her and speared a slice of cucumber on it from the salad I'd made. "He pooped in the toilet? Are you sure? Dogs don't use toilets."

"Oh, yes, they do. The smart ones do. I've seen it in videos. I'll show you some. There's one where a dog even flushes the toilet after himself.

I'm sure Pumpkin can learn how to flush, too. He's smart. He just needs to grow a little. Right now, he's too short to even reach the handle to flush."

Mom ate in silence for a little while, and I let her, afraid that if I talked too much, I'd irritate her. She was less likely to agree to anything if she was irritated.

"What will your dad say?" She sighed.

I tried to hide a smile as huge relief flushed over me. Dad was the least of my worries. If Mom said yes, he'd never say no.

"I need someone, Mom," I pleaded. "It'll be good to have Pumpkin around. You and Dad are never home."

Mom winced as if I'd slapped her.

"I mean, I'm not complaining," I added quickly.

I knew she wished she could spend more time with me. She worked so hard. And when she got home, she was often too tired and slept a lot. Dad was the same. We had lots of fun when the three of us went on vacations as a family. But most of the year, it was just me.

"I'm not allowed to have friends over when I'm home alone," I said. "I can't even open the door to anyone. But now, I won't be alone. I'll have Pumpkin."

With another deep sigh, she looked at the puppy again. He sniffed the floor around one of the legs of the kitchen table.

"Well, we're allowed a pet by the home association's rules. And he seems quiet. He hasn't barked yet."

"He doesn't bark," I rushed to assure her. "He just snorts and farts...a little."

She took a sip of her coffee, then rubbed her chin in thought. "We'll need to get a vet to look at him. He may have fleas or worms. And why the heck does he have two tails?"

I beamed. My Pumpkin was here to stay.

CHAPTER 2

Pumpkin

Ten years later.

"AWW, WHO'S A GOOD BOY? Who's a good boy?" Cassy cooed.

He wasn't a boy, not a human boy, anyway. Though the vet confirmed him as a *possible* male. But Cassy was rubbing his belly, and he would never object to any signs of her attention. Rolling over to his back, he gave her more to rub.

"You're so cute. Just look at this fluffy fluff-fluff. Look at this spoiled little puppy." She grabbed his nose and kissed his forehead.

He wasn't a puppy, either. And he certainly wasn't little. In the past ten years, he'd grown much taller, he reached higher than Cassy's waist when he stood on all four feet. If he placed his front paws on her shoulders, he was way taller than her.

Overall, he knew what he *wasn't*. The question remained what he actually *was*?

He'd discovered early on that he could access the Internet remotely, without needing a device. It put the vast knowledge of humankind at his fingertips, figuratively speaking, of course, since he had no fingers, just paws.

After years of searching the web, he'd concluded he wasn't even a dog. What he was, however, he'd failed to identify. Some parts of him might look similar to those of a dog, a fox or even a wolf, but no species fit him perfectly.

The vet had seemed as confused as everyone else when Cassy and her mom had brought him to the clinic ten years ago. At the end, she'd just told Cassy and her mom that Pumpkin must have some birth defects and abnormalities. She'd said to "enjoy him while he lasts." She'd also advised Cassy's mom against doing any x-rays or tests since...well, he wasn't supposed to *last*, anyway, so there was no need to waste money.

But there he was, a decade later, feeling stronger and healthier than ever. Maybe a vet wasn't the right doctor for him after all?

"Ooh, guess what?" Cassy made her brown eyes wider, looking excited, as if she was about to tell him a secret. "Guess what we're going to do today, Pumpkin?" She took a pause, as if inviting him to take a guess.

He couldn't reply, of course, not with words. So, he lifted his three long tails—the third one grew a few years ago—and waved them in the air, similar to the way that dogs did.

It made her giggle. She always looked so happy when he did "normal dog things." That was the main reason he did them at all. Wagging his tails always made him feel silly, but he was rewarded with the sound of her giggles that made his skin tingle with pleasure under his fur.

"Oh, you know that, don't you? The smart puppy that you are? Of course you do. You know where we're going." She raked her fingers through the soft white fur on his belly. The pleasure kicked into a new gear. It was so intense, his hind legs jerked involuntarily.

"Who likes belly rubs? This big boy likes belly rubs," she continued to murmur utter nonsense which he didn't mind at all as long as she kept scratching his belly.

He'd always liked her pets and cuddles. Wrestling with her was fun too. Lately, however, his reaction to her touch had been turning into something else. It made him wish for more. For something...something he couldn't really name.

Despite her warnings on the night he'd first hatched, she had let him sleep in her bed again the next night, and the next... They had slept together every night since. Until her bed had become his, and no one even questioned his right to be in there with her anymore.

Cassy would fall asleep with her arms wrapped around him. When she lay next to him, he made a rhythmic thudding noise in his chest and increased his body temperature a little—both seemed to comfort her.

If she woke up at night after having a scary dream, she would bury her face into the fur on his neck and splay her hand on his chest, right over the part he made thud for her. Then, she would fall asleep again, breathing evenly.

A few nights ago, something else happened, however. Cassy woke up with a moan, not a whimper. The sound seemed to reach all the way through to his gut. Something he had no control over still pulsed low in his belly when he recalled that moan. She'd stared at his eyes for the longest moment, then...she kicked him out of her bed and out of her room.

That hurt. The unpleasant feeling from the unexplained rejection still scratched inside his chest. Thankfully, she'd let him back into her bed again the following night, and things seemed to be back to normal once again.

"That's right!" Cassy exclaimed excitedly. "We're going to the park."

She jumped up, waving her arms in the air in a severely exaggerated delight at her idea. He wagged his tails harder to match her enthusiasm. She clearly loved going to that park, and he absolutely didn't mind tagging along. As far as he was concerned, he didn't care *where* she took him as long as she stayed with him.

Since Cassy started college a few years ago, she had even less time to spend with him. She wanted to be a nurse, like her mom. He loved her focus and determination in that area and was proud of her. But he was also grateful that she hadn't moved out of her parents' place, like many college students did, and hadn't left him behind. That was the advantage of living in a big city—Cassy didn't have to leave to go to college. Her campus was just a short bus ride away.

"All right." She slapped his flank. "I'll go get changed quickly, then we'll leave. Okay?"

She jumped off the living room couch and skipped to her bedroom to change out of her pajamas.

He climbed off the couch, too, and stretched his back. Going to the park allowed him to run, which he was looking forward to. The need to move turned torturous if he stayed cooped up in the apartment for an entire day.

Cassy's phone rang inside her bedroom.

AVAILABLE NOW

More by Marina Simcoe

My Holiday Tails
Married to Krampus
My Tiny Giant
My Birthday Getaway
New Year, New Planet
Mail Order Mom
My Pumpkin
What Makes an Alien a Dad?

Dark Anomaly Trilogy
Gravity
Power
Explosion

Standalone Novels
Experiment
Enduring (Valos Of Sonhadra)

The World of the River of Mists

Joyless Kingdom (Trilogy)
Somber Prince, Book 1
Joy Guardian, Book 2
Pleasure Trader, Book 3

Wingless Crow (Duet)
Wingless Crow – Part 1
Crownless King – Part 2

Fire in Stone (Duet)
Fire in Stone – Part 1
Hearts on Fire – Part 2

Serpent's Touch (Duet)
Serpent's Touch – Part 1
Serpent's Claim – Part 2

Madame Tan's Freakshow (Trilogy)

Call of Water
Madness of the Moon
Power of Rage

Paranormal Romance

About the Author

Marina Simcoe likes to write love stories with characters, who may or may not be entirely human, because she firmly believes that our contemporary world could always use a little bit of the extraordinary.

She has lots of fun exploring how her out-of-this-world characters with their own beliefs, values, and aspirations fit into our every-day life.

She lives in Canada with her very own grumpy brute, their three little kids, and a cat, who is definitely out of this world.

For illustrations, early access, signed paperbacks, and more, please join the author's Patreon:

Please Stay in Touch

Newsletter signup is on MarinaSimcoe.com:

Facebook Readers' Group:
Marina's Reading Cave
www.instagram.com/marinasimcoeauthor
www.marinasimcoe.com
www.facebook.com/MarinaSimcoeAuthor/
www.amazon.com/author/marinasimcoe
www.bookbub.com/profile/marina-simcoe
www.goodreads.com/MarinaSimcoe